STEALING GOD

James Green

Published by Accent Press Ltd 2015

ISBN 9781909624566

First published by Luath Press 2009

Author's Note

I don't suppose many writers get the chance to rewrite a book once it's been published, so I want to thank Accent Press for giving me that chance. *Stealing God* was written seven years ago while *Bad Catholics* was getting excellent reviews and being shortlisted for a Crime Writers' Association Dagger. It lays the foundations for the rest of the Road to Redemption series, but the world has definitely moved on since its first publication. When I saw I had a second chance to work on it, I took the opportunity to incorporate new themes which have a stronger relevance in today's world. Now, some years since it was written, I feel that *Stealing God* can take its proper place in the violent life and hard times of James C. Costello.

Newark on Trent, 2015

In February 1945 Germany was a defeated nation, the war almost finished. The victors, Stalin, Churchill, and Roosevelt, met at Yalta, in Crimea, to carve up post-war Europe. When it was suggested that the views of Pope Pius XII should be taken into account Stalin asked his now famous question, 'How many divisions has the pope?' The answer, of course, was none, so Vatican sensibilities were ignored. Stalin outmanoeuvred both Churchill and Roosevelt and got most of Central and Eastern Europe. The Soviet Union became a superpower.

Was Stalin right? Can the Vatican be dismissed as a serious player on the stage of world politics?

Well, just over fifty years later both Stalin and the Soviet Union were gone but the Vatican remained, arguably stronger than it had been for over three hundred years.

Makes you think, doesn't it?

The Past is a foreign country: we did things differently there ...

Life isn't fair and it can be bloody unkind. If you want the breaks you have to make them for yourself. That was Jimmy Costello's view in the old days, and the breaks he made were usually an arm or a leg, other people's of course. But things change. You do your best but then you find your best isn't good enough. You make money, lots of money, but the girl you make it for goes and dies on you. What then? Well, if you're London Irish from Kilburn you do one of two things: you humbly accept God's will and carry on or you turn your back on God and take your future into your own hands, and if your family and friends don't like it you tell them to go to hell. Unfortunately Jimmy wanted to do both and it nearly tore him apart. In the end, however, after a spell in the far west of Ireland and with the friendship of an old and wise priest, Jimmy found a way of dealing with who he'd been, who he was, and who he would become. He put himself back together and made a promise to the girl he'd worked so hard for. He'd put things right, he'd put himself right. Wherever she was he'd make her proud of him.

Jimmy applied to the Church to see if he was fitted for the Catholic priesthood. This initial enquiry got him a placement in a Paddington refuge to see if he was suitable material. But London wasn't a safe place for Jimmy and his old ways came back to bite him and they nearly bit his head off. So, in 1995, Jimmy left London, once again in a hurry, just like he'd done when his wife Bernie had died of cancer and, for a time, the madness had taken over. This time, however, he didn't hurt anyone – no one important, that is – so no one was looking for him. Jimmy put his money somewhere safe, where it would work for him, and set off for one last visit, to make peace with what was left of his family.

Jimmy and Bernie had two children, Eileen and Michael, and Jimmy had always thought of himself as a good husband and father who protected his family and made sure they would never want for anything money could buy. But as soon as they were old enough they'd both left home and put as much ground as they could between themselves and their father. Eileen married and emigrated to Australia, and Michael joined a Catholic religious order as a missionary priest. Too late, at Bernie's hospital bedside, Jimmy realised what staying with him but losing her children must have meant to his wife.

Michael survived four years of vicious civil war in southern Sudan before his order finally pulled him out and sent him to a supposedly safe place in Africa where he'd picked up something nasty which had killed him inside two months. But there was still Eileen. She had two children and lived in Melbourne with her builder husband. Jimmy had never seen his grandchildren – and Bernie never would – so he decided to go and see his daughter and her family and make whatever sort of peace and amends he could. He took his time in travelling, not because he wanted to see new places and new faces but because he didn't have high hopes and was in no hurry to have a door slammed in his face. There had always been a Christmas card with a short letter until Bernie died, then nothing. Jimmy felt it wouldn't be a long visit.

Eileen wasn't glad to see him, but he'd expected that. With the children, though, things were different. They weren't carrying any baggage from the past; to them he was Gramps, not only an English rellie but an ex-detective sergeant, someone new and different, and, to Jimmy's surprise and Eileen's disapproval, they decided to love him. Eileen's husband, Frank, was an Australian and they had met and married quickly while he was in London as part of a European trip to see the world before he settled down. Eileen had told Frank nothing about her father but he could read his wife's attitude just as well as Jimmy could. One night he took his father-in-law out to a bar and told him that what was between Jimmy and Eileen was their business, but he didn't want his children involved. If Jimmy could keep things civilised he was welcome to make as long a visit as he liked. That seemed eminently fair, so Jimmy found somewhere to rent and began to get to know his grandchildren.

Eileen allowed him to stay and for a while Jimmy was happy because he had discovered something utterly new to him: an uncomplicated life with nothing to haunt him and nothing to fight for or against. He had money so he began spending it on his grandchildren and Frank and Eileen let him. The weeks he'd intended to stay soon turned into months and then into years while the children grew and flourished. But Jimmy knew it couldn't last. He hadn't changed, he was still looking after himself, making sure he got what he wanted, and using money he'd made by bending and breaking the law to be safe, idle, and happy in a faraway country wasn't answering for the past. He'd promised Bernie he would become different, better; he had to go back and make that promise work. So, some years later than he had intended, Jimmy went back to Ireland to resurrect his application to Rome ...

ONE

The narrow side street was domestic Rome, unattractive, functional, and none too clean, the small bar halfway down was a place where locals met for a drink, a smoke, and perhaps a game of cards or dominoes. At one end the street opened out onto the busy Corso Vittorio Emanuele II where the sidewalks were full of bright dresses, casual slacks, tailored shirts, and sunglasses. The traffic, as always, churned noisily and fitfully with the inevitable sounding of horns. But in the warm spring sunshine no one wanted to think about the Eternal City's eternal chaos, certainly not the three middle-aged men sitting in the bar. They looked at home, friends having a lunch-time drink in their local. One of them looked at his watch, a man with a lived-in face, short, grizzled hair, and a rumpled shirt, who looked as if he might have been born and raised in such a street. When he spoke, however, it in was English, the accent pure north London.

'I'll have to go soon, the rector wants to see me.'

'What's up, Jimmy, smack on the wrist or a pat on the back?'

The question came from a small, balding man in a sweater. This time the accent was Australian. Jimmy smiled but didn't respond so the third man, a big man, filled the silence.

'You don't expect him to tell you, do you? Jimmy never tells

1

anyone anything if it's about Jimmy. I've been served clams in chowder that I knew more about than I do about him.' He turned to Jimmy as if inspecting him. 'Eight months since we first met and I'll tell you what we know about you. You're a Duns College student, we know because we got told. You're studying with us but you're not one of us. You come from London, your accent tells us that. You must have plenty of money because Duns students have to be self-financing here and afterwards. That's common knowledge.' He nodded to the bottle and glass in front of Jimmy. 'You like beer, not wine or spirits. And that's it, that's all of it.'

The Australian chipped in.

'Except that you don't talk about yourself.'

They were all smiling; it was banter between friends.

'That's right, Ron, he don't talk about himself.'

Jimmy finished his drink. 'What's to talk about? Anyway, neither of you came to Rome to get my life story so what's the difference?'

The big man laughed easily; you got the feeling he laughed a lot. He was wearing an overcoat and had a scarf hanging round his neck. The Jamaican accent explained why it wasn't yet time for him to get into short sleeves.

'Never mind why we came to Rome. We all know why we came to Rome, and you're right, it wasn't to talk about ourselves. But I tell you it isn't natural for people working together not to know something about each other. A careful mouth is a good thing, a secretive one is something else altogether. Secrets have a way of popping out at you when they can do the most harm.' Then he winked at the Australian before putting his elbow on the table and shielding his face with his hand. 'Confess, my son, tell me all and receive my absolution before it is too late and the fires of Hell engulf your immortal soul.' He laughed a deep, West Indian laugh. The Australian joined in.

'Take him up on it, mate, he'll go easy on you. He used to be a copper back in Jamaica so he's seen it all. You can't shock Danny.'

'That's right, you can't shock me.'

'Sorry, lads, there's nothing to shock you with. I might bore you to death though, if I ever got going.'

'Don't tell me a life lived in London hasn't had its moments, mate. I can't believe that.'

'I don't suppose London's much different from Perth if all you do is live and work there and raise kids.'

Danny laughed loudly and slapped the table with his hands, hard enough for the barman to stop reading the paper and look up and the few others in the bar to glance across at them.

'Information, Ron, information about Jimmy's dark and secret past.'

Ron joined in grinning.

'So, married with kids, who'd have thought you would let something like that slip ...'

But the laughter died quickly and Ron and Danny looked at each other, then both looked down, away from Jimmy. It was Ron who finally looked up and spoke. There was no laughter at the table now.

'Sorry, mate, I wasn't thinking. No offence intended.'

Jimmy looked at his watch again.

'None taken, lads, none taken, but the way I look at it, it's best to let the past alone. Then maybe it will let you alone.' He stood up. 'See you.'

He left the table, put the bottle and glass on the bar, nodded to the barman, and walked out. The barman didn't respond but gave Jimmy's back a half-angry look as he left. Then he looked at the glass and bottle. Why did the Englishman do that? Collecting glasses, clearing tables, was his job. What was the reason? What was he trying to do, avoid giving a tip? But it couldn't be that because he did leave tips. The suspicion natural to the Roman mind lasted as long as it took for Jimmy to leave the bar. Then the barman went back to his paper, pointedly leaving the bottle and glass where they were.

Ron looked sheepishly at Danny.

'God almighty, that was a bloody gash thing to come out with.' Danny nodded. If Jimmy had kids then he'd been married, and if he'd been married his wife was dead. Only a widower would have been accepted by Duns College to train

3

for the Catholic priesthood. 'We should have known. I tell you, mate, I felt like the floor should just open up and swallow the pair of us. I'll have to do better than that.'

'We both will.' There was silence for a moment. 'I tell you what, Ron, I didn't think it would be so hard.'

'Hard?'

'Not the study, the book stuff, I expected that, and it's not the discipline. It's what you have to become, the person you have to try and be, for others. I don't know if I can do that.'

Ron's natural cheerfulness reasserted itself.

'Come on, sure you can, we all can. You've just got to give it time. The main thing is to learn, that's why we're here. You learn by listening, you learn by reading, and you learn by your mistakes. You get better and that's the way you get where you're going.'

'Maybe so, but those mistakes hurt people, like we hurt Jimmy just now and sometimes the damage a mistake does is a lot worse and whoever gets hurt can't just get up and walk away.' The big man spoke as someone talking from painful, personal experience so the Australian stayed silent and let him talk. 'There's a price for everything, I found that out a long time ago, and I don't want other people having to pay too high a price just so I can do my learning.'

Ron thought about it.

'But it can't be helped, can it? Other people always pay the price one way or another.'

'I suppose so.'

Ron finished his beer.

'Another coffee?'

Danny pushed his cup away.

'God, no, I'm getting so I hate the filthy stuff. One is plenty.'

'Why not have a beer then?'

Danny looked at him; somehow it had suddenly turned into that sort of day.

'Because it wouldn't be a beer and it wouldn't stop at one and the price would be more than I would want anyone to pay.'

Ron had been an accountant in a firm of solicitors and was

not in any sense worldly wise, but the big man's words were not lost on him.

'Bloody hell, it's a day for finding out about people, I'll say that. Jimmy's lost a wife and you ...'

But he let the rest of it hang in the air.

'So I drink tea when I can get it and coffee when I can't,' the big smile came back, 'and I'm still trying to learn from my mistakes.'

They got up. Ron put his hand in his pocket, pulled out some coins, and put the payment with a small tip on the table. The barman looked up from his newspaper and nodded to them as they went to the door. They had left everything on the table for him to clear away. They were OK, they were the regulars.

Outside the clear sky was no more than a ribbon of blue between rooftops. Down in the street, on the narrow pavement, there was a permanent semi-gloom. The two men stood for a moment. The afternoon was free of study or lectures, it was theirs with no calls on their time. By unspoken consent they turned away from the traffic and bustle of the Corso and went the other way, towards the spring sunshine and the trees at the bottom end of the street. They'd walk beside the Tiber where it would be warm, bright, and quiet and Rome would be looking its best.

'I wonder what the rector wanted to see Jimmy about?'

'Who knows?'

And they set off, not tourists, but certainly not Romans. An odd couple.

TWO

Jimmy had also walked towards the Tiber. His most direct route would have been the Corso Vittorio Emanuele II which led to the Vatican City but it was too busy for the walk to be pleasant so he made his way through shady, narrow side streets until he came out at the Ponte Mazzini. He crossed the river which ran below him between high stone walls and broad footpaths created in homage to the Seine in Paris. The road above the river was tree-lined, quiet, and almost free of traffic, but not far away in front of him was the main road where the noise and bustle began again. He slowed his pace. What was it the rector wanted to see him about? It wasn't time for the routine monthly meeting and he couldn't think of anything that had happened which would require another appointment. He put the question out of his mind and busied himself with thoughts on a different matter, one with which he was familiar – pain.

It was hard to believe that some chance remark, like the one Ron had made in the bar, could suddenly rip open an emotional wound and make it feel as if all the hard work of healing had been wasted. The pain just flooded back. He dealt with it in the only way he could, the way the kind old Irish priest in Mayo had shown him. He accepted it. He knew he deserved it, so he didn't try to fight it. A few short years ago this pain of loss and guilt could combine so that he came close to self-destruction,

7

now a humble acceptance kept the worst of his demons at bay. His mind strayed to his theological studies; he let it, it helped.

All his life he'd heard the stories of how Jesus cured people possessed by evil spirits, first at school then on Sundays at Mass. As a child he'd enjoyed them, been impressed and a little frightened that evil spirits could get inside you somehow. As an adult he'd found such stories vaguely annoying when read out at church alongside the eternal truths enshrined in the Gospels. He sometimes wondered how the Church could mix the real Jesus and real miracles with such long-dead superstitious crap.

He no longer wondered.

Now he knew it wasn't superstition and it wasn't crap. The demons of self-destruction were very real. On arriving to study in Rome one of his first New Testament essays had been on the miracles of Jesus and he had drawn high praise for his understanding of the destructive power of inner demons. For a brief period he was regarded as a possible scholar, even asked out for a drink by a Rome-based English Dominican. But that drink and subsequent essays quickly put him back where he belonged, among the plodders.

His brain shifted again. Pain.

Why was the pain of Ron's remark so much harder to bear, so much harder to deal with, than any physical pain? As a child he had learned that it was possible to control physical pain inflicted from the outside, to feel the fist or the boot but go to a place deep inside yourself where you could hide, where physical feelings were somehow numbed or suspended. He had had to use the lesson many times himself and, as a policeman, made sure others couldn't find such a place as he questioned them in a cell or influenced their thinking in some stinking back alley. Yes, many times, too many. But with this pain he could find no place to hide, nowhere was free of it, when it came it possessed him.

Pain.

You never got to the bottom of pain. However bad it was you knew it could get worse. Of one thing he was certain, this pain wasn't something you could beat or hide from or overcome by your own efforts. The best that could be hoped for was to accept it, live with it, and ultimately find forgiveness. If forgiveness ever came.

Suddenly he realised he had stopped and was leaning on the low parapet, and gazing down into the brown water. It had rained heavily two days ago and the river was moving quickly, muddy and swirling. He stood up and looked towards the traffic on the next bridge. What the hell did it matter? He was who he was, what his past had made him. Now he had to make the best of it, what else was there? He smiled to himself. Nothing, there was nothing else. A pretty young woman was passing and smiled back at him, thinking his smile had been meant for her. She carried on and Jimmy watched her. Slim, in a light blue dress with long dark hair and high heels. Going to work or to meet a boyfriend. Someone with a life before them, things to do, people to meet, and places to go. Yet she had noticed him and smiled. That was nice, fortuitous, a piece of uncomplicated human contact. He turned and set off; the young woman had lifted him.

The quiet road ended at a bridge carrying one of Rome's main roads which, having crossed the Tiber, carried on for about a hundred metres then went into a big tunnel which swallowed its four lanes. Jimmy walked to the tunnel; once inside he lost all ability to think as his head filled with the traffic noise echoing and bouncing off the walls. After about four hundred metres he turned off the footpath and went down into a pedestrian underpass. It came out on the far side of the main road where a flight of steps took him up, back into the sunlight and out onto a wide piazza. Facing him at the end of the piazza were the massive walls and dome of St Peter's Basilica with the columns of St Peter's Square fanning out from it.

Jimmy began to walk across the piazza. On his right was an elegant hotel where people, mostly tourists, were sitting at tables, talking and drinking, soaking up the sunshine and the atmosphere. On the opposite side was a large, slab-like building which showed the world a blank, ochre wall topped by a shallow, red, pantiled roof. This was the Palazzo del Sant'Uffizio, the beginning of the Vatican and home to the

Congregation of the Doctrine of the Faith. An innocent-sounding name until you were told it used to be called the Holy Office, and before that, the Inquisition. At the far end of the Palazzo the Renaissance ended abruptly and the stuccoed walls gave way to a high, steel security fence in the middle of which were two gates. Behind the fence to the side of the gates was an equally modern and ugly one-storey set of offices. These necessities of modern civilisation stood in the space between the Palazzo and St Peter's Basilica and unashamedly jarred with everything around them as if to announce to the world, "don't be fooled by all the history, pageant, and beauty that surrounds you; we are armed and dangerous".

Jimmy arrived at the gateway where two Swiss Guards were on duty. Even after eight months in Rome he still thought they looked ridiculous in their striped red, blue, and yellow uniforms, dark floppy berets, and knee-length pantaloons. Although they looked more suited to a carnival he recognised at once the faces under the berets and the look their eyes had in them. These were soldiers, guards, and they took their job very seriously. He gave his name and the name of his rector. One of the guards went to the office inside the gate where his name was checked against a list and his face checked against a photo he had had to supply on arrival at the College. He was then waved through to the office where he was electronically swept, signed in, and given his pass. The guards' uniforms might be quaint but the security certainly wasn't.

He walked up the wide cobbled road between St. Peter's and the Palazzo towards a complex of equally ancient buildings that stood behind the Basilica. This was the Vatican no tourists saw, where the work got done, where the lives and souls of over a billion Catholics world-wide were monitored, influenced, and guided.

Why did the rector want to see him? Not a slap on the wrist. He hadn't put a foot wrong since he came to Rome, and he was sure the rector couldn't have found out anything about London … at least he was almost sure. He was being careful, but these days he knew he made mistakes. He had made one back in the bar with Ron and Danny. He had told them something about himself and they had laughed and the pain had come again.

Pain.

It always came back to pain.

Jimmy stopped outside a small side entrance to one of the big old buildings. Here an office was made available to the Duns College rector when one of its students was in training. Jimmy paused. He wanted to clear his mind before any interview began.

I can't put any of it right, I can't bring any of them back, and I can't change what I was or what I did. This is how it is now and this is what I've chosen. He looked at the ancient black door. Behind it, in an office on the top floor, the rector of the College waited. He looked at his watch. He was dead on time. Unbidden, a question forced itself into his head. What the fuck am I doing here?

But he didn't stand and think about it because he knew the answer. He knew exactly why he was there.

THREE

'Come in.'

The Duns College rector who answered Jimmy's knock was unique among the administrators of Institutions in Rome preparing men for the Catholic priesthood. She was black. No one had expected Professor Pauline McBride to take any pride or pleasure in her appointment when it had been announced. No one ever did. On the rare occasion of a Duns student being accepted for training the College appeared, Brigadoon-like, from nowhere. Once brought back to life it consisted of a temporary office, a temporary phone line, some headed notepaper, the student, and a rector who served on a part-time basis until training was finished at which point Duns College and its rector once again disappeared.

The post, though honorary, was not regarded as an honour, it was the "black spot" of Catholic academic life in Rome and when rumours of a Duns student circulated senior staff lived uneasily until the blow had fallen elsewhere. In the case of Professor McBride it was widely assumed that she would resent more deeply than most what had been done to her. After all, strictly speaking she should never even have been considered for the post. She was not a senior staff member of one of the many educational and training institutions run by the Catholic Church. She was, when not having her time wasted by Duns business, a senior member on the faculty of the Collegio Principe, founded in 1519 by Cesare Borgia to study of the relationship between Religion, Politics, and Power. The Collegio Principe, as a secular institute, had never been on the traditional rota from which Duns rectors were drawn. The consensus as to why she had allowed herself to be "persuaded" was that she had become a new and useful statistic. The Vatican had taken the opportunity, when it arose, to rectify an increasingly awkward point of political correctness. It could now point to a black female seminary college rector on its official list of senior appointments. Progress in racial equality and gender justice with the minimum of nuisance. The Vatican way.

The rector's office was a small room on a narrow, badly lit, top-floor corridor. Most of its limited space was occupied by a large, ugly desk. The bulb hanging from the ceiling had no shade and glowed weakly, shedding as much despondency as light. The single window was grimy and closed. There was no carpet on the floorboards and the walls and ceiling had been painted a slightly bilious green. In the glory-glory days of this imposing building the whole top floor would have been where the most lowly servants slept.

Despite everything, however, the rector liked the room, it suited her mood when she had to come and make use of it.

Professor McBride had an open laptop on the desk when Jimmy entered on which she continued working, ignoring him. He was glad to be able to stand for a few minutes, the wait would let him get his breath back from climbing the several flights of stairs which took you from the grandeur of the downstairs rooms to these garrets in the roof. The rector finally closed the laptop and nodded to the chair on the other side of the desk.

'Sit down, please.'

From their very first meeting she had reminded Jimmy of the headmistress of his primary school whom he remembered as a thoroughly unpleasant woman, though a nun. The resemblance seemed particularly pronounced today. Jimmy sat down on the hard upright chair while the rector busied herself slipping her

14

computer into a carrying case which she then pushed to one side of the desk. She smiled a palpably false greeting.

'It is bad enough that each month I must be dragged away from important and relevant work to waste my time discussing with you your supposed progress. I do not blame you, you understand, I merely point it out. I always think honesty by far the best policy in relationships, be they personal, political, or whatever else.' The accent was American; so was the air of superiority. For some reason Jimmy had never liked Americans; he didn't know why. He just didn't. 'Do you know what this meeting is about?'

Jimmy shook his head. How was he supposed to know? He had just been given a message to be here.

'No idea.'

'Really?'

Jimmy had the distinct impression that she didn't believe him. They both sat in silence. Professor McBride stared at him as if she were waiting for him to break down under her steady gaze and confess what this meeting was all about. She would have a long wait.

So, thought Jimmy, a meeting but apparently not set up by the rector even though it was going to take place in her office. Strange.

Despite the way she was looking at him Professor McBride wasn't waiting for any sort of confession. She was filling in the time. She had been asked to get James Costello, her student, to this office by two o'clock. She had done that. Now she waited and, with nothing else to look at, she looked at Jimmy. There was a definite air about him, if not of criminality, then an intangible something that justified mistrust. An interesting man.

'Has anyone questioned you about your papers recently, Mr Costello? In fact, have you been approached or questioned by anybody about anything?'

Jimmy shook his head.

'No. Nobody's questioned me about anything, not officially anyway.'

'Unofficially?'

'Only friends.'

'And what were they interested in?'

'Me. My background. Who I was, where I came from.'

'And who exactly are these friends?'

'Students. Two men I study with.'

'I see.' She waited. 'And did you tell them about yourself?'

'No.'

'Good.'

And there she fell silent again.

For some reason, thought Jimmy, she seemed pleased with him, with what he had said.

'Would it matter?'

'Would what matter?'

'If I had been approached, questioned?'

She seemed a little put out by his question.

'I am your rector, Mr Costello, I am supposed to take an interest in not only your academic progress but your general wellbeing while you are here in Rome.'

'Fine.'

After another few moments' silence Professor McBride looked at her watch. She decided to fill the wait with a little small talk. Her questions had been a mistake, it might have unsettled him and if it had she wanted his mind elsewhere. She did her best to smile.

'I have to tell you, Mr Costello, that if I had played a decisive role in your selection you would not now be here in training. You do not strike me as at all suitable for the priesthood, not even the diocesan priesthood.' She spoke as if being a diocesan priest had about the same standing as being an inmate of San Quentin or Wormwood Scrubs. Jimmy sat and listened. He didn't give a toss what she thought of him. All he wanted was to get on with his studies. 'I know that Duns students are given more latitude in their general oversight because they are men of sufficient independent means to serve the Church without requiring financial support of any kind. Yet if I read your file aright ...' Aright! Jimmy gave an inward smile; what a bloody poser. '... you have only a policeman's pension to live on. I must say I find that a most unusual and questionable circumstance.' She waited for Jimmy to explain.

16

Jimmy didn't dislike the woman as much as she obviously disliked him but he didn't want her as his enemy so he obliged.

'My late wife and I bought our house in London when we first married. After she died I moved away and the house was sold. It was just a small house but it fetched what I thought was an almost ridiculous price. That, with savings and two investments made many years ago, gave me the finance to take up a Duns College place. Satisfied?'

She sniffed. No, it said, she wasn't satisfied. She looked at her watch again. Someone was late.

'Well, Mr Costello, your time may be of no value but mine certainly is, so I intend ...'

But Jimmy never found out what Professor McBride intended because the ancient black phone on the desk wheezed a ringing sound. She picked up the handset, listened, then put it back and looked at Jimmy.

'Apparently you are about to be questioned by a detective from the Rome police. An Inspector Ricci is on his way up. I am to wait and confirm his identity and then leave him here to interview you.'

What the hell did the police want, thought Jimmy, but he made sure that his surprise didn't register on his face and they sat in silence looking at one another until there was a knock at the door.

'Come in.'

The man who came in looked very sharp. Around six feet, well-groomed, middle to late twenties with the physique and good looks of an Italian footballer. He wore a light grey tailored jacket with a faint pinstripe, and faded jeans. He should have looked wrong, top half almost a city suit, bottom half casual, but on him it looked just right. The three buttons at the end of each sleeve were undone and the cuffs slightly flared to show a glimpse of the dark silk lining. The pale yellow shirt was open at the neck showing a very slim silver chain. The wristwatch was white metal too. Light accessories to set off his dark skin and black hair. Designer sunglasses rounded it all off.

Jimmy looked at him: a man of two halves and already he didn't like either of them. If this was a copper he was

17

independently well off, seriously bent, or on some sort of bloody clothes allowance. The inspector took off his sunglasses and gave the office a brief once-over. For a second you got the feeling he feared for the wellbeing of his getup and might walk straight back out. Then he closed the door, switched on a smile, and came to Professor McBride who stood up. His Roman charm brought more light into the room than the window and bulb combined. He was the man you saw in adverts selling style in an aftershave bottle, encouraging young men, and the not-so-young, to spend a lot of money to look like him. They never would.

'Good afternoon, Professor. I am Inspector Ricci; you were expecting me?'

They shook hands.

'Yes, Inspector, several minutes ago.' He kept the smile going, gave a slight shrug, and didn't apologise. 'I wasn't told the reason for this meeting.' She was trying, thought Jimmy, but she couldn't get the same acid tone into her voice for this charming officer that she'd managed so easily with him. 'I have been asked to verify your identity and then leave you with Mr Costello.' The policeman turned and pointed his smile at Jimmy; it was a nice smile. Jimmy made a mental note to be careful of this man when he turned it on. It looked very practised but would work better when he had his sunglasses on because it didn't quite make it into his eyes. The inspector took out a leather warrant card holder and handed it to the rector.

While she examined it he came and held out his hand to Jimmy.

'How do you do, Mr Costello.'

Jimmy stood up for the rector's sake.

'I'm fine, thanks.'

But he waited just long enough before shaking the offered hand for the smile to melt and another look to come into the policeman's face.

Whatever this man wants, thought Jimmy, be sure to get off on the right foot – the wrong one. Make someone dislike you and you're halfway to knowing where you'll stand with him. It wasn't that he particularly wanted to antagonise the policeman, he just didn't want him thinking it was OK to get him summoned to the rector's office for no good reason he could think of.

Professor McBride held out the inspector's warrant card holder.

'Do you want me to wait, Inspector?'

'Thank you, Professor, but that will not be necessary. The matter is purely routine, one or two questions, nothing of importance. I would not want to waste your valuable time.'

'Very well. Goodbye.'

The inspector went to the door and held it open.

The rector picked up the bag from the desk and left.

After the door had closed the inspector went and sat in the rector's chair. It was funny, thought Jimmy, as he sat down on the hard chair, the number of people he had known who believed authority lay in locating your bum in the right chair.

'I suppose you would have known I was a policeman as soon as you saw me, Mr Costello? After all, you were one yourself for many years in London before you decided to give it all up and come here to be a priest.'

His English was excellent and the amount of Italian accent he allowed to remain was just right to go with his appearance and his charm. But Jimmy didn't believe in fairies any more than he believed in charming police inspectors no matter how Italian they sounded, so he made another mental note. If this smarmy bugger needed handling he would almost certainly have to be handled very carefully.

'I didn't take much notice of you but since you ask, no, I wouldn't have taken you for a policeman. You look too expensive.'

He got the false, charming smile again.

'First, Signor Costello ...' there was the briefest of pauses but Jimmy left it at Signor Costello. He didn't want this guy calling him Jimmy and thinking they could get friendly. He'd made sure they started off on the wrong foot and that's where he wanted it to stay, 'I must confirm certain details. You were a policeman in London, yes?'

Jimmy waited long enough for the policemen to be about to

19

ask his question again and then suddenly answered.

'Don't I get to be told what this is all about?' Jimmy looked at the eyes, they registered something – annoyance. That was good.

'Certainly, Mr Costello, as soon as I know the information I have about you is accurate I will explain everything. I assure you it is nothing that you need to worry about.'

No, thought Jimmy, of course it isn't. Why would being pulled in and questioned by a detective inspector worry anybody?

'You were a policeman in London?'

'Yes.'

'What was your department and rank?'

'CID, a sergeant.'

'You took early retirement?'

'Yes.'

'Why was that?'

Jimmy paused, the question wasn't routine so the answer had to be right.

'It was offered to me.'

'Why was it offered?'

'My superiors thought it best.'

'And why was that?'

'Ask them, it was their decision. I didn't say I agreed with them.'

'Would you have agreed with them?'

'They never asked.'

'But if they had?'

'They didn't.'

The policeman stopped for a moment.

'Is there something about your retirement you are unwilling to tell me, Signor Costello? I assure you these questions are purely routine.'

'Of course they are if you say they are. Look, I retired, what else is there to tell? Don't policemen ever retire in Italy?'

'Why are you being so unhelpful, Signor Costello? I merely wish to confirm the information I have been given about you. Your reasons for retirement were not at all problematic, were they?'

'I don't know.'

The inspector registered mock surprise.

'You don't know! How can you say you don't know?'

'I just open my mouth and let the words come out.'

That got a response, the temperature of the inspector's voice dropped a couple of degrees.

'You know very well what I mean, Mr Costello.'

Signor when he's OK, mister when he's pissed off. A small thing but every little helped in this kind of game.

'If I were to speculate out loud about me being problematic I would need to know who felt it was worthwhile to poke their nose into my past, what they were interested in, and why they looked in the first place. If I knew that I might be able to work out whether why I retired would be in any way problematic. For them, that is, it wasn't a problem for me and still isn't.' Jimmy waited, but the inspector didn't seem to have anything to say to he went on. 'Of course even if I knew the who, what, and why it doesn't mean I would tell them what they wanted to know, or tell anybody they sent sniffing around to get the information, even if he was a police inspector.'

He'd finished what he wanted to say, so far as he could, so he waited.

The inspector abandoned the chair and went and stood by the window with his back to Jimmy. The sun was trying its best to shine through but it was always going to be a losing the battle. The policeman took out his sunglasses anyway and put them on. Maybe they helped him to stare at the grime. Or maybe they helped him think. Then he took them off, put them away, and came back to the desk and sat down.

'All right, let's say your retirement is your own affair.'

Jimmy managed his own smile; the Italian accent had completely gone.

'The accent comes and goes, does it? When the rector was here you definitely sounded Italian even if you were speaking English.'

The inspector's smile didn't reappear. That was a good sign, that was progress.

21

'I was born in Glasgow. I lived there until I was twelve, then my family moved to Rome. At university here I studied Modern English Literature and I did a year at Leicester University as part of the Erasmus exchange scheme. The accent is just for window-dressing when I think the occasion benefits from it. It helps put people at their ease if they're being questioned in English by an Italian copper. That OK, Jimmy?' He gave the name a real Glasgow twang. 'That answer your question?'

Jimmy didn't say anything. He hadn't really asked a question. 'Look, I don't want us to get off on the wrong foot and for some reason it seems you do. So how would it be if we stop pissing around and I tell you what this is all about?'

But Jimmy decided he wasn't ready yet for an olive branch. He wanted to be firmly in the driving seat before he …

Suddenly everything changed.

What the hell was he doing? Why was he putting a wall between himself and this man? Why was he still clinging to the old rules? This was Rome, not London. He was in the rector's office, not some bloody Met nick. This wasn't trust no one, like no one, let no one get close or ever know what you're thinking. It wasn't be ready to kick the shit out of them before they kick the shit out of you. It had to have changed. He had to have changed. For Bernie's sake, for the sake of his grandchildren and the few years of happiness they'd given him.

'All right, I'm listening.'

It wasn't easy and it hadn't come out anywhere near friendly, but it was the best he could do under the circumstances. He told himself it was different now and there was no reason to worry if the police came into his life. He told himself he should try to co-operate if he could. He was a priest in training, he should want to help. That was what he told himself.

Unfortunately, he didn't believe himself.

FOUR

'I've been asked to look into the death of a visiting archbishop who died here a couple of years ago. Originally it wasn't regarded as suspicious. Now, well, let's say that it's being treated in some quarters as an open question. I'll be working independently, not in any police capacity; anything I find, if I find anything, will be off the record.' He paused for a second. 'Ask away, this isn't meant to be a monologue.'

Jimmy was angry with himself. Five years out of the job and you get sloppy. You sit at a table with people you hardly know, having a few beers, and you tell them your fucking life story. A copper you've never seen before, with no reason that you know of for talking to you, tells you he's looking into the death of some archbishop and as soon as he opens his mouth there's a question written all over your bloody face.

But then his anger switched off. What the hell? It doesn't matter any more. The Jimmy Costello who would care was dead, he died at a London hospital bedside.

So he asked his question.

'If it's police business why isn't it official?'

'I didn't say the police were involved. I said I'd been asked to look into it.'

Jimmy shook his head.

'No. That one gets right past me.'

23

'As far as the local police or anybody else is concerned I'm on leave pending medical reports.' He grinned. 'Don't worry, what I'm supposed to be suffering from won't be catching.'

Jimmy managed to smile back. There, being like other people wasn't so hard; you just had to make the effort.

'OK, you're a policeman who, at the moment, isn't a policeman. Either way I'm getting interviewed. So, once again, what's it about?'

'I don't know much, just what I've been told and what I could figure out for myself. Not long ago a high-powered but unofficial request got made to a minister. The person who made the request wanted an investigation into this archbishop's death but it had to be strictly off the record, no official police involvement, but a capable officer was to be used. I got told I should go to the ministry, which I did, and got handed the job.'

'Why you?'

The inspector shrugged.

'Someone chose me, I don't know who and I don't know why. All I know is that I got sent to the minister.'

'But you're on sick leave.'

'Someone arranged for me to be able to drop everything by creating a medical report which says I need to be given indefinite leave because I might have something and it may be serious.'

Jimmy was impressed.

'Not such an easy thing to arrange.'

'No, neither is telling a minister to set up an investigation but they both got done.'

'So the sick leave is phoney?'

'No one said as much. I keep in shape but you never know so I get checked. After the last one the doctor was a bit cagey, tests inconclusive, further tests needed. For a while I was worried.'

'I can see how you would be.'

'Then I got sent to see the minister. He knew about my medical and told me I had been given indefinite leave pending the results. While I was on leave he had a job for me.'

'Neat. Somebody took a lot of trouble to choose you.'

'They did.'

'Why? Why you?'

'I don't know. Maybe I'm good.'

'This is a special, a very high-up special if a minister's involved. In my day that would mean a superintendent at the very least and probably Special Branch, not some inspector from the plod squad.'

'Yes, that thought occurred to me as well, so I asked and it was made very clear that the whole thing was off-limits within the police community. Do as you're told and don't ask any more questions. That came from the commissioner himself, which means the original request came from a very powerful source.'

'Like who?'

'I couldn't say for certain, but this is Rome: who could tell a minister to jump through a hoop, fix a medical report, and make the police top brass keep their mouths tight shut and turn a blind eye to one of their own being commandeered?'

'It's your town, not mine.'

'How about the people we're with at the moment?'

'What people.'

'Here.'

The penny dropped.

'The Vatican.'

'The very same.'

Jimmy was even more impressed. The Church, he knew, was powerful and nowhere more so than here within its own city state.

'And the death?'

'As far as the world is concerned Archbishop Francis Xavier Cheng died a perfectly natural death and that's how it will stay.'

'Even if it turns out otherwise?'

'There will never be any official police involvement. I will keep no records and there will no follow-up whatever I turn up. Just my report to the minister. There it ends.'

'I see. It's very high-level and ultra hush-hush, so you naturally arrange to come here and spill the whole thing to a complete outsider, me.' The inspector smiled but didn't say

25

anything. Jimmy envied him his smile, it really worked. He also envied him this case. He was out of it, being a copper was behind him, finished, but that didn't stop his professional interest from being roused. He was interested, that was all, just interested. It didn't have to go anywhere. 'OK. I don't understand but at this point I guess that's how you mean it to be, so keep going. For the time being I'm still listening.'

'Archbishop Cheng was seventy-three years old and of the last thirty years twenty-two had been spent in one Chinese prison or another. He was released five years ago and placed under house arrest for one year, after which he was allowed to resume his ministry. Just over two years ago he was given permission to come to Rome to see the pope. He had been here about three weeks when he became ill and died. It was unexpected but a seventy-year-old man who's been in Chinese prisons for most of the last thirty years and still works a fourteen-hour day might be expected to have a pretty tenuous grip on life.'

'So why wait two years and then decide the death needs looking into?'

The inspector shrugged.

'Who can say? The Vatican does things in its own way and its own time. Maybe they know something now they didn't know then.'

'There was an autopsy?'

'Of course.'

'Did it turn up anything?'

'Yes and no. In the normal course of events the autopsy would have been routine. Death was caused by asphyxia, suffocation brought on by respiratory depression. His breathing failed. He was a tired, frail old man and that sort of thing happens to tired, frail old men so you'd expect a quick autopsy to confirm natural causes, end of story. But it was anything but quick or routine, it was unusually thorough.'

'Because?'

'My guess is the Chinese. They would want to know exactly what had been the cause of death. The autopsy showed that he'd been badly knocked around over the years but they'd looked

26

after him during his year's house arrest, made sure he got back to being as physically OK as was possible after what he'd been through. For whatever inscrutable reason it seems they wanted him fit and back at work. Maybe they were beginning to trust him, perhaps even getting ready to work with him in some way. Whatever their motives, they'd got as far as letting him come to Rome, and for the Chinese that's trusting a Catholic archbishop a lot.'

'You make it sound like you're an expert on China.'

'Not me, I got it all from someone who's a serious China watcher. He says maybe Cheng was a try-out as a secure, unofficial contact between Beijing, the underground Catholic Church in China, and the Vatican. Cheng had never been a member of the government-approved Church and his time in prison proved his loyalty to the pope. He would have been ideal for some sort of go-between role.'

The more Jimmy listened the more he felt himself being drawn in. He told himself it wasn't what he wanted, not what he'd come to Rome to do, but a lifetime's work wasn't so easily set aside. Part of him wanted to get up and walk out, to leave, to say it was none of his business and he wasn't interested. But his legs didn't move. He'd left it too late, he'd listened and he was interested. It was in his head now so he set his mind to work. It was unofficial which was bad and it was high level which made it worse. Unofficial meant the rules didn't apply. With the rules you got some sort of protection, and although rules could get broken they couldn't be totally ignored. And anything involving the real high-ups meant the people pulling the strings and giving the orders were fireproof. It was always the foot soldiers, the expendable ones, the inspectors and sergeants who got their balls crushed and then got screwed and mostly they never got to know the real truth about whatever it was they were getting screwed for.

That part of his mind which had wanted him to leave was almost shouting at him – have nothing to do with it, it's none of your business, all you'll do is get fucked. For God's sake get up and walk away while you can. You're not a copper now, you're a priest in training, you want to put all that behind you, you came here to change, to be someone people can turn to for help. Someone who knows good from evil and does the right thing and does it willingly. All true of course and it all made sense. But another part of his mind said, for God's sake you want this, this is what you do, what you're good at, not pissing about pretending to be a priest. That will never happen and you know it. Stop sniffing at the fucking thing and get on with it.

FIVE

'Did the autopsy turn up anything?'

'They found a trace of some sort of opioid.'

The inspector pulled out a small notebook which he flicked open.

'The nearest they could get was buprenorphine, an opioid analgesic which can bring on respiratory depression. No good to kill anyone who was fit and healthy, to do that the dose would have to be massive.'

'But a frail old man?'

The inspector nodded.

'If you had it in a form you could administer without the victim knowing, in a drink or in his food. It's not conclusive. The trace was faint and he may well have been given morphine-related drugs for pain before coming to Rome. Like I said, the autopsy showed he'd been gone over more than a few times in prison. He would almost certainly have had enough residual pain to need some sort of medication. That could account for the trace.'

'Is there anything else, anything new that's turned up?'

'Not that I've been told about.'

'So, you've got an outside possibility of cause of death and that's all you've got.'

'Apart from all the cloak and dagger business that got me

dragged into it.'

'OK. Where do I fit in?'

'Yes, now we get to you. If it is the Vatican pulling strings then I don't think they altogether trust me. It's nothing personal, you understand, it's not even professional. It's just that the Vatican doesn't trust anyone who they regard as an outsider. I think they want one of their own alongside me but it has to be someone who knows how these things work. Purple socks won't be any good on this.'

'Not a monsignor then?'

'No, a policeman, and it just so happens they have one to hand training to be a priest. You're not perfect but you're damn close. If I hadn't checked on you I'd say you were some sort of set-up.' He stopped as if a thought had struck him. 'You're not a plant, are you, Jimmy, not already a part of this?'

'Would I tell you if I was?'

That got a laugh.

'You might, if you didn't want to be dragged into it any more than I did.'

'True, but as it happens this is the first I've heard of it so, unless I was lured to Rome under false pretences, I'm exactly what I seem to be, an ex-copper who's training to be a priest.'

'In that case, you're here and can be made available so you get the job.'

'Do I get a say?'

'I didn't, and remember how high up this has to go, a minister then beyond. You want to stick two fingers up at that sort of pull?' Jimmy didn't answer. 'What would you have done if this had happened in London when you were on the Force?'

Jimmy knew the answer to that one; if the push was strong enough you rolled with it. Anyway, he'd already asked and answered the question himself so why not say it out loud and make it official?

'I'd do what you did, I'd go along with it.'

'Fine, so you're on board?'

'I suppose so.'

'I report directly to the minister's office via his senior aide. The minister passes anything I give him to whoever made the original request. But I think they want to be sure that I give the minister everything I get. They want me watched every step of the way so they're having their own trained detective watch me. Either they were very lucky or I've been underestimating the power of prayer all these years. Just when they needed it they can put their hands on a detective sergeant from the Metropolitan Police who, because he's training for the priesthood, will do exactly what he's told. If it isn't a set up what would you say that was, good luck or divine intervention?' Inspector Ricci grinned; it wasn't like his previous smile, this was genuine, you could see it in his eyes. Jimmy shrugged his shoulders, he didn't find the situation humorous. 'Either way, you're going to be my watchdog. What's it feel like to be on the staff of the Vatican already? Unofficial and unacknowledged, but fast work for a new boy who's only been in Rome five minutes.'

Looking at the friendly, grinning face and letting what Ricci had said sink in Jimmy felt a knot of suspicion form in his stomach. It was all too neat, too convenient. Things didn't fall into place like that unless they were very carefully arranged. Maybe he should have second thoughts. Did he really want to go back? Doubt, that deadly enemy of decision, crept back into his mind. Even if he wanted to do it, was he still any good after five years out of it? And did he want to run blind? He knew almost nothing, only what he's been told in this room.

'If I agree.'

Inspector Ricci's grin changed to a smile, his 'nice' smile.

'I strongly advise you to agree. I get the feeling you wouldn't like what would happen if you didn't.'

The delivery was slow, clear, and flat, and the point was taken. Jimmy was glad. This he knew about. This he could deal with. It was still his territory even after all those years; it had always been his territory.

'Is that threat just from you or is it from those friends who are so fucking powerful and mysterious?'

Ricci's smile disappeared. He'd known plenty of dangerous, violent men, men you were wise to be frightened of. Now he recognised one of them sitting opposite him. Suddenly, there it was. Christ, how did someone like that turn up in a priests' bloody training college?

Jimmy sat looking straight at the policeman's eyes. No one seeing him sitting there could have guessed that inside his head there was a voice, his own voice, screaming at him, "I told you so, you stupid bastard. Get out of this or do you actually want to be fucked?"'

Suddenly the voice stopped. With an almighty effort Jimmy switched it off. He tried to relax. Then the voice in his head, his own voice, but this time different, came back. "God in your mercy, help me, a sinner. Bernadette, pray for me. Michael, pray for me."' Jimmy's eyes became weak and slightly unfocused. His voice when he spoke was quiet, almost defeated. Whatever it was had gone back into the dark place it still lived.

'I'm sorry, Inspector, that came out wrong. What I meant was, will you please explain to me what you mean?'

Ricci didn't answer. He was too busy thinking. Opposite him was a man saying sorry. An ordinary sort of man whose face and body looked crumpled, like his clothes. A tired man with sad eyes. Yet seconds ago something had looked out from those same eyes. Something which had frightened him. Then it was gone, and here was this, this what? He had been told to expect a retired detective sergeant from the London Metropolitan CID, a man with a clean record who had been given early retirement due to ill-health brought on by stress. A man who probably drove a desk for his last few years of service. A man it would be easy for the Vatican to push around, to bully and browbeat if he didn't get into line quickly enough and do what he was told. That was all he had meant but his words had summoned up the thing that had looked at him out of those now weary eyes. This was some sort of Jekyll and Hyde. Ricci didn't understand how that worked but he understood very clearly he didn't want anything to do with it. He didn't want this man anywhere near him while he was working. In fact he didn't want him anywhere near him at all. If ever anyone was, this man was unstable, perhaps even psychotic. He got up.

'I'm sorry if you thought I was threatening you, Signor Costello. My words were perhaps ill-chosen. All I meant was that a refusal would upset whoever put your name forward. I felt that you, as a priest in training, would regret disappointing anyone in the Vatican. However,' the accent was back and so was the smile, 'I can see that you are unhappy about getting involved in this.' He moved round the desk. 'I will inform the minister's office that you do not wish to be further involved.' He put out his hand. 'Thank you for your time, Signor Costello.'

Jimmy got up.

'I didn't say …'

'It's quite all right, Signor Costello. I understand completely.'

They shook hands.

'*Buongiorno.*'

The inspector left the office. He didn't close the door.

Jimmy slumped back into the chair. He had tried and he had failed, failed miserably. The old Jimmy was still there, he hadn't changed, except on the outside; he never would.

SIX

A week later Rome held one of its glittering evenings. Old men were looking their wealthiest and young men their most beautiful. Women of all ages and none sparkled and shimmered. Power, wealth, and beauty mingled easily. The setting had all the magnificence that the occasion deserved, only innocence was absent, not wanted nor missed. In one of the brightly lit, crowded rooms, with his back to the wall in all senses of that phrase, the minister listened sullenly, his face that of a naughty boy caught out by his mother in some more-than-usually humiliating practice.

'My dear Minister ...'

The minister looked down at the champagne glass in his hand. He loathed the stuff, why did he continue to drink it? Once, about a million years ago, when he knew what happiness was, or at least how to enjoy himself, he had liked good champagne. But then he had also liked sex with amusing women and passionate men. He had liked driving fast, expensive cars, and eating fine food at the best restaurants. How and why had he let it all go? How had it all come to this? He looked up and tried to assert himself.

'Really, Monsignor, as the minister I hardly think ...'

The sleek, plump man, wearing a Roman collar and black suit, fell silent and waited with an exaggerated air of respect.

But the minister's words petered out so the sleek monsignor resumed.

'The inspector has already told the Englishman what he himself has been told and what he has already learned from looking at the autopsy. He may not want him in the investigation but what the inspector wants is not the issue. To allow the Englishman to be left out now is, I think you will agree, not a viable option.' He made a deprecating gesture with the hand not holding his champagne. 'However, being no more than a humble servant of the Church, I defer, of course, to you, Minister. If, having received the inspector's considered opinion of the Englishman's suitability, you have decided to accept his advice and dispense with him then you have made your decision. It would be presumptuous in the extreme for me to try and persuade you to alter it. That being the case I will convey your decision to …'

The minister jerked to life, splashing a small amount of warmish champagne from his glass onto one of his patent black shoes.

'No, no, Monsignor, that will not be necessary, no final decision has been made. But now, having listened to you, having weighed your arguments, having …' the monsignor waited. The minister looked despairingly past the prelate for the help he knew would not come. 'I can see that you are right. It's just that …'

And still the monsignor waited, refusing to end his misery. Having pulled the wings off the fly he denied it an easy end by stepping on it. He was, he knew, a cruel man by nature, but in this case his cruelty was not at all sinful for it had a perfectly valid motive. The minister had to be reminded that he couldn't make decisions as if this matter rested solely in his hands. He was quite free to run Italy in whatever way he and others like him saw fit. But in certain matters he was a man under authority like everyone else. The words of the New Testament were as true today as they ever were, "those who are not with us are against us". For Holy Mother Church there could be no neutrals, no middle ground for the uncommitted to occupy.

The minister finally looked at him and smiled the weak smile that was the white flag of surrender.

'Why don't you go and fuck yourself, you pious piece of useless dog shit?'

His whole being was crying out to shout those words, to shout them out so loudly that the whole glittering, pointless, bloody circus would be brought to a stunned silence. He knew that once, long ago, when he was still a man with balls and not a political eunuch, he might have actually done it. But now his words, when they came, continued in the hushed tones they had both been using and were heard only by himself and the priest.

'Of course, Monsignor, you are right as always. I will see to it.'

'Tomorrow?'

The last turn of the screw.

'Of course.'

The unconditional surrender.

'Thank you, Minister. Now, if you'll excuse me. I am rather busy tonight.'

The prelate turned and left, moving on to other business. From across the room the minister's closest aide began to hurry through the throng to see if he could breathe any life back into the corpse which was still standing, still with its back to the wall.

SEVEN

At the same table in the same bar Jimmy and Ron had beer in front of them, Danny his usual cup of coffee.

'Danny, I just don't see the problem. Jesus was human and divine at the same time, sort of half and half.'

'A mild and bitter God.'

Ron looked at Jimmy, puzzled.

'Come again?'

'Mild and bitter, it was a pub drink years ago. You mixed half a pint of mild beer with a half of bitter beer.' Ron's face remained blank. 'Mild never got to Oz though, did it?'

Danny took a small sip from his cup.

'It never got to Jamaica either. I thought you were quoting from some poem. "A mild and bitter God", sounds like it might be George Herbert, someone like that.'

Jimmy tried out his smile. He was getting better at it.

'You know your trouble? You think too much, always looking for more meanings.' He took a drink. 'Sometimes it's just about the beer.'

Danny looked at Ron. Ron took his cue.

'I wish it was always just about the beer. I reckon life would be OK if all you had to worry about was where your next pint was coming from.'

Danny grinned. Well done, Ron, the mild and bitter thing

hadn't been much of a joke, but from Jimmy any joke was a good sign and deserved encouragement.

'If we take Jimmy's metaphor of a mild and bitter God, my problem, Ron, is that the words of the Mass say that He came to share in our humanity. Let's say human beings are the mild beer.'

'So?'

'So does that mean that prior to his birth on earth Jesus was all bitter beer? No mild? In no way human? Did his humanity, the mild, only begin at the Incarnation, his birth?'

Ron thought about it for a minute.

'I suppose so. No, hang on, that's not right, at least I don't think that's right.'

Danny laughed.

'See what I mean now?'

'Not really, I'm not like you, I like to keep things simple so I don't ask the awkward questions. The way I look at it, if you're never likely to get asked the question why bother to find the answer?'

'But what if you ask yourself the question?'

Ron was stumped and fell silent but Jimmy took over.

'You know what your trouble is, Danny?'

'You already told me, I think too much.'

'That's right. You're cursed with an enquiring mind. Maybe it comes from having been a copper.'

'You were a copper too, so how come you don't have an enquiring mind?'

'I was a lot of things, but now I'm just a student. I keep my head down, do as I'm told, and don't ask any questions except the ones I'm told to ask.'

Danny took a small sip of his espresso.

'Let the dead past bury its dead, eh? Well it's not a bad rule when you get to our age. None of us is without a few things we'd rather leave behind, and with some of us maybe it's more than a few.'

Ron decided it was time to change the subject.

'Do you miss the wife, Jimmy?'

Jimmy looked at him. What sort of a bloody question was

that? But he kept any hint of anger out of his voice. Ron might be stupid, but he meant no harm.

'Every day, Ron, only every day.'

'You know, you've opened up more in the past three weeks than you did in the previous eight months. Ever since you got hauled in to see your rector, it's as if you're a different bloke. It must have been a real heart to hearter, that meeting.'

Ron wasn't really stupid, thought Jimmy; he was just a simple soul. He'd probably be a good priest because he was too thoughtless to notice what havoc a few careless words could do. He just got on with it and said whatever came into his mind.

'It was an interesting meeting in a way. I finally found out I should try and see things differently, let myself go a bit. Let people know who I am, who I want to be.'

Danny looked at him with serious eyes.

'Ron's right, you're more open now, more trusting. I think that must have been a big thing to take on. I hope it works for you, I really hope it does.' He took another sip of his coffee, but the unspoken doubt in Danny's words brought a period of silence. Then a fashion-plate of a man walked into the bar and came over to their table. He took off his designer sunglasses, slipped them into the top pocket of his short-sleeved shirt, and smiled. He had a nice smile. The three men looked at him but he looked only at Jimmy.

'Hello, Jimmy. Got a minute, outside?'

There was no accent today. Jimmy paused; let Danny and Ron know this was a copper or leave it as an English bloke who wanted a word? Leave it.

'Sure.' Jimmy stood up. 'Be seeing you, lads.' He finished the beer in his glass and pushed the half-full bottle across to Ron. 'There you are, Ron, a bonus for you.' He took his glass to the bar and nodded to the barman. The barman ignored the nod and gave his back the same suspicious look as Jimmy walked to the door where Adonis in a silk shirt and chinos waited. Outside the bar Ricci put on his sunglasses and they began walking.

'Tell me something, are you protected by God Almighty or do you just make it look that way?'

'Where are we going, to your nick?'

41

'No, I'm on sick leave, remember? I'm supposed to be getting ready to be told I'm dying. I can't swan in and out of nicks. We're going somewhere to talk, a bar, not far away but not one like that dump back there. Somewhere comfortable and quiet where you're going to tell me all about yourself.'

'Fine, if you want to be bored to death that's all right by me so long as you pick up the tab. The way you look I would guess we're going somewhere expensive.'

'That shouldn't worry a Duns student, not a real Duns student. And that's what we're going to talk about, not Jimmy Costello the priest in training, but another Jimmy Costello, the one who peeped out at me in the rector's office. My guess is that's the one who gets himself looked after by God Almighty.' He paused and took a sideways glance at Jimmy walking beside him. 'Or maybe it's the Prince of Darkness. Either way, we'll talk about that Jimmy Costello.'

Jimmy didn't like it. He had a strong suspicion that this was where it started to get messy. What should he do? Co-operate, try and be the new Jimmy, tell the truth and take the consequences or do what all his life had been the sensible thing and pull down the shutters? What was it Danny had said in the bar? Let the dead past bury its dead. It must be a quote. He was a clever bugger, Danny, probably read a lot. Jimmy decided not to think about it. Time enough to decide what to do when he found out what Ricci knew, what he wanted, and what he wanted it for. So they walked on, a crumpled, middle-aged man and a smart, youthful one.

Another odd couple.

EIGHT

The Campo del Fiori wasn't the Piazza Navona. There were no film stars, Serie A footballers, or big-time celebrities. It was a square almost hidden away from the main tourist routes and today it was crowded with brightly covered market stalls selling fresh produce to Roman housewives. Around the sides of the square were the sun umbrellas and awnings under which the customers of the bars and restaurants could sit at their tables and sip their cocktails. These bars and restaurants were where locals with plenty of money hung out. The matrons at market stalls haggling over vegetables and fruit were separated from this serious money by flimsy, decorative fences. This was where Roman style put on a display, but only for its own amusement. In one corner, gazing out at the scene, was a bronze statue of a man with a tonsure wearing a long cloak. Some long-ago Dominican friar who had been burned to death for the unforgivable sin of being right at the wrong time. Eventually giving him a statue on the spot where he went up in flames was the Catholic Church's way of making amends.

Ricci was welcomed as a valued customer when they went inside his bar. Jimmy looked around. It obviously wasn't the sort of spot that got crowded during the day so it must be more of a night-time place. Or maybe it was the sun. Drink inside on a sunny day and you missed all the action of the market, you saw no one and, more importantly, no one saw you. Ricci went to a quiet table and ordered a campari and soda. Jimmy asked for a beer.

The waiter named a few foreign brands.

'Any beer, whatever the locals drink.'

The waiter gave him a look, the sort of look he might give to a bag-snatcher who'd come in to chance his arm. The idea of beer-drinking locals at these tables obviously wounded his deepest feelings but, for Ricci's sake, he managed to force politeness into his voice.

'Certainly, sir.'

He left and the two men sat in silence until the drinks arrived. When they came Jimmy noticed the beer was imported, Tuborg. Ricci picked up his glass.

'I'm going tell you a mystery story, Jimmy, then you're going make sense of it all for me. Cheers.' He took a small drink. 'When I met you last time I didn't like you; you were not what I had been led to expect. I was told I'd meet an ex-London CID sergeant, someone who had taken early retirement due to stress. Someone who had come to Rome to train to be a priest. What I got was you, and like I said, the you I got I didn't like. I really didn't want you to work with me so I went to the minister's aide and told him you were not suitable, that you were not what I had been expecting and not what the investigation wanted or needed, that I thought you might be seriously unstable in moments of stress or pressure. I also told him I strongly suspected you were not what you seemed, that your background would almost certainly bear further looking into. Everything seemed fine. The aide agreed that this investigation was too sensitive for any chances to be taken. I could drop you and the minister would arrange that we find a new man. So I got on with things. Then, one week later, I get pulled in by the minister himself and slapped on the wrist very hard and told that you're as pure as the driven snow and that you're on this case whether I liked it or not. All that was required of me was to follow orders and do the job I had been given and under no circumstances was I ever to mention to anyone my concerns over you or your past.' He took another

44

sip. 'OK, so far?' Jimmy took a drink and nodded. The beer was good. 'Now comes the interesting part. Remember I told you I did a year at Leicester University on the Erasmus programme? Well, while I was there I met a student called Billy Campbell from Glasgow, like me. It turned out that Billy had lived quite near to where I grew up. I never knew him as a kid because he wasn't a Catholic, so we went to different schools. But both coming from the same place we started to meet and talked quite a lot. He was doing Art History. He was a good artist, could have gone to art school, but he knew he wasn't good enough to be a professional so he chose university. We became real friends, in fact I went to more Art History lectures than I went to English ones. Something else we had in common was that we were both interested in going into the police when we graduated. As it turned out we both did. We've kept in touch ever since, even visited each other, and he's been as successful in the Met. as I have here. I phoned him after I'd been hauled over the coals by the minister. I didn't like what had happened. Someone wanted to put you next to me even if that was the last place I wanted you to be. Why was that? What was so special about Jimmy Costello? So I asked my mate Billy to nose about the Met. records and maybe ask around and see what he could find out about you. But I told him to keep it very off the record and very low-key.' He took another tiny sip of his Campari. He liked to make a drink last, thought Jimmy. Was that being mean or being careful, or both?

'And he found out what?'

'Not much, nothing in fact. He told me your file was thin, too thin for a DS working north London for the years you did. He spoke to a couple of blokes who said they remembered you but that's all they'd say, they remembered you. Billy said it looked like you must have been a pretty anonymous copper who didn't do very much work.'

'We can't all be high-flying young crime busters. Somebody has to be Mr Plod and do the routine stuff.'

'Now that may be true, but I doubt it in your case because of two things. One, Billy said your record wasn't just thin, it had been filleted, and two, he suddenly got told he was being sent to the US. A special request had been made by a university for someone to give a short series of seminars on forgeries and frauds involving nineteenth- and twentieth-century artists. That was his speciality, modern art.'

'So?'

'So he lost interest in you, forgot all about you. All he could think of was that he'd been chosen to go to America and show them how good he was at his job.'

'And all this means what?'

'That someone made sure he stopped nosing about doing favours for an old friend.'

Jimmy shook his head.

'No, you've got your wires crossed.'

'I don't think so. What I do think is that I'm in trouble. You see, I didn't do as I was told and keep my nose out of your past and I think I got caught looking. So now somebody may have my balls in a vice and could be about to turn the screw and if I'm right I'm going to need help, your help.'

'Even if you are right what makes you think I can help?'

'Because your record had been doctored, officially doctored, a thorough job, not just a few sheets pulled. That's not something anyone low-level could do or get done. Also, instead of pulling in Billy and giving him a bollocking for nosing about into Detective Sergeant James Costello, he got neatly taken out of the frame and it was done by someone who could get big favours and get them quick.' Ricci let things sink in for a minute. 'Look, I'm good at what I do. I'm a good copper. Don't let all the trinkets and Armani crap fool you, that's just window-dressing.'

'Like the accent?'

'Just like the accent. I've been around and I know the score, maybe I know it better than most. I think you are or were a dangerous man with people in London who still make sure you get left alone. What sort of people are they, Jimmy? Powerful enough to do a first-class cover-up job on the file, certainly, but with enough pull to get favours from across the pond? That's pretty special. Are they doing it for love, for old times' sake?'

'Nobody loves me in London.'

'No, that's what I thought. Then what we're left with is you paid them or they're afraid of you, of what you know or what you might do.'

Jimmy took a sip of his beer.

'And which do you think, money or the frighteners?'

'Why not both? You're a Duns student. Nobody would break my legs for looking into what that means so I checked and found they only take men who are financially independent now and will be for the foreseeable future. A detective sergeant's pension doesn't come close so where did all the money come from?'

'I sold my house.'

'Do you seriously want me to believe that out of the proceeds of a house sale you were able to buy the kind of protection you're getting and still have enough left to be self-financing for the rest of your life? I know London house prices are bloody silly but no house sale would stretch round all of that, unless you lived in Mayfair. You didn't live in Mayfair, did you, Jimmy?'

Jimmy managed a genuine smile at the idea.

'No, not Mayfair.'

'And even if you did, someone who pays big money to buy a clean past and your kind of protection doesn't come to Rome and sign up for the priesthood. They go and live the high life on the Costas or wherever. What else is loot for? So, that leaves it with either you know enough to make some very important people feel very worried or you're such a dangerous bastard they don't want you coming after them. Maybe both. Remember, Jimmy, I'm a copper, I know that people don't have to look dangerous to be dangerous, so the quiet, scruffy look cuts nothing with me.'

Jimmy could feel the old times seeping back into his life and he didn't know how he could stop them; worse than that, he knew there was a part of him that didn't want to stop them.

'OK, for the sake of argument, I've got friends in London. What would you want a man with friends in London to do?'

Ricci pushed his glass away and leaned closer to Jimmy.

'If God Almighty wants to punish me then I want the Prince

of Darkness looking after me. Tell me the truth the way you see it. Am I right or wrong? Am I in deep shit here, do I need your help?'

He sat back and waited.

Christ, thought Jimmy, what's going on? Why is this happening to me? I came here to bury the London copper, to do the right thing. I want to change, be the man I should be, the man Bernie and Eileen's kids deserve. And here I am being asked to help this bloke, who may very well be in the deep shit he thinks he is, and the only way to do that is to go back to what I was. That can't fucking well be right.

He made an effort. He wasn't going to slide back without a fight.

'Look, you got a slap on the wrist, your mate got sent across to the States and I've got a thin record. It's nothing, a few coincidences.'

'If you say so. But would you call it a coincidence that my uncle's ice-cream factory just outside Glasgow suffered a fire four days ago and he got a call telling him it wouldn't be just a fire next time.'

'Who told you?'

'My cousin, he phoned me. I'm the only policeman in the family. He wanted to ask me what they should do.'

'And you said?'

'Not much, that they should go to the local police.'

'Did they?'

'He said my uncle didn't want to do that. He was treating it like it was nothing, just yobs, and he wanted it left that way, said that he could take care of himself.'

'Glasgow can be a rough town.'

'Maybe so, but wouldn't you say there's a possibility someone's decided to put pressure on me through my uncle? Or is it another coincidence?'

They both sat in silence. The waiter came over and asked if they wanted more drinks. Ricci looked at Jimmy who nodded so he ordered two more.

'So what help am I supposed to give you?'

'Use your contacts from the old days to see that my uncle is

48

left alone and tell me why I should be frightened of you. If we're going to work together I need to know who I'm working with.'

'What's in it for me?' The new Jimmy wouldn't have asked, but for the old Jimmy it was always the first question. So it got asked.

'You get the chance to do the right thing, to help me and my uncle.' Ricci finally finished his drink. If another was coming there was no point in making it last. 'And then you get to try and find out if a genuinely holy old man was murdered. If it turns out he was, maybe we find out why, and who was responsible. There's no money in this that I can see, just doing the job and doing it right.'

'That's not much, in fact it's fuck all, I never worked for …'

The words had come as if by themselves but he managed not to finish the sentence. Don't go back, Jimmy, at least don't go all the way back. Go only as far as they make you go. The drinks came. They both waited until the waiter was gone.

'Being on the side of the angels never turned a profit that I know of, not in our business. The real pay-offs are always on the other side of the street, but I guess you know that. I suppose it all comes down to whether you really are taking this priest thing seriously.'

Jimmy knew he was right. He'd been asked for help, if he took being a priest seriously then he would have to help because that was the right thing to do. But that would mean resurrecting a Jimmy Costello he wanted to bury for good and that had to be the wrong thing to do.

Shit, he thought, why is it so fucking complicated, so bloody hard? Why can't I walk away and stick to what I came to Rome to do? But that would be putting himself first, making himself the only one that mattered which would mean he hadn't really changed at all. But if he took it on he had to go back to thinking and behaving like the old Jimmy. Christ, what a mess, you're wrong if you do and you're wrong if you don't. The Catholic Church, it gets you coming and it gets you going. No wonder they said we're the experts on guilt.

'Well, are you in or out?'

Jimmy took a drink.

'So what do we do? Do you go and see the minister's aide or what?'

Ricci smiled but this time the smile reached his eyes and it didn't look at all practised. Relief usually doesn't.

'I'll see to this end. I want you to go and get the Glasgow business sorted. I can't leave Rome and I need to be sure my family aren't going to be any part of this. Can you do that?'

'I can try.'

'You must still have contacts, if it's yobs or tearaways hired to throw a scare your friends should be able to sort it out without too much trouble.' Ricci picked up his drink. 'Cheers, you made the right decision.'

He took a long pull at his Campari and soda; he wasn't being careful any more. Jimmy watched him. Like hell I made the right decision. I didn't make any bloody decision. He took a long drink of his Tuborg.

Neither of us did.

NINE

Jimmy arrived back to his apartment in the Prati, a quiet, expensive residential district to the north of the Vatican. He went to a drawer, got out a battered old notebook, and looked up the number of a pub in London. He knew he should have thrown the notebook away years ago, it was part of the past he had turned his back on. But somehow he always put it off. Now, when he needed it, there it was. Was that luck or divine intervention? He looked at his watch, in the UK it would still be lunchtime and the pub would be open. He dialled the number. A voice answered.

'Can I still contact Bridie McDonald through this number?'

'Bridie who?'

'McDonald. Bridie McDonald from Glasgow. I want to talk to her. My name's Jimmy Costello.'

'You must have a wrong number, mate, there's no one of that name here. What number did you dial?'

Jimmy gave his own Rome phone number.

'No, mate, nothing like. You're miles off.'

The phone was put down.

Two days later his apartment phone rang and when he answered it a London voice said, '10 o'clock Mass, Tuesday, St Peter the Apostle,' and rang off.

Jimmy phoned Ricci.

'I'm going to Glasgow.'

'You made your contacts?'

'I'll see what I can do.'

'But you've been in touch with people who can help?'

'I told you, I'll see what I can do.'

'Look, we need to talk …'

'No, we don't.'

He rang off.

He didn't need Ricci pumping him for information he didn't have. He'd made a contact. Whether it would do him any good he had no idea but it was the best he could do. Tomorrow he would go to morning Mass and light some candles. If there was a priest available he might go to Confession. It was a big risk contacting Bridie so it was best to be prepared. There was nothing else he could think of so he went into his bedroom, pulled out an old black holdall from the wardrobe, and began to sort out his packing.

The budget flight left Ciampino in bright sunshine, it had been clear skies all the way until the flight reached the North Sea where thick clouds below the plane shone in the sunlight. The final descent to Edinburgh took the plane down through the cloud into a dark, wet afternoon and looking out of the rain-streaked windows the passengers' thoughts turned to raincoats and umbrellas. They taxied to a standstill and everybody on the crowded plane got up and started opening and emptying the lockers above the seats. The doors at the front and rear opened and the slow, shuffling exit of passengers began. This was a budget flight so it didn't include protection from the weather at either end of the journey. Going down the steps which had been wheeled to the doors, Jimmy turned up his coat collar against the wind and the squally rain. Once on the tarmac, he didn't hurry as some passengers did. His legs felt stiff and the weather made him feel even more dispirited than he had been when he'd set off from Rome.

It was all very well for Ricci to say 'use your old contacts'. What Ricci didn't understand was that if he got in touch with any of the old contacts, the ones who had fixed his file and kept prying eyes away, he would be a dead man very quickly. His safety lay in staying well away from those contacts. But he needed to know who was doing what. As Ricci had said, it was one thing to fillet a file and get a petrol bomb thrown through a window, quite another thing to fix a visit to the States to lecture on art crime.

By the time he got out of the rain, his hair and coat were wet. He thought of the Rome sunshine he had left only hours ago. He ran his fingers through his hair and began to climb the wide, carpeted staircase up to the Arrivals terminal.

'Bloody weather,' he muttered.

'Get used to it, pal, this is Scotland.'

The Glasgow voice belonged to a smiling young man in a smart, black overcoat who was carrying a small suitcase. Jimmy stood still against the stainless steel handrail and watched the man's back. It was nothing, it couldn't be. Why would anyone be put on the plane? Anyway no one knew which plane he would be on. I'm getting paranoid, he thought. Then he remembered the old joke, just because you're paranoid doesn't mean they're not out to get you. He came out of the stairway into a wide, well-lit walkway that led towards the baggage hall. He had nothing in the hold of the plane so he walked through Nothing to Declare and on until he went through the doors into Arrivals.

Crossing the Arrivals hall he tried to make his mind find the old routine.

Be careful but not so careful that you're slow. See what's there but only take notice of what matters. Don't get noticed, don't … don't … He heaved a heavy sigh then said, 'I'm getting too bloody old and tired for this crap.'

He was passing an elderly lady in tweeds. She gave him a sharp look and moved quickly away.

Talking out loud to myself. Yes, I really am getting too bloody old and tired for this crap.

But this time he upset nobody because he said it to himself. He tried again to remember the rules. Don't make mistakes but know when mistakes have been made, your own or anybody else's …

He left the main terminal and bought a ticket for the City

Shuttle, the double-decker bus which ferried people to and from the centre of Edinburgh. One was waiting so he got on and asked the driver if the bus passed the railway station.

'Haymarket or Waverley?'

'I'm going to Glasgow.'

'Go with Haymarket. You can't miss it.'

Sitting in the bus looking at the window and watching the rain drops running down, Jimmy went over things.

Ricci got angry when he wouldn't tell him what he planned to do, thought it meant he didn't trust him. He wasn't altogether wrong. But the truth was, when he'd set up the meeting he didn't know himself how he would handle it. Now he had arrived he still wasn't sure.

Another couple of passengers got on the bus, showed their tickets to the driver, stowed their big cases in the luggage rack, and sat down. Jimmy looked at his watch, three o'clock. He looked out of the window. Everything was blurred by the rain and it was dark enough for early evening.

Tomorrow was Tuesday. He should have plenty of time to get settled into a B&B or hotel, find out where the church was, and give it a walk-by to get the layout sorted in his mind. Another passenger got onto the bus, pushed a suitcase onto the luggage rack, and sat down. The driver closed the doors and the bus moved away. Once clear of the airport roads it went up the slip road onto the main dual carriageway and headed for the city.

The driver was right. You couldn't miss Haymarket station, the bus stopped right outside it. Jimmy bought a ticket, went down to the platform and waited. When the train came, he got on, put his holdall on the seat beside him and watched Edinburgh slip by as the train picked up speed.

How rusty am I, he wondered? Well, it was too late now to change his plans. He'd committed himself. He just hoped he hadn't committed himself too far.

TEN

Jimmy found somewhere to stay near the station and then took a taxi out to the church. St Peter the Apostle was a modern church on a quiet road of well-established detached houses standing in their own substantial gardens. This was where post-war Glasgow money had come to live in their architect-designed homes, a leafy suburb for like-minded people with incomes that meant they could afford the best.

He asked the taxi to wait while he went and checked Mass times. The church's side door was unlocked even though it was half-past seven in the evening. If people round here stole they didn't do it on the cheap by sneaking into churches and raiding the poor box. There were better ways to steal from the poor. Jimmy gave the surrounds to the church a once-over and chose a couple of places where he could look at the front of the church without attracting too much attention. Then he went back to his taxi and asked to be taken to a decent Italian restaurant somewhere near the station. Once he'd had a good meal and a couple of beers he went back to his room. Everything he could do he'd done. Now it would all be down to Bridie. It had been a long day and almost as soon as his head hit the pillow he slept.

The heavy, main double doors were shut and the few people who went in to morning Mass used the same side door that Jimmy had checked the previous evening. He'd seen Bridie arrive in a black Mercedes driven by a middle-aged woman. The car had disappeared behind the church and a few minutes later Bridie and her driver had both reappeared, talking. They were a couple of well-off, pious, Catholic biddies going to week-day morning Mass, except they weren't dressed like biddies. The driver was smart and sombre in a well-cut suit. Bridie was expensive and brassy, her skirt still too short for her age and legs. Both carried thick prayer books.

Jimmy waited until the Mass was under way then walked across the road, went behind the church and into the car park. The Mercedes was there with a few other cars. Morning Mass, unless the priest was a zealot, would last no more than half an hour, maybe only twenty minutes. There was nothing to do but wait so he put his hands in his pockets, leaned his backside against the front wing, and waited.

After twenty minutes the first person came into the car park, a young woman. She gave Jimmy a look which said, "and what do you think you're hanging about for?" but didn't take it further. She got into a snappy little red sports car and drove off. Soon after that a husband and wife came out and walked past the car park, then a single middle-aged woman. Mass was over. Bridie and her driver came round the corner; they couldn't miss him but neither bothered to look. They were talking and before they got to the car Jimmy could make out what Bridie was saying. She had a carrying voice.

'... so I said to Father Leahy, Father, I've done the White Elephant stall for ten years and if you want Mrs Mac to help me you can have Mrs Mac do the whole thing because I don't need her help or anyone else's.'

The driver pulled her door open.

'The cheek, telling you that you need help to do your stall.'

Bridie opened the passenger side door, got in, and pulled it shut. The engine started and Bridie's window slid down.

'What the fuck are you standing there for, Jimmy Costello? If you came to see me get in unless you're thinking of running alongside.' Jimmy opened the back door and got in. 'I'll take you back to your hotel and you can tell me what this is about on the way.'

'We could talk here, Bridie. I don't need a lift and it won't take long.'

'You're getting a lift and it had better not take long. Where to?' Jimmy gave the name and address of a B&B. The car slid away across the car park and out onto the road.

'Know the way, Norah?'

'Where's it near?' The question was for Jimmy. She looked at him in the mirror.

'The station.'

'Which one?'

'Is there more than one?'

Bridie turned round.

'Stop fucking about. Which station?'

'I don't know. I just got somewhere near the station when I came in from Edinburgh.' Norah nodded and Bridie turned away. Jimmy had felt uncomfortable about this meeting ever since he'd decided to arrange it. Now, with Bridie at close range, he knew he was right to be uncomfortable, in fact he was right to be bloody shit-scared. Norah looked at him in the mirror again.

'I'll take you to Queen Street station and drop you there.'

'Queen Street. Fine.'

The car turned onto another, busier road and headed towards the city centre.

'OK, Jimmy Costello, what do you want?'

Bridie didn't turn round when she spoke so Jimmy talked to the back of her head.

'A factory out at Cumbernauld got a petrol bomb thrown through the window recently. It was an ice-cream factory owned by …'

'Johnny Fabrizzi. I heard about it, a bunch of young hooligans pissing about. It was nothing.'

'Maybe, maybe not, and if not I need to know where the idea originated.'

'That's a fucking queer way of putting it. Why not just say you want to know who did it?'

'Because I don't want to know who did it?'

'No?'

'No. I don't care who did it.'

Bridie paused for a moment.

'OK, so now I know what you don't care about. What is it you do care about?'

'Who wanted it done?'

'Why do you care, are you trying to get whoever it is off Johnny Fabrizzi's back? Is that it?'

'No. If Johnny Fabrizzi does business in this town he takes the chances that go with it same as everybody else. He'll have to look after himself as best he can. If somebody's putting the arm on him, let them get on with it. It's nothing to do with me.'

'So what is to do with you?'

'That's something new since my time, Bridie, something for nothing, free information. I didn't know the Freedom of Information Act applied to your kind of business.'

The driver looked in the mirror and Jimmy gave her his best smile. She looked away and would never know what that casual-looking smile had cost him in effort. Thank God he'd practised.

'Still a smart fucker. No one knocked that out of you yet?'

'Not yet. Look, I'm just calling in a favour. When I gave you Jamie to take home you told me to ask when I wanted something. Now I want something so I'm asking. Why I want it is my business.'

'Like fuck I told you to ask.'

'OK, a man in a pub said the actual words. But it was the same pub I used to let you know I'd got Jamie's body and it was the same pub that set up this meeting. As far as I'm concerned the words came from you. If I'm wrong stop the car and I'll get out and you won't see me again.'

'I can make fucking sure I don't see you again any time I like.' She wasn't joking and she wasn't boasting, she was stating the simple truth. Jimmy felt the knot of tension tighten in his stomach and knew he had to stop it creeping into his voice. If Bridie got a whiff of weakness he was dead. She didn't work with weaklings, she stamped on them. All the old fear was right back with him now. He remembered how he had ridden with her in her Mercedes those years ago in London, how he had got out and she'd told him to kneel down. Then her man Colin had shot him in the back of the head. This time, if the same thing happened, it really would be the gun at the back of his head that went off, not some other gun. This time he wouldn't wake up with only his trousers soiled. He wouldn't wake up at all because what would be left of his face would be on the floor in bits of his own brains.

'Well, Bridie, what's it to be?' were the words he said, 'Oh God of mercy keep my bloody voice calm,' was what he was praying. Bridie turned and looked at him.

'I'll see what I can do. If I can do anything you'll have it tomorrow at the latest. What's your number?'

Jimmy gave it to her.

'Want to write it down?'

She ignored him and turned to the driver.

'What stall did Mrs Mac do last year?'

'The bottle stall, remember? She helped Molly O'Dowd. It didn't make nearly as much as it usually does. Molly couldn't understand it, it seemed to go as well as she expected.'

Bridie laughed.

'The devious young bugger. He wants her on my stall because he knows I'll spot her if she dips into the takings. Well, Norah, maybe our young Father Leahy's not as green as he's cabbage-looking after all.'

'What do you think, take her on and see what happens?'

'No, what's the point? If she lifts some cash and I catch her he won't do anything. Her husband does the parish accounts so Fatherr Leahy can't risk offending him by accusing his wife of being a thief. And I can hardly have her legs broken, can I? No, if she's light-fingered let her get on with it somewhere else.'

'If her husband's an accountant why does she do it? She can't need the money. Is it an illness, do you think?'

'If stealing's an illness then Glasgow's been in an epidemic for as long as I can remember.'

They both laughed. Jimmy sat back and stopped listening as the two women continued discussing the forthcoming parish bazaar.

I'm no bloody good at this any more, he thought; it's got to be done properly or not all. A half-hard bastard is no bastard at all. If I get by with Bridie it will be on the back of what she remembers, the man I was, not the man I am now. I'm just too fucking old and tired. Who the hell does Ricci think I am, James bloody Bond? If his uncle's in trouble let him sort it out himself. I'm going to have my hands full just staying alive.

The car turned into George Square and pulled up in front of the station. Jimmy leaned forward.

'I'll hear from you then?'

'Fuck off.'

Jimmy got out and the car pulled away. He went into the first bar he came to and ordered a double whisky. He didn't like whisky but just now beer wouldn't do what was needed.

He drank the whisky as soon as it came, waited until the harshness had settled from his throat, then ordered another. With the second he took his time.

Why am I part of it? That was what made no sense. What sort of Alice in Wonderland scenario put a trainee priest, even one that used to be a copper, alongside the suspicious death of an archbishop?

If Bridie came across and it turned out the ice-cream factory got torched on someone's orders then … then what? He took another long sip. It had to be London. Or maybe it would turn out to be just some hooligans like Bridie said, nothing more than young tearaways trying their hand at extortion. Why not? Everyone has to begin somewhere. He finished the last drops of his drink, got off his stool, and left the bar.

Outside he felt better. The meeting with Bridie had gone well after all. Now it was time for a late breakfast. Jimmy headed to his hotel which was not so very near the B&B whose name and address he had given to Bridie. Yes, he'd managed to stay careful. Maybe he wasn't such a tired old has-been after all.

ELEVEN

It was about eight o'clock that night when the phone in his hotel room rang. Jimmy went across and picked it up. The message was brief and to the point, there was no introduction, no preamble of any sort.

'It was ordered. They were told to fire-bomb the place then make the call. They were given the number and told what to say.'

'So who ordered it?'

'They don't know and they were asked thoroughly. The best they could come up with was that the man was English, fiftyish, and seemed official, like the police.'

'The police?'

'Like the police. Kids like that only know two kinds of people, their own and the police.'

'What about the local force?'

'What about them?'

'Did they get involved?'

'No, they wrote it off as hooligans.'

'But it was an out-of-town job farmed to local nobodies.'

'Yes, and that's it, that's all of it. Understood?'

Jimmy understood.

'Yeah.'

Whoever it was rang off. Jimmy slowly put the phone down.

'Shit.'

He'd suspected the fire was ordered and now he knew for certain. Ricci had been caught looking and the petrol bomb was London's way of telling him to take his nose out. That left his mate who'd suddenly been invited to America. They wouldn't have done both even if they had that sort of pull which he doubted. So who arranged that little stunt? Well, he'd done what he came to do. Ricci wasn't going to do any more digging into old files so his uncle would be left alone. The bad news was the call had come to the hotel, not the mobile number he'd given her. Did that matter? She'd come across with the information so maybe it didn't, but with Bridie you never could tell. He sat down heavily on his bed. He should have stayed in Rome. Ricci's family troubles weren't anything to do with him, he'd pretty much guessed what it was all about. He hadn't really needed to come and make certain. But he knew that wasn't the real reason he'd come, not all of it anyway. A petrol-bomb with a threatening call alongside his mate getting taken out of the frame had set his mind working like it used to and he'd liked the feeling it gave him. The idea of coming back and taking on Bridie had given him the old adrenaline rush. It was maybe a last chance to … Then the phone rang again.

'Your lift to the airport is here, Mr Costello. I'm afraid I'll have to charge you for the two nights even though you'll not be staying after all. Your bill will be ready when you come down.'

'Thanks, I'll be down in a few minutes.'

Jimmy began to gather his things and stuff them into his holdall. He hadn't ordered a car so it had to be Bridie's people waiting for him downstairs. There was no point in running. Even if he got past whoever was down there how long would he last in Glasgow with Bridie looking for him? It was her turf and she knew it like she knew the inside of her handbag. He finished pushing his stuff into the holdall. What choices had he got? The answer came at once, none. All the choices were Bridie's now, she was the one who'd decide if he'd finish up as a permanent Glasgow resident, maybe in the same cemetery as two of her sons, more probably dumped on some derelict site. He went to the door, switched the light out, and left.

Downstairs Bridie's driver from church was waiting, still wearing the same smart suit. Jimmy paid his bill and followed her out of the hotel to where the black Mercedes was parked. There was no one else in it. Jimmy looked around. What was there to see, why look? What's the point of being careful at the wrong time?

'Get in.'

He threw his holdall onto the back seat and got in beside the driver. It wasn't a long journey and it wasn't to the airport. She took him to Queen Street Station.

'I thought you were taking me to the airport?'

'The airport's over thirty miles away. If you want to fly somewhere go to Edinburgh and fly from there. I'm not your taxi. I just deliver you to the station and give you a message.'

'Why is it called Glasgow airport if it's bloody miles away from Glasgow?'

Jimmy was trying hard to hide his relief and not piss his pants, saying something, anything, helped. If the driver was annoyed at his stupid question she wasn't about to show it. Jimmy liked her, whatever it was she did besides driving Bridie he guessed she would be good at it.

'Finished being funny?'

Outside the car were people and lights. Nothing was going to happen here. Now he knew he was safe the tension disappeared, he didn't need to hear his own voice to know he was still alive.

'Yeah, finished.'

'OK, here's your message. We don't like people who bring their London shite up here and cause trouble, especially when they've come to ask a favour. It's bad manners. Maybe somebody will teach you a lesson about that, it could get you into trouble, know what I mean?' Jimmy didn't answer. He guessed the question was rhetorical. 'There's no more favours for you here, Costello, there's nothing here for you or your London friends, ever. Tomorrow morning if you're still in Scotland, anywhere in Scotland, you're dead and if you're stupid enough to come back you'll wind up like Jamie, and you know how Jamie wound up.' He knew. 'Now get out.'

Jimmy did as he was told, watched the car pull away, then

looked around but as the people flowed past him on their way in and out he asked himself, what the hell am I looking for? This is a railway station, who am I going to see? If Bridie had someone following him until he was clear of Glasgow he knew he wouldn't spot them unless they were attached to him by a rope. If someone was there then there was fuck all he could do about it so he went into the station, found the toilets, and gratefully relieved himself. Then he bought a ticket to Edinburgh Haymarket and headed for the platform.

While he sat in the train waiting for it to pull away he thought about Bridie. How the hell do you figure a woman like that? A violent, Mass-going biddy who runs serious crime and a stall at the parish bazaar stall. He wondered what she thought about it all, her life, her family, her business, and her Church. If she ever thought about it. He specially wondered why she went to Mass in the mornings. But then he thought, it's cost her two sons so I suppose she's got a lot to pray about, we all have. The train began to pull away from the station, out into the night, and Jimmy switched off his brain. Time to rest. Later on, back in Rome, he would do the thinking. He closed his eyes and tried to doze.

At Edinburgh airport Jimmy walked to the nearest departures screen. There was no flight to Rome but there was the last KLM City-hopper going to Schiphol. From there it wouldn't be a problem to get to Rome. He went to the KLM desk, bought a ticket, checked in, and went through the security checks into the departure lounge. In one of the bars he looked at the beers and ordered a Tuborg. The main rush of the day was over. Most of those waiting were people like him who had to take a late flight, tired, quiet people, ordinary people who, if they looked at him at all, would see just another tired traveller waiting for his flight and having a beer. He grinned to himself and then took a sip. He'd done well, it had been a good outing, worth the effort even though it was no more than he'd expected.

'Never touched me, Bridie. Never bloody touched me.'

TWELVE

The flight landed at Schiphol just after midnight local time. Once there Jimmy had a choice, a flight to Florence which would get him on his way within the hour or wait just over two and a half hours and fly direct. He was out of Scotland so there was no hurry, but the idea of hanging round an airport for a couple of hours didn't appeal so he opted for Florence.

At Florence Airport he checked his options at travel information and found he had the same choice, hang around and catch the first Rome flight just before seven which would get him into Fiumicino at seven fifty-five or get a taxi to Florence station and catch the five-thirty train which would also get him into Rome at the same time, seven fifty-five. He was knackered, he didn't want to hang about in another airport so he opted for the station. Once there he could get a bit of breakfast, then on the train stretch his legs and sleep, maybe. Also, the train put him into central Rome, not out at the airport. The train made sense.

In Rome he chose a taxi from the station rather than the face the Metro. It dropped him off in a tree-lined street bathed in the sunlight of a beautiful morning where people were on the move going about their business. He was home. He paid off the taxi, went up to his apartment, threw his holdall onto the settee, took off his jacket, kicked off his shoes, then went into the bathroom.

He had made it back safe and sound and done what he'd set out to do. Now all he wanted to do was wash the travel off his face and hands, get into bed, and sleep. There had been a young family near him on the train with a baby that must have been teething because it cried nearly all the time. He'd dozed when he could but hadn't been able to get any real sleep and his body was crying out for it. He went into his bedroom, drew the curtains to shut out the morning sun, dropped his clothes on the floor, and went to bed. Four hours later he woke feeling much better. He showered, shaved, dressed, and made himself some coffee. He sat down and made a call. Ricci was quick to answer.

'Yeah?'

'I'm back, it's sorted.'

'He'll be left alone?'

'I did what I could.'

'But he'll be left alone?'

'Look. I've had four hours' sleep in two days. I got home this morning and I've called you. Your uncle's all right, he's nothing to do with us any more, nothing will happen to him. That's it.'

'OK. Thanks.'

Ricci rang off and Jimmy put the phone down.

Ricci wasn't as good as he'd like to think, he let his personal feelings get in the way and that had made him sloppy. The firebomb was somebody was warning him off, but not from any investigation of a dead archbishop. It was about him nosing about in old files. He'd let his thinking get mixed up. Jimmy got up to make himself another coffee. It was a small fire, only closed a part of the factory and only for one day. Not like getting his mate sent to the US. That was different. That was the sort of thing God Almighty organised from Rome. The fire was just London's way of saying keep out of Jimmy Costello's past, or your uncle will pay the price. Well, Ricci wouldn't be doing any more sniffing in records so it was over, finished.

He looked at his watch. It was just after one and he felt hungry. He would go out, walk in the sunshine for a bit, get rid of the last of the damp, depressed feeling he'd picked up in Scotland and had travelled back with him. Then he'd get a plate of pasta and after that come back and think. There was a lot to think about. He finished his coffee. He felt better, almost happy. He was back doing something he'd been good at. This would be his last outing as a detective, a farewell, a swan song, before he got down to his training and put his past behind him for good. And if it was his last case he'd make damn sure he got a result. Yes, he felt a lot better.

Never touched me, Bridie, never fucking touched me.

THIRTEEN

Jimmy woke in a bed in a room which seemed full of machines with dials and cables. A clear plastic bag hung from a stand at his bedside feeding fluid to his left arm. There was a window with the blind drawn and a low light was glowing in the ceiling. He felt no pain, he didn't feel much of anything. He guessed that was because he was shot full of stuff. He lay there trying to remember what had happened. He got as far as leaving his apartment but then it all went blank. The door of the room opened slightly and a nurse put her head round. Jimmy turned his head and looked at her. She came in.

'How do you feel?' She spoke good English but Jimmy didn't feel like answering. She smiled at him. 'Rest, Mr Costello, rest and get well. We were told to take very special care of you so don't let us down. Get well.' She checked the fluid bag then put a cool hand on his forehead. 'You're doing fine.'

She left the room and Jimmy lay still. There was nothing to think about, so he didn't think. He went back to sleep. When he next opened his eyes Ricci was sitting in a chair by the bed looking at him. He wore a light sports coat and an open-neck blue shirt with his sunglasses in the top pocket.

'Hello, Jimmy, welcome back.'

'How bad is it?'

'Pretty bad. They certainly messed you up, a few ribs broken and the doctors were worried about your spleen for a while. The biggest worry was whether your head injuries had done some real damage. But you're a tough old bird, with rest you'll be OK.'

'How long have I been out?'

'You were out cold for two days, that was the tricky time when they thought they might lose you. Then you sort of came round. They say you rambled, kept waking up and trying to tell them about someone touching you or not touching you. It didn't make much sense that anyone could make out, not the way I got told anyway. Then you started sleeping properly. You've slept for nearly two days, now you're awake and the doctors say you'll make a full recovery.'

'I don't remember talking to anyone.'

'I don't suppose you'll remember much of anything for a while. But it will come back, just give it time.' Jimmy looked at the ceiling. The light was still dimmed. He felt tired again. 'Your wallet was gone, your watch, and your phone. Was this what it looked like, a mugging, or was it something else? You live in a classy neighbourhood, not many people get attacked in that part of the city.' Jimmy tried to shrug but stopped as the pain shot through him. He grimaced. 'Stay still, any moving will hurt. You got messed about quite a lot and they're reducing the pain killers now you're on the mend so be ready to suffer.' He smiled, his real one, the one that reached his eyes. 'Maybe they were Roma fans and thought you supported Lazio.'

Jimmy could see he was doing his best to lighten things up so he smiled. Smiling didn't hurt.

'I wasn't wearing a Lazio shirt.'

'Maybe you just look like a Lazio supporter.'

'What's a Lazio supporter supposed to look like?'

'I don't know, ask a Roma fan. Football isn't something I'm interested in.'

Jimmy felt better for talking. He guessed Ricci knew that, or maybe the doctor had told him to get him talking, to wake him up a bit.

'Where was I found?'

70

'In the lobby of your apartments, beside the stairway. A neighbour found you.'

'They were waiting for me?'

There was no smile now. They were back to business.

'Must have been. You've got a very good address and good security goes with a good address. If they were inside the building then they weren't casual thugs hanging about on the off-chance. Was it anything to do with the trip to Glasgow?'

'Maybe. Maybe somebody wanted to remind me of a message.'

'A message? The one that went with the fire at my uncle's place?'

'No, another message. One I was given at the station before I left.'

'It must have been quite a message, it could have killed you. Couldn't your old contacts have protected you?'

Suddenly Jimmy didn't feel better any more, the pain had started building.

'Don't you understand, you stupid bastard? The business about your uncle was to warn you off looking into my record. You were caught looking, remember?'

Ricci obviously didn't understand.

'But if they're protecting you in London why the beating here?'

'That came from one of my old contacts, the one I went to Glasgow to see. She didn't like my manners. That's the sort of relationship we have. If I try and talk to them, they try to kill me, but this one owed me a big favour so I'm in hospital and not in the morgue.'

'Sorry, Jimmy. With what I found out and what I guessed, I thought you had contacts, people over there who could protect you.'

'They're only interested in protecting themselves. I know too much and if, for one second, they think I might tell anyone what I know I really will be a dead man.'

'I see.'

'No you don't.'

'You're right, I don't. If you're such a threat why aren't you dead already?'

'Because they tried and they found out I'm hard to kill.'

'They tried?'

'In London, a few years ago. The one who ordered it is dead, so is the one he sent to do the job. So are a few other people. But I'm still alive and if they're sure I'll keep my mouth shut they'll leave me alone. After the London business I deposited some stuff, life insurance. They'll have guessed I'd do that so now it's important that I stay alive or die in the right way.'

'The right way being only after they've got their hands on your insurance.'

'That's right. Now you know my fucking life story.'

The pain was getting worse. Whatever he was shot full of was wearing off and if Ricci was right another dose wasn't coming soon.

'Now I know.'

Jimmy closed his eyes and tried to shut everything out. It didn't help. He felt tired. Totally used up. The pain seeped into his mind but his brain reacted by closing down. As he fell asleep his last thoughts were, "Dear God, let it all end here. I've had enough".

Ricci got up and pressed a button. A nurse came.

'He seemed better, he talked. Then he changed, I think the pain was getting worse. Then he closed his eyes and went to sleep or passed out.'

The nurse nodded and left. After a while she came back with a doctor who checked his pulse, looked at a few dials, then gave the nurse some instructions.

'Don't worry, Inspector, he's doing fine. He'll be sitting up out of bed in a couple of days and should be out of here in a week.'

'Thanks, that's good news.'

The doctor left.

Ricci went back to the bed and looked at Jimmy.

'Get well, Jimmy, there's still work to do and we're the ones supposed to be doing it.'

Then he left and Jimmy slept.

His body was busy getting well so he could go back to work.

FOURTEEN

Doctors make mistakes, but in Jimmy's case their diagnosis confirmed Ricci's assessment. He was a tough old bird and mending quickly. Ricci was his only visitor and came at the end of most days. He would bring Jimmy up to date and they would discuss progress. At this stage it was all that Jimmy could do. They had both agreed that what they needed was a better picture of Cheng.

'I'm stuck here but it's not a two-man job. There's got to be paper on him, files, archived articles, official memos.'

For four days Ricci read everything there was to read on Archbishop Cheng, wrote up notes, cross-referenced, checked, and then wrote up more notes, and each evening visited Jimmy to go over what he had found.

During the days Jimmy rested and thought about the case, about the information Ricci had brought him so far.

Cheng had been born in Guandong Province in southern China but the family moved to Portuguese Macau during the Civil War, and Cheng was educated by the Jesuits. When he left school he applied to join the order, was accepted and sent to Rome for training. In Rome he was a star student, tipped for a top flight career but after ordination he asked to go back into Mao's People's Republic as a parish priest. He dug his heels in and in the end got what he wanted.

He went and China simply swallowed him up. There Ricci's paper trail had dried until 1971, when his release was officially announced. He'd served five years of re-education through hard labour under the careful direction of the Red Guards, another victim of the Cultural Revolution. The only reason his release was noticed was that the Father Cheng who had gone into prison was Bishop Cheng on release. He'd been elevated by the Vatican while he was being 're-educated'. Then nothing again until 1978 when he was re-arrested at the tail end of the Cultural Revolution for anti-patriotic behaviour and acting as a spy for a foreign power, official code for any Catholic priest loyal to the Vatican. This time the sentence he served was ten years. His refusal to sign up to the government-sponsored official Catholic Church meant that he spent a further seven years in prison at one time or another. But one more Catholic bishop being arrested or released wasn't news except to a handful of specialists, dedicated China watchers. To them, which members of the Catholic hierarchy were in favour and which were in prison was as good a barometer as any to the power struggles within the ruling Communist Party. As a simple rule of thumb Bishop Cheng was invaluable. If he was in prison, the hard-liners were on top. If he was out the reformers were calling the shots.

By the end of the century China was changing fast and ready to play its part as an economic superpower. In 1999 they got back Macau from the Portuguese and during the run-up to the final official handover it was noted by the government-controlled press that a senior Catholic cleric who had grown up in Macau but served all his priestly life in the People's Republic was visiting his family. That was Beijing's way of saying to the world that any member of the Catholic Church, even the unofficial Catholic Church, had the same freedom of action and movement as any other citizen who had served the Chinese people loyally and for so long. Now officially recognised, Archbishop Cheng was photographed with his family and local Communist officials.

Ricci had shown Jimmy a copy of a newspaper photo. In it there was a small, smiling man who looked shy and insignificant in clerical black but who, even in the news photo, gave an impression of deep inner peace and strength.

Archbishop Cheng's trip to Macau was a success and was the beginning of his official rehabilitation during which neither he nor the government ever referred to his years in prison. To the Vatican and to the Chinese government Cheng was a small piece in a long and hard-fought political chess game. After Macau the game had moved into a new phase and Cheng's role changed accordingly.

His visit to Rome figured widely in the national Chinese media, a signal to the people of China and to the West that a new tolerance was growing which could even encompass unofficial Catholic prelates. His return to Rome should have been the crowning moment of his rehabilitation but it didn't turn out that way. Not long after he arrived he fell ill and died two days later in what now could appear to be suspicious circumstances.

It was the end of another day. Ricci was sitting on the side of the bed. He put down his notes. Jimmy was in his pyjamas sitting on the chair beside his bed. He looked at the notes. A man's life in a few pages.

'Poor old sod.'

'Poor old sod indeed. As a Catholic I ask for divine mercy on his soul, as a rationalist I say that if there is a God he is at best indifferent to human suffering or at worst uses humanity as a plaything to service a rather nasty sense of humour. What do you think, or being a good Catholic don't you allow yourself to dwell on such things too much?'

'I don't dwell on them at all. We die. God or no God, it's the same for everyone.'

'True.' Ricci left the metaphysics and moved on. 'I reckon we've got all we're going to get on him, we know him as well as we're ever going to.'

Jimmy agreed.

'So, who would want him dead?'

Ricci shook his head.

'At the time of his death Archbishop Cheng was universally loved and respected, that's it, that's what everything I've read says.'

'What about the autopsy?'

'Checked and checked again. The results of the autopsy were inconclusive. The best guess is that the old man died of natural causes brought about by previous ill-treatment and general debility due to age. There's nothing I can find that might make him a target.' They sat in silence for a minute. Ricci reached down, ran his fingers through his pages of notes, and then looked back to Jimmy. 'Maybe it was just a case of natural causes.'

'It's all a load of fucking bollocks, that's what it is.'

There was no doubt in Ricci's mind that Jimmy was ready to be discharged. Inactivity may have made him irritable and angry in the way he expressed himself but Ricci wholeheartedly agreed with the essence of his assessment.

'Well, if it's a murder it's the best one I've come across. No suspects, no motives, no hard evidence. No reason at all for it to have happened. Nothing.'

Jimmy let his anger rise. He always hated it when a case hit a brick wall.

'What the hell are we supposed to be looking for? And why me? That's what sticks in my throat. Why drag me into this?'

'To keep an eye on me?'

'That doesn't stand up, they could have got a dozen locals to keep an eye on you if they'd wanted to. But you get told to bring me in on things and when we meet you don't like me …'

Ricci smiled his genuine smile.

'I didn't know you then.'

'You don't know me now. You only think you know me.'

'Have it your own way.'

'Anyway, you don't want me on the case and you say so. What happens?'

'I get smacked on the wrist, warned off, and get stuck with you anyway.'

'And because you got your mate to look at my file and ask awkward questions some Glasgow hooligans throw a petrol bomb into your uncle's ice-cream factory. I go and look into it and get put in here. We're not doing very well so far, are we?'

'You know, you're a hard bloke to figure. We're supposed to be working together.'

'We are working together.'

'Then why not tell me you'd guessed it was a message from your old friends in London?'

'And that would have been enough, would it? You'd have settled for my guess and left it alone?'

Ricci took the point.

'No, probably not.'

'So I went. Let's leave it at that.'

It wasn't the whole truth, Ricci was sure of that. Jimmy hadn't gone to Glasgow just to confirm what he already knew. There was something else, but whatever it was, it was Jimmy's business so he left well alone.

'There's one idea I've come up with. Cheng trained for the priesthood in Rome and when he finally comes back, bing, he cops it. Could it be something to do with when he was here doing his training?'

'No, I don't see it. Training as a priest doesn't make you the sort of connections that get you killed and certainly not decades later. I don't say you're wrong, you might have something but I doubt it.'

Ricci doubted it as well.

'Then that only leaves the Chinese. Cheng has been in China all his working life and at daggers drawn with the authorities. If he was killed the Chinese must have done it or had it done.' Jimmy nodded his head in a tired way. He had nothing better to offer so it had to be the fucking Chinese, besides, he was too tired to argue or think of anything else.

'I suppose so, who else is there?'

'You should get back into bed, Jimmy. You look as if you've about had enough for one session.'

Jimmy agreed. He tried to stand but didn't quite make it and fell back into the chair. Ricci went to him, took his arm, and managed to get him up and back into bed.

'Oh Christ, I'm not up to this sort of thing any more. I have my hands full just looking after me, there's not a lot left over for anything else.'

'You'll feel better in a day or two. You need rest, that's all.'

But Jimmy wasn't convinced.

'Don't expect too much. I'll do my best but I can't promise my best will be good enough.'

'You'll do OK once you're fit and well. And remember, you were right about my uncle. I didn't think it through, you did. I thought family, you thought copper. I guess I'm more Italian than I thought I was. Maybe there's not much of the Glaswegian left in me.'

'Thank God for that, if the Glaswegians I've met are anything to go by. As for thinking family, you made the same mistake anyone would make if one of their own got targeted. If it had been my daughter or her kids in Australia you'd have had to be the one doing the thinking for both of us.'

But Ricci knew Jimmy was just saying words. You didn't help anybody by being sloppy. Being sloppy got people hurt.

He picked up his notes from the bed.

'You rest, Jimmy, rest and get well and then we'll get back to work properly.'

Jimmy closed his eyes.

'Maybe. But I tell you something …'

But Jimmy didn't tell Ricci anything. His voice faded and he slept. Ricci waited a moment then left the room closing the door quietly behind him.

Jimmy was a tough old bird all right, but even the toughest wear out eventually.

FIFTEEN

Jimmy was up and dressed, except for his shoes and socks. He couldn't find his shoes. The socks didn't matter so much, he could do without socks but he couldn't go out with no shoes on. He looked under the bed and saw a pair of black lace-ups. His shoes were tan slip-ons. He pulled the shoes out and tried them anyway. They were too small. He threw them on the bed. He opened his locker. It was full of shoes, someone had filled it with shoes, but they were all ladies' shoes. The door opened and the nurse came in. She was Chinese.

'I need my shoes.'

She smiled and held a pair out to him. They were blue suede platform shoes.

Jimmy took them and the nurse left.

Why had he taken them? Why had she given him them? They couldn't be his shoes.

The door opened and the doctor came in. He was an American and black.

'You must leave now, Mr Costello. It is time for you to go.'

'But I can't find my shoes.'

'Then look for them outside, Mr Costello. Find your shoes somewhere else and then you can go home. You must leave so we can clear up.'

The doctor gestured to the room. It had suddenly become

littered with shoes. Jimmy sat down and picked up the nearest one. It was left-hand, laceless, leather boot with a steel toecap. He put it to one side and picked up another. It was a …

Then he woke up.

Of course it had to be the Chinese, or Professor McBride, or maybe the bloody pope. Who else was there?

He got out of bed. He felt better. He began to walk and found the pain was almost gone. Yes he definitely felt better. And he wanted his breakfast. He pressed the button by his bed and after a few minutes the nurse appeared. She wasn't black or Chinese.

'You look better today, Mr Costello, that's good, we were told to take special care of you and see that you made a full recovery.'

'Yes?'

'Oh yes, you're a VIP around here.'

'A VIP? That's nice. What's for breakfast? No, it doesn't matter what it is, just bring it, will you?'

The nurse smiled.

'Yes, you're better. I'll get you your breakfast.'

'And can you get me a phone?'

'No, we don't allow phones in these rooms. Patients in these rooms are supposed to be too ill to make or receive calls.'

'Then can you make a call for me?' The nurse looked doubtful. 'It's to Inspector Ricci of the Rome police. He's the one who has been visiting me.'

The nurse smiled.

'Give me the number.'

Jimmy gave it to her.

'Tell him I need to see him now. Tell him it's urgent.'

'Is it?'

'It is to me.'

The nurse gave him a smile and left; Jimmy resumed his walking.

Why not stick with the Chinese? They would do well enough until someone else turned up. Why not the fucking Chinese?

Jimmy got his breakfast and Ricci turned up an hour later.

'You said it was urgent.'

'It is.'

'OK, I've come running, let's hear it.'

'When we started this we agreed that all we had to go on was Cheng, right?' Ricci nodded. 'Well we were wrong. We have something else.'

'What?'

'Me.'

'You?'

'Me. Whatever's going on I'm part of it. I got dragged in for no reason that I or you could see and when you tried to kick me out you found you couldn't. For some reason I'm part of it.'

It was a thought. It was somewhere to go, something to work on.

'OK, so how are you connected to Cheng?'

'I'm not, I can't be.'

'But you just said …'

'No, I said I'm part of it, and whatever it is it's not just Cheng's death.'

'You're sure there's nothing in your past, no common denominator, no link to Cheng?'

'There's nothing.'

'Something or someone you know? You have to be connected to Cheng or the Vatican somehow.'

Jimmy shook his head. He lain in bed for longer than he cared to remember and gone down that road, gone as far as it went.

'No, nothing.'

'Then it's a brick wall and Cheng is still all we've got.'

'No it's not.'

'Why not?'

'If part of this is about me we need to know, don't we?'

'If you say so.'

Ricci saw a look that had come into Jimmy's eyes. Not quite the one that had frightened him at their first meeting, but close, too close.

'So why don't we just ask? Why piss about wasting our time trying to work it out? If we're working for the good guys let's ask them. If they won't tell us, we'll tell them to go and fuck themselves and their investigation.'

Ricci thought of trying his smile and decided against it. Jimmy wasn't going to be lightened up or jollied along on this.

'They've got you mad at them now, haven't they? You look like you could be a bit of a handful when you're mad.'

The look went out of Jimmy's eyes.

'Maybe, once, back when Moses was in the fire brigade and Pontius was a pilot. Now I just want to ask the tricky bastards what's going on. Either we're on the same side and we help each other or we're not.'

'OK, we'll ask. So what do we do, kick in the minister's door and say, "why is Jimmy Costello mixed up in this?"'

'That's one way but I've got another.'

'Go on.'

'What have we got so far on Cheng's death?'

'Next to nothing.'

'No, wrong. We've dug around as much as we could and we came up empty. We got nothing and nothing was all we were ever going to get even if we went all over Cheng like a cheap suit. If it was murder then it was done by people who can kill an archbishop in Rome, leave the body lying about, and still be sure of total immunity. There was always going to be nothing to find and we found it.'

'What are you saying?'

'Who could do that, kill an archbishop here in Rome and be sure it would never get back to them? Who has that kind of resources?'

There weren't a lot of choices.

'You're saying this is political?'

'Why not? And if it isn't then let's make it that way.'

'Talk sense, Jimmy, I'm not in the mood for riddles.'

'You've already said it. It was the Chinese. Why not? They kick the shit out of Cheng for God knows how many years then suddenly rehabilitate him. Why? To show him off as their pin-up of the tolerant new China, a place that's open for business. But he's still a threat, he still won't toe their line, and he still represents a challenge to their authority. So, like I say, they build him up, use him to show that they're all good guys now, even go so far as to let him come to Rome. Once he's here and the PR job is done he's dead, natural causes, very sad. The Chinese keep their good-guy image and get rid of Cheng in a way which means no one can point the finger at them. What do you think?'

Ricci thought.

'It's not exactly a fairy tale but it's still a long way from any sort of convincing argument and it still gives us nothing.'

'It gives us enough to do what it has to do.'

'Which is?'

'We go to your minister and tell him it was the Chinese, end of story, end of case. You get well again and go back to being a copper and I go back to my training. Good night, Vienna, show's over.'

'I see. If you're right and this is as much about you as Cheng's death and they need you to stay involved they won't let you walk away any more than they let me kick you out.'

'That's right.'

'And if it is just Cheng's death then we've done as much as can be done, we're finished and we can walk away.'

'Right again. One way or another …'

'… we'll get told and be able to move on or move out.' The room door opened and a nurse came in. Ricci turned to her. 'It's OK, nurse, I'm about to go. Just give me a few more minutes.'

'Not long. Signor Costello is much better but he still needs his rest and strictly speaking there should be no visitors at all in this part of the hospital at this time of day.'

Ricci put on his most charming smile.

'Gone in a couple of minutes, promise.'

It bounced off the nurse and hit the floor with a thud.

'Two minutes. No more.'

And she went out leaving the door open.

'No sale for your charm there.'

'Jimmy, there's a problem.'

'Just one?'

'Look, maybe you're right but how do we do this? You might be able to barge in and say "It's the Chinese, end of story.

Now I quit". That's fine for you, you get to go back to being a student priest. But what about me? I go back to what? However we wrap it up if I say, "we're done now, go fuck yourself" to the minister then I'll be lucky to go back to work as a traffic cop.' He paused. 'You can see what I mean, can't you? Your career as a copper is over, mine's just taking off. It's a big ask for me to go along with it your way, a very big ask.'

Jimmy smiled. His smile was getting better, he'd been practising it while he was stuck in hospital. Now it nearly went all across his mouth.

'Being on the side of the angels always is a big ask, isn't it? Wasn't that something you told me?'

Ricci took the point.

'OK, it's easy to tell someone else to do the right thing. It's not so easy to do it when you have to pay the price yourself. Maybe right and wrong never look quite so clear-cut when you're at the sharp end.'

'Don't worry, I don't need you to do much, you won't get any crap on your record. I'll see to it that you stay as neat and clean as your nice, sharp clothes.'

'And you, will you stay clean?'

'Me? Who the hell would notice or care if Jimmy Costello picked up another bit of crap. I stopped smelling of roses long ago when ...'

'Moses was in the fire brigade and Pontius was a pilot.'

'Get me out of here tomorrow morning and set up a meeting for as soon as you can. Now piss off. I'm tired and the nurse says I need my rest.'

Jimmy climbed onto the bed, lay down, and closed his eyes but Ricci didn't leave.

'About Glasgow.'

'What about Glasgow?'

'You're sure it's finished, my uncle will be OK?'

'Why shouldn't he be?'

'Because according to you someone there nearly had you killed because you went and looked into the fire. What if they decide to do the same to my uncle? Do you think they might?'

'How the hell would I know? Your uncle's nothing to do

with the case so it's nothing to me one way or the other.' Jimmy turned over. 'Close the door on your way out.'

Ricci left, closing the door quietly behind him and walked on through the hospital. He would set up a meeting with the minister's aide, but from now on he would trust Jimmy about as much as he trusted the aide, which was only as far as he had to. By the time he was out of the hospital and walking to his car he had made a decision. He had been right the first time. He didn't like Jimmy Costello after all.

SIXTEEN

When Jimmy came to Rome he'd rented his furnished apartment from a couple who were making an extended visit to their son in South America. It was in an expensive residential district north-east of the Vatican and had been furnished with plenty of nice things; naturally the couple had worried about getting the right kind of tenant. For them an English ex-policeman in Rome training for the priesthood had been the answer to a prayer. It was too big really for just one person but Jimmy liked the convenience of the location, being able to walk into central Rome. For longer journeys Lepanto Metro station was only five minutes' walk and St Gioacchino's Church was nearby so if he wanted to go to morning Mass it wasn't a problem. He went most mornings, except when he, Danny, and Ron went together to eleven o'clock Mass at Chiesa Nuova before going to the bar for a drink. All in all he didn't mind what it was costing him, he could afford to pay for comfort, convenience, and privacy.

He sat in the kitchen sipping his coffee. He was tired after the journey from the hospital which reminded him that he was recuperating from a bad beating and wasn't ready yet to go ballroom dancing. There was a buzz from the street door. He went to the intercom. It was Danny.

'Come up. Top floor, the door will be open.' There was no

"glad to see you" in Jimmy's invitation. Nobody had visited him in hospital except Ricci. It wasn't that he'd wanted visitors, if he'd been asked he would have told the nurses to turn away any that came. But that wasn't the point. Nobody had come to be turned away, not Danny, not Ron, not anybody.

Danny appeared at the door and Jimmy took him into the living room where he motioned to an easy chair and they sat down.

'What's been going on, Jimmy?'

'I was in hospital, that's what's been going on. If you'd bothered to ask you'd have known.'

Danny laughed his deep laugh.

'Oh, I asked. When you suddenly dropped out of sight I asked. You'd been given permission to make a short trip back to the UK on urgent family business, which sounds a bit thin seeing as how you told us not so long ago that you'd got no family in the UK. Then I ask again, are you back yet? They tell me you're back but you got mugged and put into hospital. Ron and I came to see you but we got told you weren't having any visitors for as long as you were in there. No one. Why were you so off-limits? Was the mugging so bad?'

Keeping everyone away must have been Ricci's idea, though God knows why he did it.

'They did a fair job.'

'I tried to come and visit a couple of times but the answer was still no one allowed.'

'I didn't know that. I just thought I didn't have any visitors.'

'I phoned every morning, all I could get was, "Mr Costello is as well as can be expected". Then today they said you'd been discharged so I came round here. Look, I don't want to know why someone was keeping you under wraps, if that's what it was, that's your affair. I just want to know if you're OK.'

'Thanks, Danny. I'm OK. A bit fragile still, but like a bloke said, I'm a tough old bird and I've been knocked around before. I'll be fine. How are things going with you?'

'Not so well.' You could tell by the way he said it that it was going to be something serious. Danny paused before going on, getting himself ready. 'I'm giving up at the end of this term. I tried but it's just not for me. I wanted to tell you before anyone else because,' he paused again, looking for the right words, 'because I think we might have become friends. Because I think there's something I recognise in you that I know is in me.'

'About being a copper?'

'No, something about living with who we are, about accepting the person we find we've become. I think we're both looking for something. Not a new start, there's never a completely new start. The past doesn't let you go that easily. But trying to change, trying to make sure the future is different. I thought becoming a priest might be a part of building a future I could be happy to live with. Maybe you did as well. In my case I was wrong.'

'Do you want to talk about it?'

'No. It won't help to drag it out and show it about.' He laughed. 'It's no big deal. I'll survive. I'll go back to Jamaica and get myself a place. I'll get by on my pension and savings and go back to being just another old sinner. One more bad Catholic in need of God's love and mercy.'

They sat in silence.

'Coffee?'

'No, I hate the muck.'

'That's right, I forgot. You say it whenever we go to the bar. Why do you drink it if you don't like it?'

'It's a penance.' They both laughed. The seriousness had gone. Now they were just talking. 'Each day I have to say three Hail Marys, and drink at least three filthy coffees.'

'It must have been a real serious sin.'

'I'm a Jamaican who hates coffee. That's not just serious, it should be mortal. But there's no mortals these days, are there, Jimmy? Nobody's sin sends them to hell any more. Everything's venial now, all little sins. The days of big sins and big sinners are over. Everybody gets forgiven ever since somebody discovered that God's love is unconditional. You can't deserve it, you can't earn it, you get it whether you like it or not.'

'Like fluoride in the water.'

Danny laughed loudly.

'Spot on. And if God's love is unconditional his forgiveness has to be as well. So we all get forgiven whether we ask for it or not. Like fluoride in the water.' Then the laughter died away. 'Except that it isn't like that, is it? Most people don't want to think about whether they need forgiveness because they never look at themselves too closely. If they did they might not like what they see.'

'Listen, it was nice of you to call but I'm a bit tired.'

Danny got up.

'Sure. I just popped round.'

Jimmy got up and put out his hand.

'Thanks, Danny. I'm sorry you're packing it in.'

'Look after yourself, Jimmy, and take care.'

'I will. See you around.'

Danny left and Jimmy closed the door behind him. He went back into the living room, picked up the phone, and dialled.

'You get that meeting with the minister's aide? Good, when is it? Pick me up. Never mind that, let me deal with it. I said I would. Don't worry, I know what I'm doing. Just get me there, I'll do the rest.'

Jimmy put the phone down. Two days before the meeting to rest up and get ready then it was back to work. He went into the bedroom and drew the curtains and lay down on the bed. Danny's visit had unsettled him, that was why he had bustled him out. What Danny was doing, what he had said, was too close to home. While his doubts all stayed in his head he could deal with them but Danny had laid them out for him and he could see that what was true for Danny was probably just as true for him. He lay still wondering whether, after this Cheng business was over, he'd go back to training or do like Danny and pack it in. His mind circled the question but not for long. He was tired and in a few minutes he was asleep.

SEVENTEEN

'They won't let you in. You can't just walk into a government office and get a meeting with whoever you like.'

'We'll see.'

Ricci had picked Jimmy up at 9.30 and was now driving through the mad Roman traffic. A passing car swerved in front of him. Ricci pumped the horn a couple of times, a reflex reaction. Everybody pumped the horn.

'Just being with me won't get you in. Being a police inspector doesn't give me any pull. I'm not even a minor civil servant to these people.'

'We'll see.'

Ricci drove on. If Jimmy wasn't going to tell him he wasn't going to tell him.

'OK, have it your own way.'

'Like you had it your way so I got no visitors?'

Ricci gave him a quick, surprised look.

'That wasn't me, that was the hospital. At first they wouldn't even let me in to see you but when they were sure you were out of danger and going to be OK they changed their minds and made me an exception. But they were right, if they hadn't done it I would have seen to it. You'd been rambling. If you had visitors you might have said something.'

They drove on in through the busy traffic. It was the big

scooters that made Roman traffic different. All the bloody scooters in the world seemed to be on these roads and on cue a powerful black one, ridden by a woman whose leather-mixture jacket and pleated skirt clashed violently with her vivid yellow crash helmet, cut up a Suzuki rider who retaliated by revving up his big bike and roaring past her, causing shock waves of braking, swerving, and hooting. A Barbie girl in a tight white top, sunglasses, and jeans, with masses of curly black hair spilling from under her helmet, calmly slid her scooter into the openings the manoeuvring caused. Then everything subsided back into the normal horn-laden chaos.

Jimmy wondered why there were so few accidents. One day of this madness in London and the roads would be strewn with crash-helmeted corpses. But for Rome this was purely routine.

Ricci pulled across the traffic and turned down a side street which in turn took them into a narrower street behind a big government building. On one side were the high, unlovely backs of the government offices and on the other, high blank brick walls. Warehouses, maybe, or factories, whatever they were they didn't set a high premium on light, not on this side anyway. They came to an arched entrance originally designed for coach and horses, it was still big enough for a car or small van to get in, but nothing bigger. Ricci turned in and stopped. Immediately beyond the arch was a modern barrier blocking the access to a wide, deep, cobbled yard. Once this yard had rattled to coach wheels and horses' hooves and would have had plenty of stabling adjacent to it. Today tyres made almost no noise and the stables were gone. In their place was a guardroom not dissimilar to the one behind the security fence at the Vatican. A soldier in army fatigues appeared from the low building; he had a clipboard in his hand and an automatic rifle slung round his shoulder. He came to the car. Another face watched them from the guardroom window. Ricci slid the window down, showed his ID, and gave his name. The guard took the ID, checked the photo, and checked Ricci. Then he checked his list, gave Ricci back his ID, and looked into the car at Jimmy. Ricci also looked.

'OK, now what? Do you get us shot or what?'

'Does he know who you're here to see?' Ricci nodded. 'Then tell him you have an unscheduled visitor with you, give him my name, and ask him to OK it with your man inside. Tell him you apologise for not being able to give him any notice. Do it all slow and easy.'

The soldier stood impassively, he may have understood what was said but if he did he didn't register any kind of response. He just stood while Ricci spoke but a second guard came out of the hut and walked to where she had a clear field of fire at the car. Her automatic was in her hands but held, for the moment, casually. Ricci finished speaking and the guard went back into the hut. The other guard just stood in the same place but now she wasn't holding her weapon so casually and the barrel was pointing at the car. After a few minutes Clipboard came back. He spoke to Ricci who turned to Jimmy.

'He wants to see some ID. For God's sake, say you've got some.' Jimmy put his hand slowly into his inside jacket pocket, took out his passport, and passed it to Ricci who passed it on. The guard looked inside it, looked in at Jimmy, then he handed the passport back to Ricci, and said something to the other guard who didn't respond but kept looking at the car. Ricci handed Jimmy his passport while the guard wrote something on the list on his clipboard. 'He's adding your name. He says to get a temporary pass inside at the reception desk.'

The guard raised the barrier and they drove into a courtyard where a few cars were already parked and three large, commercial bins stood against a wall. As Jimmy got out of the car he wondered how they got emptied; the entrance would never take a refuse lorry big enough to handle them, even assuming a refuse lorry could get down the narrow street as far as the entrance. The yard itself managed to retain some of the elegance of a bygone age, it was clean with three old stone troughs by the walls which had once watered horses but now acted as planters for well-tended displays. With a little imagination you could imagine carriages on the cobbles and liveried servants bustling about. But the back of the building was different. It was several storeys of grimed-over brickwork with small windows and festooned with cabling conduits. There were also several big, ugly air-conditioning boxes and plenty of black drain pipes. This was the side of the building where the waste came out and the likes of Jimmy and Ricci went in.

They walked across the cobbles; the guard who had come out of the hut watched them all the way, the muzzle of her gun tracking them until they reached a heavy, black door. They went into the building, along a dim corridor with a bare stone floor, through another door into another corridor where the floor had some hard-wearing covering and better lighting, then through yet another door into what was obviously the main reception area.

This was front-of-house, where the people who mattered came and went. It was all style and elegance. The ceiling was high and elaborate. The floor was still stone, but now it was marble, inlaid with patterns. The two guards who stood not far from the entrance wore smart uniforms but both had their automatics in their hands and watched as Jimmy and Ricci were electronically swept by a civilian who had been by the door as they came in. Once they were waved on the guards lost interest. From the moment the car arrived at the barrier, and maybe before in the narrow street, they had been watched. It was the Vatican all over again but on a larger scale: everything looked Renaissance except the security, which looked and felt very modern.

Ricci led the way to a small desk where again he showed his ID and got checked off on a list. He clipped his pass to his jacket top pocket and began the business of getting a temporary pass for Jimmy. A phone call was made, the passport brought out again and taken away. There was the inevitable wait but finally Jimmy got his passport back, a pass was issued, and they crossed the hall to the lifts.

Their man was on the third floor which made him important. His office was high enough to be out of the noise of the street but not so high that the rooms had become small. They walked down a thickly carpeted corridor and stopped at a door. Ricci knocked and they waited.

'Knock again.'

'He heard. He'll tell us to come in when he's ready. He's

probably pissed off for having to OK you without notice and then having to wait while we got your pass.'

After a short while a voice called them in.

It was a spacious, baroque room with large windows letting in plenty of light. From the ceiling there hung two elaborate chandeliers surrounded by roundels of delicate plasterwork. The rest of the ceiling was covered with a painting of well-fed, naked young ladies who were about to get up to naughty things with some small men who had pointed ears, pointed beards, and goats' legs. The whole thing was framed at the walls by fancy gilded plasterwork. In each corner of the plaster decoration was a chubby naked cherub looking down and smiling broadly as if thoroughly amused by what was going on below. Things changed abruptly below the gilding. The walls were painted in a neutral colour and devoid of any decoration, no patterns, no pictures, no mirrors, only one severely elegant wall clock with a barely audible tick. The floor was also neutral, covered with a light-coloured carpet, the sort you put down if it wasn't going to get trodden on by feet that saw a lot of street work. The few pieces of furniture were ultra-modern chic with two smallish abstract bronzes on chrome stands to add a dash of contemporary culture. It was all as if someone had wanted to make the strongest possible contrast with the ceiling which spoke of pleasure and dalliance during a time when office chic hadn't existed and what interested artists was never abstract.

Jimmy liked it all. It appealed, especially the centrepiece, a large desk with thick chrome legs and a black, leather-covered top. It was all vaguely ridiculous and the cherubs, he felt, still saw the funny side. The man behind the desk obviously didn't. Either he was chewing a wasp or he was angry and about to let them know it.

He rapped out something in Italian. Inspector Ricci's voice was apologetic, almost humble.

'Signor Costello speaks very poor Italian.'

The minister's aide looked at Jimmy. The wasp gave him trouble again. He should stop chewing it, thought Jimmy.

'Sit down.'

There were no chairs at the desk, only two either side of an incongruous, delicate wooden table that had a crystal vase of fresh flowers on it. They dutifully collected their chairs, put them in front of the desk, and sat down.

The cut of the aide's dark suit did its best to hide his chubbiness and was so expensive it almost succeeded. He had a fullish face and curly, fair hair. Jimmy pigeonholed him at once, real plaster-gilding material, pure Cinquecento, a bad-tempered cherub in a sharp suit, as vaguely ridiculous as the office which he fitted to perfection.

'Perhaps you can explain, Inspector, why Mister Costello has to be present and without any notice?'

It was Jimmy who answered.

'Because as far as I'm concerned the investigation is over.' The aide slowly turned his disapproving gaze. 'Inspector Ricci doesn't agree. I phoned him this morning and told him to pick me up and bring me so that I could tell you personally. Inspector Ricci made it clear that my coming unannounced was highly irregular and I almost certainly wouldn't be admitted, but I insisted and threatened to withdraw completely from the investigation unless he brought me. So here I am.'

The aide looked back to Ricci.

'I am not satisfied, Inspector, that you have ...'

'It was the Chinese.' The cherub's eyes snapped back to Jimmy. 'On the basis of the evidence we have been given and as a result of our own enquiries which have been as thorough as circumstances have allowed I have come to the conclusion that either Archbishop Cheng died of natural causes aggravated by many years of systematic ill-treatment or he was murdered by an agent of the Chinese government because he represented a threat to their internal security.' Ricci looked down at the backs of his hands. They suddenly seemed to have a fascination for him. 'There being no further information available to us I consider our investigation to be at an end. I am quite happy for Inspector Ricci to put in a dissenting report from my conclusions but my decision on this matter is final and I now consider the matter closed. I also consider that, having given my fullest cooperation, I am now free to return to my studies.'

That was that. Now it was up to the cherub.

The aide's eyes were still angry but now there was something else: doubt. He turned back to Ricci and said something in Italian. Ricci looked at Jimmy and began to speak slowly but his expression made it clear that it was Jimmy's hand and he had to play it out.

'The minister's aide says ...'

Jimmy didn't wait.

'I didn't ask to be part of this and I understand that Inspector Ricci actively tried to have me removed but was overruled. As I said, we have done all that can be done with the information we have been given. Either you can accept my conclusions or ...'

It was crunch time. Jimmy let his last word hang and looked at the aide.

'Or?'

'Or you arrange a direct contact between me and a representative of whoever originated this investigation and arranged for me to be involved. If I am to continue as part of all this,' Jimmy paused; he wanted to be sure he created the right effect, 'there are certain questions I need to ask and they cannot be asked through intermediaries or functionaries.' The choice of words couldn't have had more effect. The aide looked at Jimmy with cold fury in his eyes, but before he could speak Jimmy had stood up. 'Good, now that's done I'll go. Thank you, Inspector, for bringing me. Goodbye, Mr ...?'

But the aide didn't volunteer a name. He just looked at Jimmy with a stare in which anger and loathing were nicely blended with pure amazement. A well-dressed cherub who'd bitten into a bad oyster in his favourite restaurant. Well, at least the wasp was gone.

Jimmy turned and left the office, walked back along the corridor, and went down in the lift to Reception where he handed back his pass and left the building through the main door, the one that the people who mattered used.

Outside, in the sunshine, he felt great. He hadn't felt this good for ... oh, how long? Well, a very long time indeed.

He walked along the street smiling. Forgotten Games of the Past: Squashing the Snotty Bastard.

The smile became a grin. No, he hadn't felt like this since

Moses was in the fire brigade and Pontius was a bloody pilot.

EIGHTEEN

They walked into the restaurant. Ricci ignored the welcome; he wasn't in a mood to be polite to waiters.

'You did well to walk out.'

'He took it badly, did he?'

'What do you think? "Cannot be asked through intermediaries or functionaries." For God's sake. Nobody must have talked to him like that since,' he paused trying to find the right words and failed, 'for a very long time. You couldn't have offended him more if you'd punched him on the nose.'

'I couldn't do that, it would spoil his face.'

Ricci gave him a sideways glance. He said odd things and did odd things. He was a difficult man to pin down.

They sat down at a table and Ricci ordered two coffees. Jimmy watched the waiter go. It was the same one as before and he had given him the look again.

'I see I'm still a bag-snatcher,'

There it was again.

'And what the hell is that supposed to mean?'

'Nothing.'

'Then why say it?'

Ricci's mood didn't lighten so Jimmy looked around. It still wasn't busy.

'Why do we have to come here? Why can't we go

somewhere else, somewhere ... well somewhere that's not like here.'

'You mean somewhere cheap and dirty like your bar?'

'I like it. At least it's not a morgue like this place.'

'And I like it here because here it's on expenses.' Ricci decided that what was done was done, and anyway, it hadn't gone so very badly. In fact it had been quite a show. 'I need to be a regular in a few places like this so I can blend in.'

'So what is it you do exactly, when you're not busy dying from something terminal and running unofficial investigations for the minister?'

'I suppose there's no harm in you knowing. I work in the ...' he paused, looking for the right words; this time he found them, '... what might get called in London, the Glitz Squad.'

Jimmy laughed,

'The Glitz Squad. What's that?'

'It's what it says. I operate on any case where there is or might be Beautiful People involvement.'

'What, celebrities and that?'

The coffees came. They waited until the waiter had gone.

'You don't know Rome, it's not like the London you worked in, it's a different world. High fashion sits at the same table with lowlifes and you can't always tell the difference. Crime follows the money and if the money wears glitz so does crime. Underneath all the glamour and the gushing the usual nasty things go on, maybe even more so. The rich are always targets and the super-rich are super targets. And they didn't get or keep their money by being kind and gentle so sometimes it gets rough. I get plenty of work and believe me, I earn my pay.'

Jimmy thought he probably did. 'So how rich is super rich?'

'In your world you'd call them the haves and have-nots. In my world it's the haves and have-yachts.'

Jimmy liked it.

'That's good.'

'I got it out of an English newspaper.'

'And does all your gear come on expenses?'

Ricci nodded.

'Has to; I couldn't afford the shirts, never mind the rest of it.

102

But it's more than just dressing up. The way I dress, anyone who knows about clothes and stuff will figure there's no way on God's earth I could do it on a policeman's pay and that must mean I'm a self-serving, dishonest bastard who gets what he wants any way he can, so I just naturally fit right on in.'

'So how about politics and politicians? Are you used to dealing with people like Charlie Cherub?'

'Charlie Cherub?'

'Your man from this morning.'

Now it was Ricci's turn to like it.

'Yeah, it fits. I meet them socially sometimes. I don't usually deal with them though, politicos are normally off my patch. Charlie Cherub, what made you think of it?'

'His office, the ceiling mostly.'

'You know, up to now I took him seriously, senior personal aide to the minister and all that. I thought of him as a big hitter. I don't think I can any more. From now on he'll always be Charlie Cherub.'

'Believe me, whatever he is he's not a big hitter.'

'How do you know?'

'Because I got in.'

'And what does that mean?'

'If he was half the man he thinks he is he'd have had me turned back at the barrier; better still shot.'

'If he hadn't OK'd you we might both have got shot. Those guards aren't for show. They'd use their guns if they thought they had to and leave any questions for somebody else to deal with.'

'I should hope they would. Armed guards who ask questions when they should be shooting would be no bloody good at all.'

'What would you have done if he had sent you packing?'

'Gone away and tried something else. As it was I got in and that means either he's not very hot on security ...'

'Which he is.'

'... or he knows I have to be on board, that I'm important to whatever's going on. He was being careful. He let me in to see why I was there. He wanted to be sure that whatever I was up to he would be in a position to cover his back.'

'And that's it, you bet on him being careful, on him wanting to cover his back?'

'I've met his sort a hundred times and more, they all run true to form. They're successful, they get to go right on up, but they never make it all the way to the top. They get to be the deputy this or principal assistant that. They're usually cleverer than the people they work for, often quite a bit cleverer, but they're always second-raters. The bottom line for them is: always make sure you have a way out from under if things go pear-shaped. They never carry the can, they're never the one to blame. And that means they won't commit, not fully. They haven't got the bottle to match the brains. So you'll always find one of them in the kitchen but they never get to be the chef, and if things get too hot they don't take the heat or help put out the fire, they put all their talents into getting out clean. When you need them most, they'll just not be there.'

'And you guessed he'd be like that?'

'No, but it was worth a try and as it turned out I was right. Once I was in I knew what I was dealing with so I just let him have it between the eyes and walked away. No sense in overdoing it. It's like making a hit. Keep it simple, keep it clean, and walk away.'

Ricci looked down at his cup. He didn't appreciate the comparison.

'You sound as if you speak from personal experience. Is that one of the things that got filleted out of your record?'

It was a straight question.

'You don't have to have done something like that to know how it's done.'

It was an evasive answer.

Each took a drink of their tiny espressos. Ricci put his question behind him.

'OK, you did what you did and I took the flak.'

'Did it amount to anything?'

'Not really. Huffing and puffing, threats of reports to my superiors.'

'But you got out clean, you put it down to me like we agreed? You got my ultimatum with no warning just like he did and you both did what you thought was for the best?' Ricci nodded. 'Good, in that case you're in the clear because if you were wrong to bring me along with you then he was wrong to let me in and, believe me, the way he will tell it he won't be wrong.'

Ricci agreed.

'After he'd let off steam at me he chewed you up but it'll come out OK.'

'I told you it would.'

'So, what happens now?'

'We wait until we get contacted. When we get the meeting with our man from the Vatican, if it is the Vatican, we ask our questions. If we find there's anything to chase, we're off and running.'

'What do we do till we get the call?'

'See your China watcher again. I want to know if there's still something we might not know about Cheng.'

'Like what?'

'He went into prison first time as a priest and came out as a bishop. When and why did that happen? When he surfaces in Macau he's an archbishop. Again, when and why did it happen? Was it Vatican support for someone under the cosh, was it for services rendered against the People's Republic, or was it part of some sort of diplomatic game? If it was part of some diplomatic chess game then were all the moves over with Cheng once he got rehabilitated?'

'So exactly what is it I'm looking for?'

'How should I know? Ask your China watcher.'

'Ask him what?'

'How should I know? I'm not a bloody China watcher.'

They sat in silence. Then Jimmy had an idea.

'How about, was he still an archbishop when he died?' Ricci obviously didn't understand. 'Cheng got made a bishop in secret, then archbishop in secret, so why not a cardinal in secret? Could that be why he'd come to Rome, to get the red hat on the quiet, to get bumped up to cardinal but without any publicity so as not to offend the Chinese?'

Ricci frowned. 'It's a good thought.'

105

'If you asked the question do you think your China watcher could answer it?'

'Maybe. Would it be important?'

'How the hell would I know? I don't even know why I'm doing this. But if I'm only going to be allowed to know diddly-squat about what's going on, I want all of the diddly-squat. We'll sort out if any of it's important later.'

'OK, I'll look into it. What are you going to do?'

'I'm going to rest. I mend quick but not as quick as I used to. And I've got to arrange some proper leave of absence with my rector, make up some sort of cover story like you've got. My not being where I should has already been noticed and questions asked. I'll need to fix it so it's not going to be a problem.'

'Will your rector kick off?'

'I doubt it. She doesn't like me, doesn't consider me a suitable candidate for the priesthood. She hates any time of hers that I take up so if I drop out for a while that'll be like an early Christmas present for her.' Jimmy stood up. 'You'll pay if it's on expenses?'

'Sure.'

Jimmy left and Ricci watched him go.

How the hell did a man who could talk with easy familiarity about blowing someone's brains out get onto a priests' training course?

But he stopped himself thinking along those lines. It served no useful purpose to speculate about how Jimmy had turned up in Rome. If his record had been fixed and he got vouched for by the right kind of people it could happen easily enough. What mattered now was whether he brought something special to the inquiry, and he did. He'd got in to see the minister's aide and maybe got them a meeting with someone who could throw some light on what they were actually involved in. And he had done it like he said, with no mud sticking on anybody but himself.

Ricci smiled. He used his nice smile even though there was no one there to see it. Watch out, Jimmy, if that aide gets a chance to do you some harm he'll jump at it. You made him look bad this morning and he's going to have to do some very fancy talking not to come out of things with a black mark against him. You were bang on about his sort; their greatest duty is their greatest joy, the delegation of blame. When someone puts them in the firing line it's the unforgivable sin and one they never forget.

Ricci was honest enough, now he was talking to himself, to admit that he had a little of that same attitude. Maybe even more than a little. Take care, Jimmy, because if Charlie Cherub turns up the heat on you don't look to me for help. Like you said, I'll be well out of the kitchen.

He looked at his watch; time to get moving. He would set up a meeting with his China watcher and ask about that cardinal business. He put some money on the table, pushed the bill into his pocket and got up. He wondered what the pay-off would be at the end of things. If it was important, and it looked like it was, he wanted to be the one on the receiving end of any congratulations and commendations, even if they were only unofficial. If there was anything else, if the shit started flying, well, Jimmy wouldn't mind being on the receiving end for that; he'd said as much.

After all, he was going to be a priest, wasn't he?

NINETEEN

'That's it, "Call at my office at three tomorrow afternoon," he said nothing else?'

Ricci turned the car into the narrow back street behind the ministry building.

'How many times do you need telling?'

They stopped at the barrier, a guard came out with his clipboard. Ricci showed his ID, gave his name, the guard checked his list, gave Ricci's ID photo and his face a good look, then asked a question in which Jimmy thought he caught his own name.

'This is Signor Costello.' Jimmy gave his passport to Ricci who passed it on. The guard checked it then bent down and looked into the car, this time giving Jimmy a good once-over, then he looked at the passport again, then went back into the guardroom. They could see him talking to the other guard.

'Is it me or have things tightened up a bit?'

Ricci turned away from watching the guardroom.

'It's nothing, your name's on the list alongside mine. It's just that your ID isn't official, just a passport. He's being careful.' The guard was on the phone now, looking out at them while he talked. When he put the phone down it was the woman guard who came out and gave Ricci the passport and opened the barrier. This time she hardly touched her gun at all. They drove in and parked the car in the same place as last time. Jimmy got out and noticed that the three bins were open and had been emptied. They went through the back door, along the corridors, and on into the reception area where they were once again met and swept before they picked up their passes. Then they went up in the lift, along the silent corridor, and knocked at the aide's door.

'Come in.'

It was a woman's voice. Inside there were the same two chairs but this time in front of the desk and sitting behind the desk was Professor McBride. She gave them a steady look.

'Come in, please, and close the door.'

Ricci closed the door and they sat down. McBride didn't speak, she waited, so Jimmy broke the silence.

'Professor, what are you doing here? What we're here for is nothing to do with Duns College.'

'Only very indirectly, Mr Costello. You are currently assisting Inspector Ricci, who is officially on sick leave, in an unofficial inquiry. You are doing this at the request of the minister who, in turn, is acting at the request of an unnamed party. But you are also currently a Duns student so, in that respect but in that respect only, it could be said to be Duns College business. And since you have brought the matter up I think I should point out that for a Duns student to become involved in such a bizarre course of action without seeking the necessary permissions is irregular in the extreme, not to mention how incompatible with your studies such an involvement must be. As to whether it is at all fitting for one training for the priesthood ...'

'Excuse me, Professor.'

'Yes, Inspector?'

'We were told the minister's aide wanted to see us. If you could please explain?'

'There you're wrong, Inspector. All you were told was to be here at three. You were not told that the minister's aide would be the one you would see.'

'But I naturally assumed ...'

'Then I'm afraid you assumed wrongly.'

110

Jimmy asked the question.

'Why are you here?'

'Because, Mr Costello, you asked to talk to someone in authority in this matter. Apparently you have questions you wish answered. I will answer them in so far as it is in my power so to do.'

So to do! Still a prat, whatever hat she was wearing this time.

'Professor, I don't like being pissed about, not by you, not by the Vatican, not by anybody.' Jimmy noticed Ricci stiffen slightly in his chair, but he didn't care. 'I'm here because somebody, I thought the Vatican, wanted my help. So far all that's happened is that I've been pissed about.'

'Does being savagely beaten and put into hospital come under your heading of being pissed about? I would have thought it rather more serious.'

She was smiling, enjoying herself. Jimmy relaxed, he smiled as well.

'No, you're right. That wasn't being pissed about. But it wasn't the Vatican or the minister who had me put in hospital, was it?'

'No. Neither the minister nor the Vatican are in the habit of putting people in hospital.'

This time it was Ricci who moved things on.

'Professor, will you please explain?'

'Certainly. Mr Costello made it clear that unless he received more active co-operation he would withdraw from the inquiry. It has been decided, at the highest level, that his services should be retained so I have been asked to liaise in this matter.'

'You, Professor?'

'Does that surprise you, Inspector? I wonder why? Is it perhaps because I'm a woman? Or is it because I'm black? Please feel free to be frank.'

Ricci became confused.

'Of course not. I just expected that, well, from the Vatican, I expected ...'

'From the Vatican you would expect a man, a priest, probably a monsignor at the very least. Someone with a touch of red about them to lend authority. Well I'm afraid all you've got is me and not a touch of red to be seen anywhere. So, what can I do for you?'

'Why me? Why am I so important?'

McBride looked at Jimmy then at Ricci, then back at Jimmy.

'I am happy to answer that question, Mr Costello, but I have been asked to give my fullest co-operation. My answers will be quite forthright. I will hold back nothing. Are you both happy that I speak freely about you in front of each other?'

Ricci didn't mind. He knew he was as clean as a Sunday in white socks.

'It's OK with me.'

'And you, Mr Costello, is it OK with you?'

Jimmy hesitated. It wasn't OK with him, but what could he do? His past was no business of Ricci's, and he was pretty sure Ricci would use anything he heard if ever he felt he needed to. The question was, would he ever need to? The next question, a very big question, was how much did she know? If she knew ... The new Jimmy took over. What does it matter? Let Ricci know. Just get on with it, you were the one who wanted to know why you're in this. Let the woman tell you.

'Sure, go ahead.'

'Very well. The investigation you are carrying out is a highly sensitive one and might have far-reaching consequences.'

'If it shows that Cheng's death was not due to natural causes.'

The sharpness of Jimmy's interruption surprised Ricci but that wasn't what McBride took exception to. So far as she was concerned he could ask all the questions he wanted in whatever manner he chose. What she did take exception to was the way Jimmy used the name.

'Archbishop Cheng.' She paused, to make her point then continued, 'And it is not quite that simple, Mr Costello. Even if there were only a suspicion of foul play, credibly established in the minds of various interested parties, the repercussions could be considerable. In fact, were your investigations to leave the death as an open question that might be far more damaging than

112

a confirmation that Archbishop Cheng's death was the result of a deliberate act.' Jimmy noticed she didn't say murdered. He was listening as carefully to her as she was to him. 'When it became apparent that Archbishop Cheng's death might have to be re-investigated the first concern was to ensure that full control was retained over the investigation, especially its outcome. Seeing as there was no way of knowing what the outcome of any enquiry might be it was essential that nothing was begun until it was certain that the whole process could be properly handled right from the beginning in whatever way was deemed best.'

'Handled?'

'Yes, Inspector, handled.'

'In what way, handled?'

'Presented in such a way that all interested parties were satisfied.'

'You mean you wanted to manipulate the whole thing?'

'If you prefer. The investigation and its conclusions on the archbishop's death will be presented, if and when they are presented, in a way that ensures that the repercussions, should there be any, will do as little damage as possible or as much good as possible to those most interested in the matter. Surely you as a policeman are not unused to such things. For the police to manipulate, or handle, information in the way it is released is, I am sure, not something new to you.' Ricci didn't like it but he couldn't argue with it. 'And you, Mr Costello, are an essential ingredient of the future management of the outcome of the enquiry should it prove necessary to manipulate it, as you are also, Inspector.' She looked from one to the other. 'You are a matched pair.'

'Never mind what sort of pair we are. Why me in particular, why am I so special?'

'As the outcome of any enquiry into Archbishop Cheng's death was unpredictable we needed to be in a position to endorse or to reject the outcome as we saw fit. The enquiry had to be as thorough and professional as the sensitive nature of the case would allow, which meant two detectives with proven abilities. However, our requirements went beyond professional

113

skill. One of the detectives had to be above suspicion, with no trace of corruption attached to him. If we wished to endorse the findings we wanted to be able to point out that the investigation had been led by an officer of experience and integrity and that its findings were above suspicion with no question of any failure of method or thoroughness, nor of any tampering with or distortion of the evidence.' Jimmy began to feel uncomfortable. He knew what was coming. 'The other detective had to be someone whose presence as part of the enquiry would, on investigation, render any findings absolutely unreliable. Someone whose record, when properly looked into, showed him to have been a thoroughly corrupt officer.' She let it sink in. 'We began our search for a suitable candidate for the latter role in Rome, but the few officers drawn to our attention were not up to the job as detectives. We widened our field of search, but how true we found the old saying that you can never find a really corrupt policeman when you want one.' She looked at Jimmy and smiled. 'Then you turned up, Mr Costello. Your second application had come to Rome and my attention was drawn to the fact that you had been a detective sergeant in the London Metropolitan Police. I thought it worth following up because you were a Catholic and therefore more traceable for us. Also you had been given early retirement, which might or might not mean something. When I was told your official file was remarkably slim and uninformative about your career I realised we might at last have what we were looking for.'

She paused. If she was going to hang him she wanted to give him the chance of saying a few last words.

'Nobody objected to you nosing about in police personnel files?'

'Good heavens no, Mr Costello. The questions were asked by people who thought they were making genuine enquiries on behalf of Rome about someone applying for the priesthood. It was the sort of thing the Metropolitan Police would bend over backwards to facilitate. Your friends who had fixed the records were, for once, quite out of their depth and unable to intervene. You cannot take the Catholic Church down an alley and kick it into submission. Well, actually you can, and in certain parts of the world people still do, but not in London, Mr Costello, in London we get co-operation.'

'OK, so you got told about my record, that it wasn't anything special.'

'How true. According to your official record, what was left of it, you hardly existed as a policeman. Considering how long you had served that was very encouraging, so further enquiries were made through your old parish in Kilburn. Those enquiries revealed the sort of man you had been. Serving and retired policemen who remembered you confirmed the extent to which you were feared. We got a very clear picture of you, Mr Costello. You can hide your past from officialdom in many ways but you cannot erase the memories of ordinary people. Our picture was drawn from the memories of people you probably never noticed but who noticed you because you were a man to be avoided, a man to fear. You were, Mr Costello, just the man we were looking for because, whatever else you were, everyone who had any knowledge of you professionally agreed that you were an excellent detective. And there you were, suddenly dropped into our lap in our time of need. Good luck or divine intervention, Mr Costello? Which would you say it was?'

Jimmy knew the answer to that one.

'I wouldn't say.'

'You came to Rome for your preliminary interview and were eventually accepted. The interview panel, lacking the information to which I had access, had no reason to reject you as a student, especially as Sister Philomena gave such an excellent report on your placement. Fortunately for me the selection process is a slow one, especially when it involves a Duns College student. I was also able to slow it down even further by arranging that certain papers were temporarily lost.'

'I wondered why it took so long.'

'A nuisance for you, of course, but necessary for me to make sure you were the sort of man we needed.'

A thought occurred to Jimmy.

'Was the placement part of your fix?'

'Fix?'

'Was it some sort of set-up? Did Philomena know anything
115

about what you were up to?'

'Good heavens, no. Our resources do not run to setting up false placements, real ones are hard enough to find. It was a perfectly normal placement after a preliminary enquiry – and you weren't even on my radar at that time. The fix, as you call it, was only delaying your final application to keep you in the system so that you would be in Rome when we needed you. It was fortunate that you did so well in London though. Had anything gone wrong during your time with Sister Philomena it would have been a nuisance for us here. But the placement proved satisfactory so you came to Rome for your extended interview which, given they only had access to information you had supplied and Sister Philomena's report, you naturally passed, and eventually, somewhat later than would normally be the case, you began life as a student.'

'Didn't anyone think it odd that my application took so long?'

'Oh no, These things take as long as they take, weeks, months ...'

'Years?'

'Yes, that is unusual, but not unique. We were glad you proved to be so very patient. It would have been awkward if you had chosen to withdraw and go elsewhere to pursue your vocation.'

'Yes, I can see it would have been awkward.'

'Purely as a matter of interest, where were you?'

'Ireland, the west of Ireland. There was a priest there that I knew.'

'Ah yes. There was an enquiry from an Irish priest about the delay in your application.'

'He said he'd try and help.'

'I'm afraid he was told, politely but firmly, to mind his own business.'

'He told me to be patient.'

'Good advice, I'm glad you took it. And when you finally came to Rome you were exactly what you thought you were, a student priest, until we wanted our investigation to begin. That is why I brought you to Rome, to ensure that if it becomes necessary anything you and Inspector Ricci find can be written off as compromised and unreliable due to your dubious and almost certainly criminal past. That, Mr Costello, is why you are necessary, to give us an avenue of denial.' There was an uncomfortable silence. Even the aide's chic clock ticked in what seemed a shocked manner. McBride sat still and when it was clear that neither Jimmy nor Ricci were inclined to say anything she went on. 'I hope that answers your question, Mr Costello. I don't think I left anything out.'

Nothing much, thought Jimmy. Only a few dead and broken bodies in London that Philomena had left out of her report. Nothing that would spoil the placement and upset her plans.

'No, I think you covered the ground. Would you answer two more questions?'

'Of course; it's why I'm here.'

'If we find that Cheng's death ...'

'Archbishop Cheng's death.'

'... is suspicious, how serious is it likely to be?'

'Serious enough to justify all we have done and are prepared to do in the future. And we are prepared to do a great deal. I cannot exaggerate how serious this matter could become. Your second question?'

'Is Inspector Ricci any good as a detective and is he really as squeaky clean as you say he is?'

Ricci looked uncomfortable. He had recognised in Professor McBride a heavyweight, an establishment hard case and probably as clever as they come. She would know him as well as she obviously knew Jimmy and, though he had nothing to hide professionally, somehow that didn't fill him with confidence.

'Oh, yes. Inspector Ricci has his eye on considerable advancement and wouldn't dream of jeopardising his promotion chances by getting his hands dirty. And although he hasn't your skills as a detective I think you will find him a useful assistant in the inquiry.'

Ricci's attitude changed in a flash: she had touched him in a sensitive place.

'What do you mean, assistant?'

'Oh, come now, Inspector, you have been assistant to Mr Costello's lead in this from the moment you started to work together. That we are in this room together having this meeting is down to Mr Costello's judgement, experience, and strength of purpose. You were both carefully chosen not only for the reasons I have given but to complement each other in your work. I realise that you are a serving inspector, albeit on temporary sick leave, and that Mr Costello, before retirement, never rose above sergeant, but rank in this matter is immaterial. Mr Costello leads. That's final.'

Ricci was out of his seat.

'If he leads, I quit. You've just been telling me what sort of policeman he is, corrupt and dangerous, and now you want me to ...'

'Was, Inspector. I have told you what he was, not what he is.'

'Was, is, what's the difference?'

'All the difference in the world, I should have thought. Please, Inspector, sit down.' Ricci sat down, his anger had run out of steam and reason was seeping back. This woman had clout, she would make a bad enemy.

'When this investigation is over, whatever the outcome, particular thanks will be expressed to the minister for his co-operation in setting up this inquiry. He in turn will express his thanks to whoever in the police assisted him. For obvious reasons, you will be the one whom they will be told led the inquiry. Officially, Mr Costello's role will be entirely subordinate to your own.'

Reason was fully back in the driving seat.

'What if you need to discredit the findings? Who gets to do that?'

'That will be your affair to manage as you see fit. You will need to arrange it so that Mr Costello's involvement, though a minor one compared to your own, was sufficient to severely prejudice the outcome. You will also need to explain how and why you became suspicious of him. But all that can be arranged if it becomes necessary. I'm sure you will deal with it perfectly well, if it has to be done at all.'

Jimmy sat there listening as they talked about him. It was funny, he didn't mind, he didn't mind what Ricci knew or what he thought. It was all true and as bad as it sounded. It was because it was true that it didn't matter. Jimmy put away all that she had said about him. It was as it was. Now he knew why he was here. He would do what he had to do as best he could, not because it was what anybody wanted, but because a good and possibly holy old man deserved the truth about his death to be known. That at least was something good and honest he could do. All the rest could wait.

Ricci was all reasonableness now.

'OK, if it's all unofficial anyway which of us actually leads doesn't matter one way or the other.'

'How sensible of you. Now, are there any more questions?'

It was time for Jimmy to be a detective, and a bloody good one. So, he got to business.

'If Archbishop Cheng was murdered it was done by people who were certain they could get away with it. There's no direct evidence, no motive, nothing. If they exist they're invisible.'

'I would have thought that narrowed the field considerably.'

Ricci cut in.

'Not at all. One invisible man is no easier to see than a crowd of invisible men.'

Jimmy liked it.

'He's right. So what we need is a way in. Something that we can see, something that is Cheng-related.'

McBride sat back.

'You have looked into his life, his background, as fully as you can?'

'Yes.'

'And you have studied all the available evidence of his death?'

'Which is just the autopsy report and some paperwork, none of which gets us anywhere.'

'Which is not just the autopsy report and the paperwork.'

'What else is there?'

'His funeral. Did you look into his funeral?'

No, they hadn't looked into his funeral. The body had been

119

flown back to China as soon as the autopsy had been completed and there was no way that they could follow it even if they'd wanted to.

'If we had looked into the funeral what would we have seen?'

'Hardly anything, Inspector. You would have seen almost nothing.'

'If there was nothing to see how can ...'

'Wait a minute.'

'Yes, Mr Costello?'

'It was a small affair?'

'Almost non-existent. Immediate family from Macau and two officials from Beijing.'

'From Beijing?'

'Yes Inspector, two officials from Beijing.'

'And it took place where?'

'Not in his cathedral. It took place in a small parish church belonging to the Official Catholic Church. One priest from the Official Church presided then the archbishop's body was taken to his cathedral where he was quietly buried. No one, not even family, were present at the interment.'

If she was taking them somewhere, why pussyfoot around, why not just say what she wanted them to know?

'Make your point, Professor. I've told you, I don't want to be pissed about any more.'

If the words and the way they were said bothered her she didn't show it.

'He came to Rome as a recognised figure in the Chinese media, a glowing symbol of their new openness and tolerance. He was buried in a silence that was almost deafening. There was no media coverage of any sort, not a word about his death, other than that he had died.'

'So what does that mean?'

'Ah, now that question I cannot answer.'

'Can't or won't?'

'Can't, and before you speak again, Mr Costello, I assure you that I am not in any way "pissing you about". I cannot tell you why Archbishop Cheng's funeral was such a low-key affair,' she made the point by pausing, 'but was nonetheless attended by two senior officials from Beijing.'

Whatever she was pointing at, it was passing Jimmy by. But Ricci picked it up.

'So he was more than an archbishop when he was buried. He was someone Beijing were prepared to recognise as a senior Vatican official.' He turned to Jimmy, 'He was a cardinal. He had to be.'

'I never said he had been made a cardinal, Inspector. That is your assumption.'

Jimmy looked at Ricci. A cardinal. Did it matter? And why was Ricci so sure?

'What makes you think so?'

'Because the Professor just said Beijing sent two officials, senior officials. Why two, why any at all if it was such a hole-and-corner affair, the funeral of someone the state wanted buried and forgotten?'

'OK, why?'

'It was a message to the Vatican, "we acknowledge his rank even though we cannot give him a public burial".' He turned to McBride. 'For Beijing that would be some concession, yes?'

'If you are correct, yes it would be a very significant concession.'

'Then he was a cardinal?'

'I cannot tell you what I do not know, Mr Costello, and I do not know if Archbishop Cheng had been given the red hat. I could speculate as Inspector Ricci has done but I am not a detective. I deal in facts and leave speculation to others.'

'Fine. If you can't be sure then find us someone who can.'

She thought about it for a moment.

'Would you both step outside for a moment while I make a phone call?'

They left the office and stood outside the door in the corridor.

'Well?'

Ricci pretended not to know what Jimmy meant.

'Well what?'

'You know what.'

121

Ricci knew.

'Listen, you were a bent copper, you were a dangerous man, now it's caught up with you and it's being used. I don't care what sort of copper you were and I already guessed you could be a dangerous man so nothing's changed. I just hope you were as good a detective as she thinks you were.'

'So you'll get your brownie points if we get a result?'

'Yes. She's right, I want to go all the way and if this helps, fine. I'll follow your lead so long as your lead takes us where I want to go.'

'And then, if she says so, you'll drop me in it?'

'With the greatest of pleasure, Jimmy. It's where you deserve to be after all, not swanning about playing at becoming a priest or doing the Vatican's detective work.'

'Ah, the moral high ground. I bet you spend a fortnight there each year just to remind yourself how nice the neighbours will be when you get to live there permanently.'

'Fuck you.'

Jimmy didn't care about Ricci. But that was the point, he should care. Any normal person would care. If he wanted to be a normal person he had to try and care.

'Look, we have to work together, we don't have to like each other but we have to get on with each other. So what say we just do this like it's a roster thing? The list's gone up and we've been put on a case together. Let's just do it.'

Ricci thought about it. It was the only sensible way, they were a team, that's all. They'd been put together to do a job and it was in his best interests to see it well done. He'd worked perfectly well often enough with men he hadn't liked. He'd even worked well with a few men he reckoned were crooked enough to hide behind a spiral staircase.

'OK, what's done is history. We just get on with the job in hand.'

'That was good, by the way, about him being a cardinal because of the boys from Beijing. I should have seen it.'

'Not really, you'd already guessed it, remember? You were past it and looking for something else.'

He's right, thought Jimmy, I'd half guessed it. But did his

being a cardinal make him worth killing, and if it did, why did he have to die in Rome?

TWENTY

The office door opened.

'Come in, please.'

They all went back in and sat down. When she spoke it was very deliberately.

'I have asked your question and I have been given a response. The Vatican can neither confirm nor deny that the late Archbishop Cheng had been given a red hat by his Holiness.'

Jimmy felt his anger rising.

'Neither confirm nor deny. What sort of answer is that?'

Ricci, however, seemed satisfied.

'I see.'

Jimmy didn't.

'Well I bloody don't. I thought we were going to get answers, straight answers.'

McBride repeated it for him.

'I have been told to say that the Vatican can neither confirm nor deny that the late Archbishop Cheng had been given the red hat by his Holiness.'

'I heard you the first time and it still doesn't mean anything.'

'Leave it, Jimmy.'

There was a command in Ricci's voice, so Jimmy left it. He didn't like it but he left it.

Ricci got up.

'Is there anything else about Archbishop Cheng you can tell us?'

She turned the question over in her mind. The truth was always tricky. Anything else about Archbishop Cheng or the case? Hmm.

'Nothing that I can think of.'

'In that case we'll be going. Goodbye, Professor, and thank you.'

Jimmy got up. He didn't know what was going on but obviously Ricci did.

'Goodbye, Inspector, goodbye, Mr Costello. Just tell the minister's aide to let me know if you need my help again.'

Professor McBride didn't get up, she just watched them go to the door. Ricci went out but Jimmy paused.

'You'll sort out leave of absence for me?'

'It's already done, Mr Costello.' Jimmy nodded, of course it was. 'But we should discuss the arrangements. They are reasonably straightforward but you should be fully aware of what they involve. Could you come to my office tomorrow at ten?'

'Sure.'

He left and closed the door. When he caught Ricci up in the corridor he asked his question.

'What did it mean, the "neither confirm nor deny" stuff? How does that help?'

'Because it means he was a cardinal. It's Vaticanese. It's their way of saying yes when they can't say yes.'

'I see, so all we've got that's new is his being a cardinal?'

'There's nothing else unless you're prepared to go to China and start digging, literally as well as metaphorically.'

They took the lift down, handed back their passes, and went back to the car where the guards checked them out. Soon they were back in the Roman traffic where Ricci picked it up again.

'So now we know he was a cardinal. I don't see how that gets us anywhere.'

Jimmy was looking out of the window watching Roman drivers trying to kill each other. He turned and answered absently.

'If it was murder it tells us it wasn't the Chinese. Why give him such a big build up then kill him and why kill him in Rome and if it was them why the senior officials at the funeral? It's all too elaborate, too much trouble, and it makes no sense.'

Jimmy turned back to watching the traffic and thought about it. Cheng as a cardinal was the only new thing they had, but he didn't like it. Murder for him had always been simple, either an act of impulse or follow the trail until you found out who benefited most, which usually meant follow the money. But if this was murder it wasn't an impulse killing, it was a planned, and it probably wasn't going to be about money. He tried to see some way in which the cardinal thing could get them started and go somewhere.

Ricci did some horn pumping as a white van cut him up then got back to the subject in hand.

'It's all we've got so let's fill in what we can and see if anything comes out of it.'

'Like what?'

'Well he must have got his red hat here in Rome before he died. That means only Cheng and the pope knew he was a cardinal. No one else, except maybe just a few top bods in the Vatican.'

'And?'

'And if no one knew about it how can it be part of the reason he died, unless you're prepared to put the pope in the frame? Unless ...' Ricci left it hanging. But Jimmy wanted it. Anything was better than nothing.

'Unless what?'

'No, it's nothing, it can't be.'

'Try me, we're not exactly dripping with places to go on this.'

'Well, you figured it out first, Jimmy.'

'Me?'

'Yes, remember, you said first a secret bishop, then a secret archbishop, so what else might have happened that nobody knew about? Well, now we know. He *was* a secret cardinal.'

'But if no one knew.'

'You guessed. Why shouldn't somebody else guess? Why

127

couldn't someone else work out it would happen.'

'What? They killed him because he might be a cardinal?'

Said out loud like that Ricci remembered why he hadn't wanted to say it. He now wished he hadn't.

'I told you it was nothing. It can't be.'

They drove on.

Jimmy looked out of the window. This was all new waters for him, a million miles away from anything he'd ever done before, but he'd still have to use the old methods since they were the only ones he had. So he began. Use your experience, Jimmy. Do the same things, follow the same routines, ask the same questions. Forget it's the Vatican, forget it's Rome, forget it's political. Just ask the same questions. Was this an isolated killing, was it just Cheng? It's not a normal killing, so is it related to anything? Have there been others like it?

'How many others?'

'How many other what?'

'Cardinals who've died suddenly. How many other unexpected deaths in, say, the last two years?'

Ricci gave a low whistle and braked slightly as a Fiat sports car cut in, apparently intent on cadging a lift on his front bumper. Jimmy's question made him forget to pump the horn.

'It's a bit rich, isn't it, murdering cardinals?'

'Well, if we're right, one's been done, so why not ask if there're any more?'

'All right, if you think it's a question worth asking. You lead in this, remember.'

'I'm seeing McBride tomorrow to sort out my leave of absence. I'll ask her who I need to see to get the information.'

'What do you think she'll do for you, arrange something terminal like they did for me?'

Jimmy gave a small laugh.

'The way things are going I think I may already have something terminal.'

The car came to Jimmy's district of quiet, tree-lined streets, pulled into his street, and stopped outside the Café Mozart. He got out of the car. He was tired again. No, not tired, weary.

'I'll let you know how I get on.'

Ricci nodded and the car pulled away. Jimmy went into the apartment block and went to the stairs where he had so recently been deposited like a piece of broken rubbish.

'Do it right next time, you bastards. Do it right and finish the fucking job.'

TWENTY-ONE

The small room on the top floor was as depressing as ever.

'Sit down, Mr Costello.' Jimmy sat down. 'I'm afraid I have been guilty of a little subterfuge.'

'Oh yes?'

'I didn't ask you here to talk about your leave of absence.' The room was stuffy. It was high up in the building and there was no air-conditioning so any warm air rose and, as the window didn't open, stuck, stale and oppressive. Jimmy began to feel not just crumpled but tainted somehow. McBride obviously wasn't affected by the room. She was wearing a smart dark blue jacket and skirt and a plain white blouse with an open collar. She was all neatly pressed and just back from the laundry. 'I asked you here to tell you something. Something about yourself.'

'I know all I want to know about myself, Professor. There's nothing I want to hear from you.'

'That's true. It is not something that you'll want to hear, but I think you do need to hear it.'

'If you say so.'

He didn't care. It was going to be nasty and it was going to be true and there was nothing he could do about it. Saying it out loud wouldn't change any of it.

'Yesterday I explained why you are here in Rome. What I

didn't explain was that I had strong reservations about using you. Other councils prevailed, however.' Fastidious bitch, thought Jimmy, set me up in this shit then distance yourself from the smell.

'Not bad enough, or too bad?'

'Not well enough, Mr Costello, not nearly well enough.'

He wasn't ready for that. It had come at him from nowhere. 'That my opinion was overruled in your selection is obvious from your presence here.'

He wasn't sick, what was she on about? It was true he didn't bother with check-ups, but that was because he didn't care if there was something there. He had watched Bernie die from something that hadn't shown itself until it was too late to do anything and Michael had died from something that killed as soon as it showed. You died, that was all, the way didn't matter. What was the point in getting formally introduced to what was going to kill you? But he wasn't sick right now. He knew that for certain because he had just come out of hospital and he had been cleared as OK to leave. If there was anything the matter with him they would have spotted it. But something about McBride made him ask.

'What's the matter with me?'

'In my opinion you would do well to seek psychiatric help.'

He couldn't fault her for being different. Given what she knew about him or had guessed, she could have accused him of being many things but he hadn't expected it would be that he was a nutter.

'I'm mad, is that it?'

'Mr Costello, I have no medical training whatsoever, but I have spent most of my working life studying people who operate the levers of power. The men and women who decide the fate of others. My special field of study has become those who have great power but whose behaviour and motivation could be classed as abnormal.'

'For instance?'

'Dictators, those who lead totalitarian regimes, heads of terrorist organisations, all the ones you would expect, but also presidents, prime ministers, and, sadly, religious leaders of all faiths. I study people who perpetrate injustice on a grand scale. I study people with power.'

'And power corrupts?'

'Absolutely. No one who has real power can ever be sure they will not succumb to the misuse of that power or that it will not influence their mental state.'

'What's that got to do with me? You don't think I ever had any real power, do you?'

'No, I don't think that. Let me explain what I mean by using as an example Saddam Hussein in Iraq. Saddam was a dictator who, in his political life, had to be utterly ruthless and totally without pity or remorse. He had to care for no one nor trust anyone. In fact he had to be a monster. But he was a loving husband and father, kind, trusting, and caring. A father to be relied upon, that his family could turn to. In order to be able to live such conflicting lives he had to be two different people. He had to live a schizoid-inducing duality sustained in one case by an unshakable and fanatical belief in the rightness of his actions, and in the other by a profound love for and commitment to his family. Saddam the dictator was able to believe in his love for the Iraqi people yet still do terrible things to them, to individuals, groups, and whole communities, to anyone he saw as a threat. I'm afraid it is not uncommon for those who have a fanatical love of abstract humanity to inflict great cruelty on real people.'

'Is that what you spend your time doing, watching mad dictators trying to conquer the world? Why not just watch old Bond movies?'

'Semyon Frank predicted the terrible cruelty of Bolshevism long before the October Revolution. George Bush's famous, or infamous if you prefer, War on Terror could be said to be the same thing in different clothes. The justification of evil acts is often some greater good.'

'Well I'm not Saddam and thank God I'm not George Bush and I was never fanatical about my work as a copper. Corrupt, yes, I give you that. But fanatical? No.'

'No indeed. You were never fanatical as a policeman, just, as you say, corrupt. Your fanaticism lay in your effort to be a good Catholic, to be a good husband and father, to be a good parishioner. You had to be obsessive about that to sustain the duality you had imposed on your life. The Good Catholic in your private life, the Corrupt Policeman in your working life. To sustain those mutually incompatible personalities was only possible so long as you took the template of your police life from a small group of highly successful but deeply dishonest officers. They were corrupt and, to some extent, they were allowed to be corrupt. They were seen as a necessary evil. You chose to go the same way and, so long as an official blind eye was turned, you could believe it was an acceptable part of an imperfect system, that there was some form of greater good which justified your individual acts of violence and dishonesty.'

He waited. She had been spot on so far and he didn't want to know where this was going. But it was something he knew he had to hear.

'And my home life? My life as a good Catholic?'

'I know nothing of your wife, Mr Costello, but I am pretty certain she was the one you looked to for the validation of your image of yourself as a good Catholic. Not the Church itself and certainly never any priest. I would guess she was all that you believed a good Catholic should be: devout, believing, loving, loyal. That she stayed with you, cared for you, accepted you, was the endorsement your private life needed for you to sustain it. Once she was gone, your world simply fell apart. My guess is that before she died, maybe during her illness, you glimpsed what being your wife had cost her, knowing as she did what sort of man you were as a policeman. That realisation brought you to the edge and after she died you suffered the inevitable psychotic episode. You almost killed two men whom you thought represented all that had gone wrong in your life. You were acting out a psychotic fantasy in which you had cast yourself as Nemesis. Those two men you so savagely attacked were a message to all the others that they could be reached by justice, even if they were beyond the reach of the law. That one of them was a powerful criminal who would have done you great harm after he came out hospital was what gave you your honourable early retirement. Where you should have gone, of course, was to prison.'

'Prison would have been a death sentence.'

'You aren't suggesting early retirement and a pension to save the Metropolitan Police embarrassment was justice for what you did?'

No, he wasn't saying anything about justice. He didn't want to say or hear anything more, because she was right. He was hearing the truth about himself and it gave him almost unbearable pain to be confronted by what he had known since he sat at Bernie's hospital bedside. What he had buried so deep that he could pretend he didn't know. Now she had calmly shredded his emotional defences and told him that the only two things his life had achieved were making his wife suffer so much and for so long, and turning himself into some sort of sick monster.

'Are you saying that what I did to those animals was because I was sick, mentally sick?'

'I told you, I have no medical training nor experience. I am making an interpretation of what happened on the basis of years of study. I couldn't say whether your condition made you clinically insane but I doubt it. You thought you were acting rationally and you carefully planned what you did. I'm sure you would have been found, for criminal prosecution purposes, quite sane. But what you did was the action of a very disturbed mind, a mind which I think is still very disturbed.'

She had to be wrong, please God, make her wrong.

'So how come I'm here, how come you got overruled?'

'My field is the politics of power, not psychiatry. There were two people on the panel which conducted your extended interview who were specialists in the field of mental health. Their view was that your going to Ireland after you left London and living quietly, going to Mass and choosing a kind old priest as the person you talked to, all showed remorse, a willingness to repent, to confront what you had done. Your decision to make amends for your life by applying to become a priest meant that you were no longer a danger to yourself or others and open to recovery.'

'But you disagreed.'

'I know how well a condition such as I have described can be hidden, camouflaged. The world I study is increasingly peopled by those who achieve great power but whose inner evil remains hidden until it is too late to restrain them and the monster emerges. Sadly I sometimes think that our world today owes more to the Book of Revelation than to the Gospels. I am quite sure you could appear to have begun your recovery and yet be someone who was still motivated by something that might not be fanaticism but is certainly sufficiently obsessive to be dangerous.'

'You think I might still be a fanatical Catholic then? That applying to become a priest was part of some obsession?'

'No, I think the goal you now pursue with such single-mindedness, a single-mindedness that could become dangerous, is to make your life right.'

'Right?'

'Right in a way you think your late wife would accept. I think you are determined to become a good man and you are prepared to do whatever it takes to become that good man. If you pursue such a goal without regard for the consequences either for yourself or others, you will re-create your old duality. You will try to embody the old saying that out of evil cometh good. It is a good thing for you to want to be a different person, one your wife could have loved and been proud of. It is a bad thing to destroy yourself and possibly others in the attempt.'

She was still right, of course, she knew him better than he knew himself, but suddenly the anguish which had been filling his mind left him. She knew and she had made him face it. It was no longer hidden, no longer denied, buried deep within him, festering. It was out in the open. Please God it could now be dealt with, and not in his way, but in a way Bernie would have wanted it.

'So what can I do?'

'You need a friend, Mr Costello. You have tried to go on living your life in your head with only yourself as judge and jury on what you are doing and how you are doing it. You are trying to fight the evil in your life entirely on your own. If you continue you will at some point break down and you may suffer another, but more severe, psychotic episode. This time if you try to kill someone you may very well succeed. If so then you will spend the rest of your life heavily sedated in an asylum or be tried for murder and serve the rest of your life in a secure establishment for the criminally insane. Either way there will be no question of a recovery.' It was the way she said it that made a cold hand clutch at his heart. She was so certain, so matter of fact. He knew she was speaking no more than the simple truth but that only increased the horror at how far he had continued to travel the road of his own destruction. 'You need a friend, someone to take the role of your late wife, to support you and help you, someone with whom you can share your thoughts and feelings, someone you do not close out of one half of your life. You must learn to live one life and to live it outside your head, to live it with and among others.'

He thought about what she was saying, about what she meant.

'Will it be you? Will you be my friend?'

'Good heavens, no. As I said before I didn't want you for this work. I thought you unfit and I still think you unfit. Also I don't like you. You are not a nice man, Mr Costello, not at all nice. But putting all that to one side, I can't help you because I am far too busy. I've already said I resented the time our monthly meetings took up and kept me from my work. The meetings were necessary of course because I wanted to monitor you. Your progress or otherwise as a student was, as you now know, irrelevant, but your mental state concerned me so I had to give time to meeting you.'

She had put him on the floor and now she was busy kicking the shit out of him. Oh well, what she was only doing with words he had done often enough with fists and feet. If you're going to put someone down make sure they stay down. It was a universal rule. It obviously applied as much to people who worked for the Vatican as it did to corrupt coppers or North London gangsters

'So that's it. That's what I have to do, find a friend?'

'I can only advise you, and remember, I have no medical knowledge whatever. You are free to dismiss the interpretation

I have put on events. I didn't think you suitable for this investigation but, as I said, I was overruled. How is the enquiry going by the way, any progress?'

Her voice hadn't changed. It was still coldly matter of fact but she'd finished with the dangerous headcase who was on the way to becoming criminally insane, now she was talking to the clever detective who was supposed to be good at getting results.

His reply was automatic. She was entitled to ask so he answered. There was no question who had taken the lead role in this relationship.

'Maybe. We need to know how many other cardinals, if any, have died in circumstances similar to Archbishop Cheng's over the last two years, unexpectedly but apparently of natural causes.'

'I'll send you someone who can give you all the details you need. Anything else?'

'What about Ricci?'

'What about Inspector Ricci?'

'As a friend.'

'I will give you a word of advice about Inspector Ricci. He has a talent for the kind of work he does. He moves among people whose lives are built around extravagance, around show and display. False, constructed lives for false, constructed people. He can see through their show with an almost amazing insight. He can see the real person behind the façade. He can pass as one of them without becoming one of them and he can cultivate the right friends. He will go far, but he will not go as far as he expects. I told you, he has a spotless record. What I didn't tell you was that he keeps it that way because when he gets to the top he wants no skeletons in his cupboard to hamper him in enjoying his power and authority. He may even have political ambitions. If and when you find yourself in circumstances where you need Inspector Ricci to commit unconditionally, be careful, he may very well not be there. I tell you this because you must work together and work well. Yesterday he found out about you. Today you find out about him.'

'And when do I find out about you?'

Her answer was a smile but nothing else.

'I hope, Mr Costello, you are now fully and irrevocably committed to this investigation and we will have no more of the "it was the Chinese" nonsense.'

'How do you know it was nonsense?'

'In the same way you do. If you are to make progress I suggest that you open your mind to the wider possibilities.'

'Which are?'

'These days it is not only governments and multi-nationals who can influence international affairs.'

'Do you have anybody in mind?'

'More importantly, do you? As I said, keep your mind open to all the possibilities. Now, if there is nothing else I must conclude our meeting.'

She stood up, so did Jimmy. The interview was over.

'Thank you, Professor.'

'Not at all, I have been asked to give you my full co-operation. I hope you feel you are getting it.'

'Oh, yes, I feel you're holding nothing back.'

'Then goodbye.'

He was dismissed.

He left feeling numb and shell-shocked.

No, he thought as he descended the stone stairs, she was holding nothing back. No one could accuse her of that.

TWENTY-TWO

The library had once been the dining hall in the Rome residence of Gioffre Borgia, youngest son of Pope Alexander VI. He was considered at the time and thereafter by history as a very minor Borgia. His only rumoured excursion into family-like behaviour was the apparent murder of his elder brother Giovanni because he was having an affair with Gioffre's wife, Sancia. His father, Pope Alexander, had to use his divine authority and publicly exonerate him. Gioffre subsequently remarried, retired from Rome, and had four children by his new wife Maria de Mila. He chose to live in the small town of Squillace on the Calabrian coast which he held as a vassal of Naples and which his descendants ruled after him in comparative peace until 1735. Well away from Roman politics and intrigue he came to be considered a good man, for a Borgia, and in his will he left his small Roman palazzo to the Church on the understanding that his soul would be prayed out of Purgatory and into Heaven in no more than a year. The Church had accepted the gift on the grounds that, for a Borgia, he hadn't been at all such a bad man.

The room which was now a library was small for a princely dining hall, probably capable of seating no more than forty to fifty people, but when the palazzo was turned into a college it was thought perfect to house their library. This it had stayed. Ricci's China-watcher loved the room. He loved the rich plaster decoration of its ceiling, the leaded windows with stained glass decorations above and between the dark wooden shelves which were still filled with leather-bound books. He especially loved being alone in this room, which he frequently was when he visited. But he was under no illusions. One day it would be taken over for some other use and the volumes archived, hidden away. Their content, if considered of any value, would be digitised and databased and put online or stored on some electronic retrieval system. But until then he would use the room to sit, think, pray, and sometimes doze.

He was sitting beside a small table in a comfortable leather chair. Opposite him sat Inspector Ricci, waiting for an answer. Finally it came.

'Definitely.'

'He was a cardinal?'

'Certainly.' He paused for a moment. 'In my opinion.'

'Are you sure?'

'Certainly.'

'Thank you.'

'In so far as it is possible to be certain.'

Ricci fidgeted. He didn't want to press the old man but he wanted a straight answer.

The China-watcher was a tiny, delicate, oriental man with wispy grey hair, who wore in a black suit that was shiny with age, and a Roman collar. The large chair made him seem even smaller than he was. He looked very old, except for his eyes which shone with either mischief or delight. Or maybe it was both. Ricci got the feeling that if handled in the least bit roughly, he might break, like some flimsy, porcelain trinket.

Ricci tried another tack.

'What makes you so sure he was a cardinal?'

'Because he came to Rome.'

'But last time you told me that he was probably sent to Rome by the Chinese to see if he could be a link between them, the Vatican, and the underground church.'

'Yes, that is what I told you.'

'So how does coming to Rome make you sure he was a cardinal? You said it was the Chinese who wanted him here.'

'Archbishop Cheng was sent to Rome by the Chinese. I have given you what I think is their reason.'

There was another pause.

'And?'

'You never asked me why Archbishop Cheng was summoned to Rome.'

'Summoned to Rome?'

'By the Vatican. You never asked me why the Vatican wanted him here.'

'And should I have?'

'That is not for me to say, your reasons are your own. I have been asked by a friend to answer your questions which I have done to the best of my ability.'

Ricci sighed; it was tough going. The old priest watched him. His wrinkled face was creased with a smile. He was enjoying himself.

'Please tell me, Father Phan, why was Archbishop Cheng summoned to Rome?'

'To be given his red hat by the pope personally.'

'So he was sent by the Chinese for one reason and summoned by the Vatican for another reason.'

'Unless both parties had wanted Archbishop Cheng in Rome he could not have come. His visit was arranged by a joint agreement.'

'So Archbishop Cheng was summoned here to be made a cardinal as well as being sent here on behalf of the Chinese government?'

'No.'

'No?'

'No.'

Ricci sighed again. It was getting tougher.

'No, he wasn't made a cardinal or no he wasn't here on behalf of the Chinese government?'

'Yes.'

Ricci almost swore out loud but fought down the impulse.

'Yes?'

The smile widened slightly to a grin.

'Yes. No is the answer to both questions.'

Watching the man opposite the grin slightly widened. Fr Phan hadn't had so much fun since a rather silly CIA agent had tried to pump information from him about a high Chinese government official whom it was rumoured had become a secret Catholic.

Ricci sat back. He was beaten.

'I give up, Father. You've defeated me.' He'd have to wait and let the old priest do it in his own way. He would help when he was ready, he just wasn't ready yet. 'Tell me, Father, how did you become a China-watcher?'

'When I was eighteen I was sent from Vietnam to Hong Kong to represent a French business based in what was then French Indo-China. While I was in Hong Kong Dien Bien Phu happened, the French were sent packing, and I was left stranded. My family came from what became the Communist North. I couldn't go back so I decided to do what I had, for a time, been thinking about. I applied to be sent to Rome and trained for the priesthood. I was accepted and after six years was ordained and went back to Hong Kong. My family were not among the million or so North Vietnamese Catholics who had managed to go South; I lost touch with them. China was playing Big Brother to the North Vietnamese government, so watching China and Vietnam was one small way of feeling that I was keeping in touch with my family. I kept on watching until I was told by a refugee from my home town who had got out in the mess that was the end of the American war in Vietnam, that my family were dead, killed in an American air raid. I stopped watching Vietnam but kept on watching China. It was something I was good at and the Church wanted me to do it, so I did it.'

'And you're still doing it?'

The old priest nodded. Now he was ready to answer. He had wanted a bit of fun and a little talk. Now he'd had had both he was ready to tell the inspector what he wanted to know.

'Archbishop Cheng would have been made a cardinal *in pectore* when he was last imprisoned.'

'*In pectore*?'

'*In pectore* is Latin. It means literally "in the breast". It
144

means Archbishop Cheng was created a cardinal in secret. When that happens it is known only to the pope. Not even the cardinal so named is necessarily aware of his elevation. In any case he cannot function as a cardinal while his appointment is *in pectore* because it is only used in situations where the individual or their congregation need to be protected from any reprisals the elevation might cause. It is used when the individual is functioning, if at all, in a dangerous situation.'

'So Cheng was already a cardinal when he came to Rome, but he may not have known it?'.

'No, he would have known. He would have been told as soon as his position in China began to be regularised, as soon as there was no danger to him or his people. The Chinese government, however, would almost certainly not have known. It was a move in the game that Rome was saving.'

'Why?'

The little priest shrugged.

'I don't know, I watch China not the Vatican.'

'But others in the Vatican would definitely have known?'

'Oh yes, there would have had to be others, to arrange for Archbishop Cheng to be told but in such a way that the Chinese government would not get to know.'

'So it was still secret?'

'Secret, yes, but no longer known only known to the pope.'

Ricci nodded.

'I see.'

'And although Archbishop Cheng was sent by the Chinese he was not really here on their behalf. He was sent as a sign to show Rome that Beijing was prepared to trust him. If Rome chose to use him as a contact in some way, the Chinese were showing they were open to negotiations. When he arrived in Rome he was seen by the pope. What they talked about is known only to them.'

'And the Chinese, if in some way they could have found out he was a cardinal, might they have wanted him dead and wanted it to happen in Rome, not China?'

'No, they very much wanted him alive and I would think it mattered little to them whether he was an archbishop or a cardinal. If they cared at all they would probably have favoured it.'

'So why the ultra low-key funeral?'

'They didn't want anyone else to know that they hadn't known. It was a matter of face-saving, both domestic and international. They had begun to build up Archbishop Cheng as some sort of symbol of the new China, a China that encouraged individuals with talent and flair. A China that was safe to invest in and work with. But they didn't want anyone thinking that the new China had gone soft or sloppy. The Vatican would have told the Chinese on Cardinal Cheng's death of his elevation. That would have been necessary for his funeral.'

'Why?'

'A cardinal is always buried with his coat of arms and red hat on the coffin.'

'And the Chinese were told that?'

'Almost certainly. That the man in question had died and was no longer a part of their complicated manoeuvres was neither here nor there. The Vatican had made a move they hadn't seen or countered and that was unacceptable to Beijing. They had to respond so they arranged the funeral in the way they did. The form it took was a rebuke to Rome but the attendance of two senior officials acknowledged the status of the man. Faced with a difficult problem they simply decided to bury it.'

The grin was back and Ricci realised Father Phan had made a joke.

'Buried it, yes, I see.'

The priest grinned and nodded.

'A little joke, inappropriate perhaps. We are talking about the death of one who might have been a great man, but who was undoubtedly a holy one. I allow myself a little fun from time to time,' a pause and another grin, 'between friends, you understand.' Ricci understood all right, it was another joke. They'd only met twice and the priest had had a little bit of fun at his expense on both occasions. 'Inspector, I have tried to tell you what you want to know. I was asked to co-operate by someone I trust. Many people seek me out and ask me things. I don't always tell them what they want to hear. I am afraid that trust, real trust, is not a common currency among those who seek my knowledge. Alas they often think that they can use me and the information I can give them.'

'Use you; how?'

'The Catholic Church is frequently in a position to know far more accurately than the diplomatic or intelligence services of most Western governments what is the real situation on the ground in certain volatile or hostile parts of the world. We often have people and resources in the places where it would be very dangerous for the personnel of Western governments to go, so their intelligence or diplomatic services come to the Church and ask it to give them information or get information for them. The Catholic Church is seen as a reliable source by many Western governments and because of that I have many contacts both in China and in the Western intelligence and diplomatic services. I am always happy to be channel of information in both directions if it promotes the common good. I share my information only if I can be sure, insofar as anyone can ever be sure, that it will not be used to do harm, but to inform and thereby improve relationships. I am sometimes asked, as a favour, to find out things, or to pass on or get information. If I trust the person, I try to do as I am asked. Mine is a world of favours asked and favours given. It is all unofficial and off the record, as have been our conversations. I must hope you will do no harm with what I have given you. It seems of no particular importance to me but I have learned over many years that the value of information is not necessarily apparent to the one who provides it. Its value is known more accurately by the one who requests and receives it.'

The old priest looked at him. There was no smile now and the twinkle had gone from his eyes. The speech was over, it was time to go. Ricci got up. He put his hand out to the old man who took it. It was like holding an incredibly delicate figurine. Was it just because he was Vietnamese or was he really as old as he looked?

'Thank you, Father Phan, you have been most helpful.'

The priest nodded but said nothing. Ricci turned and walked

away.

So, people had known about Cheng being a cardinal before he came to Rome and becoming a cardinal in the way he did had upset the Chinese. Jimmy had guessed but others might not have needed to guess. That meant the next step was to find out who knew of Cheng's elevation and might any of them have slipped that information to the Chinese? The list of people who knew would probably be very short. The shorter the better. At last he was beginning to get a good feeling about this inquiry, that it might actually be important, that it might get him somewhere. If the link his China watcher had given him then who knows, it might just turn out to be the Chinese after all.

TWENTY-THREE

Danny looked around the café. Upmarket tourists of all ages were enjoying themselves, seeing and being seen, getting a sniff of Rome's *la dolce vita*.

'Why did you drag me here? Why not meet at our usual place?'

'I wanted to be somewhere different, with people who were enjoying themselves.' At the next table a party of young Germans were laughing and talking loudly and photographing themselves and each other on their phones. 'What's the matter, don't you like to see people happy?'

The noise of the nearby laughter rose. Danny turned and the laughter died a little.

'Noisy bastards.'

'Take it easy. They're just kids.'

'What the hell are you up to, Jimmy? You suddenly disappear and the next thing we know someone's put you in hospital. No one's allowed to see you, then, when you're out of hospital you drop out of classes. Leave of absence, we get told, Duns College business not anybody else's. In other words, clear off. But here you are still in Rome and all well again. So what's going on?'

'Is anybody else interested in me?'

'Not really. They're all too tied up with their studies.'

'Nobody that you know of been asking any questions?'

'No, nobody asking except me.'

'What sort of copper were you, Danny?'

'Me? I was Traffic.'

'Traffic.'

'You sound disappointed. What sort of policeman did you want me to be?'

'Oh, not any particular sort, I just thought you would have been at the more serious end. I'm surprised you stuck to Traffic, that's all.'

'A good guess. I only did the last five years in Traffic, before that I was in Narcotics.'

'What got you moved to Traffic?'

'Two bullets, and I was damned lucky they didn't get me moved to the cemetery.'

'It's nasty work, narcotics.'

'And dangerous, man, don't forget the dangerous, and the one who put the bullets in me was about the same age as these noisy bastards. They're not kids at that age any more.'

'No, I suppose not. What rank were you?'

'A sergeant.'

'Never try for higher?'

'No. I never wanted the responsibility. Maybe that's why I'm finishing here, giving it up. Since I came I've begun to realise that if I became a priest how much I would have to be responsible for people, advise them, judge them. It's not for me.'

But Jimmy wasn't interested in Danny's problems today. He had other things on his mind.

'Did you ever do any undercover work?'

'No, just catching the bad guys and getting convictions.'

'Getting convictions?'

'You know how it works. You know they're guilty, you just want to hear them say it. You do what you have to so they say it out loud. I'm a big man and not naturally violent so I got brought in sometimes. I could hurt people enough but not hurt them too much.'

'Needs a nice judgement.'

'If you've done it you'll know. With me nobody died, nobody got put into hospital. They were bad guys and like I said, we just needed to hear them say so.'

'So you got shot?'

'On a routine bust, dropped my guard and took two bullets. The guy using the gun was dead before he hit the floor but by the time we'd got him I was on the floor too.'

'And then?'

'Then I got better and I asked to go to Traffic. I was finished in Narcotics. Getting shot had scared the shit out of me and I knew that if I had to go back I'd be looking out for myself when I should be looking out for someone else. And that's no good, Jimmy, is it? When you go for the bad guys you do what has to be done any way it has to be done, and you commit. If you're looking out for yourself, someone else will get hurt. So I went to Traffic and no one got hurt. I served five years to get a pension, then quit, thought about what I wanted to do, and finished up here.'

'No wife?'

'No, no wife. I had a partner though.'

There was a gleam in his eye and a smile on his face.

'Oh yes?'

'A steady partner.'

'So what happened there?'

The smile widened to a grin.

'When I started thinking about coming to Rome we broke up.'

'I should bloody well think so. What did she say when you told her?'

'Nothing. Her name was Appleton and she was white rum, and when we went to bed she was the one inside me not me inside her.'

He laughed, so did Jimmy.

'You used to hit the bottle. Oh well, lots did and they still cut it as coppers.'

'But when you're not a copper any more and don't have to wash the day out of your mind to get to sleep, then you just become a drunk. I didn't want to end up like that so I gave up the rum and set about thinking what I did want to be. There, now you know my life story, you inquisitive bastard, so answer my question. What the hell are you up to?'

Jimmy had thought hard about what Professor McBride had told him and had come to a decision. She was right, he needed a friend. He might also need someone looking after his back if things went pear-shaped and at the moment Ricci was the only one doing the looking. But most of all he needed someone to be there if he began to lose it in his head. He wanted someone to be there who could stop him if he cracked up again. He didn't want to end his days banged up in some Italian psycho-bin. If Danny was up to what he wanted then he wanted him as the friend who would watch his back, the friend who would stop him falling off the edge.

'It's like this …'

TWENTY-FOUR

The waiter who brought the drinks didn't give Jimmy a second look this time. If a good customer like Inspector Ricci brought him then he was something horrible you couldn't do anything about. Jimmy, he had decided, must be treated as an Act of God.

'She's set up a meeting with someone who can tell me about any other cardinals. How did it go with you?'

Ricci took a sip of his Campari and soda.

'Good, although the guy is a bit of a bastard. He jerked me about before he unbuttoned, but he delivered in the end. Cheng was made a cardinal last time he was put in prison. He didn't know because it was an *in pectore* job which means only the pope knew. He would have been told when the Chinese started putting him back on his feet but the Chinese weren't told. The Vatican was saving that for a rainy day. When Cheng died the Chinese got told and they took it badly, hence the ultra-low-level funeral. They didn't know and hadn't guessed and that represented a loss of face in their political chess game with the Vatican. The Vatican had put one over on them so they decided to bury the whole thing.'

Jimmy smiled.

'They buried it. I like that.'

'Yeah, funny.'

'So, your watcher reckons that if Cheng was told when they started rehabilitating him it means somebody had to tell him which means a few people here in Rome had to know even if the Vatican was keeping it secret.'

Ricci nodded.

'That's right, we guessed, but whoever killed him could have been told.'

'What about the Chinese; what does your man say?'

Ricci shook his head.

'My man says not but the way I look at it, if they were told they might have decided to do something about it.'

'Kill him? A bit extreme.'

'Maybe but if this is between the Chinese and the Vatican then we're way out of our depth as to what might or might not happen.'

'True, but even so I can't see being a secret cardinal as worth killing for.'

'No, me neither, but it's something.'

'An outside possibility at best. What if he'd lived?'

'How do you mean?'

'What did your man say about Cheng being a cardinal if he'd lived?'

'That the Chinese didn't care what he was: bishop, archbishop, cardinal, and if they were going to keep building him up then he looked better as a cardinal. The watcher says they just wanted to save face, not let anyone know they'd missed a trick. Other than that they weren't interested.'

'Sounds better than killing him.'

'Unfortunately, yes.' Ricci put his hand into his pocket and pulled out a mobile phone and put it on the table in front of Jimmy. 'Take it.'

Jimmy shook his head.

'I bought another one after the mugging.'

'Well now you've got this one as well.'

'I don't want it. I forget to take them with me or I lose them and when I've got one with me I forget to switch it on. I don't like the things. They go off when you don't want them to. Anyway I never have anyone I want to call.'

He pushed it back to Ricci who leaned forward and pushed it towards Jimmy.

'Well now you do have someone to call: me. I'm not working with a partner I can't contact. I phoned you three times this morning, where were you?'

'In the apartment.'

'Well why didn't you answer?'

'I have that meeting today, lunch with someone who can tell me about dead cardinals and it wanted thinking about so I didn't answer the phone. I didn't know who it was. It could have been anybody.'

'It was me and you have to answer the bloody thing to find out who it is. That's what phones are for. I can't hang about waiting until you've stopped thinking when we need to meet. I wasted a whole morning because I couldn't get you.' Jimmy looked at the mobile. Ricci was right of course, but he didn't like the idea of someone being able to contact him whenever they liked. 'Nobody else will call you because nobody else knows the number. If this one rings it's me.'

Jimmy picked it up and looked at it.

'I suppose it does everything: makes the tea, wipes my bum, gives me access to the bloody internet, and does my tax return.'

'Never mind what it does, it rings and you answer it.' Ricci took out another mobile and dialled. The one in Jimmy's hand started to ring, the tone was a jingle version of the 'Ride of the Valkyries'. Jimmy looked at Ricci. 'Never mind that, we can change it. That's my number on the screen.' He ended the call. 'If it rings it's me, you answer it.'

'OK.'

'Mine is the only number on the log. Press call and you'll get me. Try it.'

Jimmy tried.

Ricci's phone rang. This time the tone was Verdi. Jimmy gave Ricci another look and they put the phones away.

'What about the Wagner? I'm not having bloody Wagner going off where people can hear it.'

'Don't bother about that. I'll do it before you go.'

'I want it to just ring, like a proper phone, just ring.'

155

Ricci sounded doubtful.

'I'll try. It's got about fifty ringtones but I don't think it does just a ring. Look, I'll sort out something before you go.'

'If it doesn't just ring then no Verdi either.'

'OK, I'll sort it.'

'In fact no opera of any sort.'

'For God's sake, I said I'd bloody well sort it out before you go. Now, how do we find out who knew Cheng was a cardinal?'

Jimmy took a sip. It was a snotty bar but this beer was all right.

'He has to be right, your China-watcher? You think he really knows how the cardinal thing was all done?'

'If you mean, is it official, is he quoting some official record, then no, he's guessing. But it makes sense. So how do we find out who knew?'

'We don't yet.'

'Why not?'

'Because that wouldn't give us motive, and what we need is a motive. The best way in for us would be if he wasn't the only one. If there were others we get a connection and that might give us our reason. Either we're looking at Cheng on his own, in which case end of story, or we're looking at Cheng as one of …'

Jimmy stopped, then took a slow sip.

'Got something?'

'Listen, if Cheng is a one-off we're stuck. Even if we find out who knew he was a cardinal that won't lead us anywhere. The only ones who might have cared were the Chinese and we can't say "it was the Chinese", not again.'

'So?'

'So we stick with what we can do.'

'Which is?'

'The "more than one" theory. If it's wrong, it's wrong and we tell your minister, sorry, we got nowhere. You get well and go back to being a copper and I get on with,' he paused. When this finished there was nothing to get on with. 'I get on with whatever I get on with.'

'OK, so what if there's more than Cheng? Who would want

to kill some cardinals and why?'

'That's what I was thinking about this morning.'

'And you came up with?'

'As I understand it cardinals do one thing no one else does: they choose the pope. Right?'

'So?'

'So say someone, a government maybe, wanted to be sure to get the right kind of pope next time round, a pope who would see things their way.'

'The right kind of pope? What the hell is the right kind of pope?'

'A pope who's, well, one who's on your side, one who's ... Look, I don't know what sort of pope but it's what cardinals do so let's just say, for the sake of argument, somebody wants to fix a papal election.'

'Are you being serious?'

'I'm trying to be.'

Ricci shrugged and took a sip.

'OK, it's your bright idea. Carry on.'

'You want to control that choice, but you can't get at the cardinals when they're actually doing the election; they meet in conclave locked away in the Vatican. So, before they get locked away, you get as many as you can thinking your way and then you take out a few key players so your men on the inside can influence the likely outcome.'

'Brilliant! There's only one small flaw. It's rubbish, total, bloody rubbish.'

'Go on, why is it rubbish?'

'First, it doesn't even come close to giving anyone a result worth killing for. Let's say you could get a few cardinals thinking your way, which probably does happen, you might have an influence on the outcome but that's all, just an influence. And if someone's prepared to kill cardinals they'll want to be absolutely sure of getting what they want, not just a possibility. Then there's the timing. If you kill a few selected cardinals, and I don't see how you can risk killing more than a few, it doesn't get you anywhere because it doesn't get you an election. You have to wait until the pope dies to get an election

157

and that could be years and by that time there would be new cardinals, things would have changed, and it would be back to square one. Like I say, it's rubbish.' Jimmy agreed but he said nothing. When you only had one avenue to explore you didn't give it up easily. 'I don't know how many cardinals there are, there's plenty here in Rome and more scattered across the world, so how do you get at enough of them to make your idea come even close to working? You couldn't do it. A big enough outfit might be able to buy a few but that's all and you'd still not be close to getting the pope you wanted, even if the sitting tenant conveniently died when you wanted him to so you got your election.' He paused. 'Or are you suggesting that they're going to kill the present pope as well?'

Jimmy was silent.

Ricci waited for him to say he agreed the idea was rubbish and took another sip of his drink.

He hadn't meant it seriously, killing the pope.

'It's been tried.'

They both thought about it.

Ricci surfaced first. He was angry; this wasn't anywhere near where they should be going.

'No, it doesn't work. I don't care who you are, you don't kill the pope. For one thing he's too well protected, ever since that Turkish bloke had a go at John Paul. But even if you did pull it off and got the election, that still doesn't mean you get it to go the way you want. It's still all too chancy. No, it's got more holes than a Swiss cheese. Fix some cardinals, kill some others, then take out the pope and run a fixed papal election, and all for what, a sympathetic pope? It's just bloody fantasy. It makes *Alice in Wonderland* look like grim fucking realism.'

'Call it what you like but if whoever McBride sends says that it may not be Cheng on his own, if there are others, it's something and it's all we've got. It may be rubbish, but it's the only thing we can follow up on. Unless you want to pack it in right now?'

Ricci looked at him. So this was the great detective, the one who took the lead. He didn't know whether to laugh or weep. The man was following a fairy story.

'Come on, Jimmy, don't tell me you're serious about this; it's just wasting time.'

'If the man I talk to at lunch today says Cheng had company then I'm serious.'

'You're wrong, Jimmy. It could never happen.'

'The Twin Towers attack could never happen but that didn't stop it. These days it not just governments who can make big things happen, there's others out there who are organised, funded, and dedicated enough to do things so that everyone has to sit up and take notice. And they're crazy enough to try something nobody else would even dream of trying.'

'Oh yes, like killing the pope? What would that get anybody?'

'What if there was a chance, only a chance but still a chance, it could get them a pope who was really sympathetic to the Palestinians, prepared to side with them and with Islam against Israel and the Americans?'

God, thought Ricci, his mind just keeps on going until he comes up with an answer. But then, why not that answer? Was it really a fairy story? It was all about terrorism these days. Everyone's a player in that game one way or another and no one plays by any rules except do what has to be done. If terrorism was involved then anything became possible. Ricci rallied himself.

'No, you're wrong, Jimmy. Definitely off beam.'

Jimmy shrugged.

'If you say so.' They sat for a moment. The chance of a pro-Palestinian pope, a pope who believed the Catholic Church should put a higher price on justice than American dollars? The chance of a Muslim-Catholic alliance? Was it possible?

'But if you're not ...' Jimmy waited. 'Well, I just hope it's Cheng's on his own, that's all.'

TWENTY-FIVE

'No, really, Mr Costello, not pasta.' Jimmy looked at him. Why not pasta? This was a restaurant and this was bloody Italy, so why not pasta? 'If you will be recommended by me try the *saltimbocca*. I assure you, you will find it the best in Rome.'

Jimmy shrugged. He didn't care, he wasn't paying and he wasn't that hungry.

'What is it?'

The monsignor smiled a bland smile, but though the blandness was perfectly practised he couldn't altogether hide the sneer.

'It is veal beaten very thinly with a layer of Parma ham spread over it and then fried in butter. Simple and, like all simple dishes, the outcome is primarily dependent on the quality of the ingredients rather than the talents of the chef. Like people, don't you think?'

'What?'

'Like people. The outcomes individuals are capable of achieving are primarily the result of the quality of person rather than of the skills they have acquired. A good man can achieve good things, a great man, great things.'

'I'm not with you. I thought we were talking about food, about what we were going to have for lunch.'

The bland monsignor switched off the charm at the plug and

spoke to the waiter who had been silently standing by the table waiting for their order.

'Two *saltimbocca* and a bottle of the Pecorino.' The waiter nodded, removed the menus and some redundant cutlery from the table, and left. The monsignor decided he should, as host, fill the silence while they waited. 'I hope my choice of wine is satisfactory for you, Mr Costello. You mustn't be put off by the name,' he held up his hand as if Jimmy was about to say something; he wasn't, 'it is indeed called Pecorino but it is *not*, I assure you, anything to do with the cheese. It is a little-known, rare grape variety from the Abruzzo which, under the right conditions and in the right hands, can produce a very acceptable wine. I am a personal friend of the producer and when he has a drinkable vintage he lets me know and I ask the proprietor here to buy a few cases. I find it an excellent lunch-time wine and very inexpensive. To live modestly is to live well, don't you think?'

While the monsignor was holding forth about his choice of wine Jimmy noted that, as the waiter had taken the order and gone, it actually didn't matter a toss whether the wine was what he wanted or not.

'No, not really.'

That got in amongst you, thought Jimmy, as the bland monsignor's eyebrows went up.

'Really! You do not think that to live modestly is to live well? I'm surprised, you didn't strike me as someone who would approve of excess.'

'Not that, the wine.'

'The Pecorino? You do not like my choice?'

'No. But not because it's got the same name as a cheese, it's because I don't like any wine much. I'd prefer a beer.'

He could see that what his appearance had begun when they had met, his lack of taste for wine had cemented. He had now gone so far down in the opinion of the monsignor that a dredger couldn't find him. But as far as Jimmy was concerned, with blokes like him, that was the best place to be.

'I'll mention it to the waiter when he brings our order.' The monsignor busied himself with his napkin. Finally he surfaced.

'Is there any particular brand of beer you would like? Please say, I'm not a drinker of beer.'

'Just what comes to hand.'

'I see.'

The monsignor took in the other tables and smiled to one or two of the diners. Jimmy watched him; this was the man that Professor McBride had sent to tell him about cardinals. He was obviously a see and be seen sort of bloke, a mixer, but if he moved in a gin-and-tonic world Jimmy's guess was that he was the tonic and not the gin. He was another minister's aide type, right-hand man to someone who hadn't got his brains but hadn't, like him, lost his balls. Jimmy also looked around. It was a calm and elegant place. The tables, of which there were many and all in use, were spaced so that a low voice at your table meant your conversation stayed at your table. It was all white linen, bentwood chairs, and restrained décor. A place of understated elegance for quiet money. The monsignor, having scouted the tables, was ready to return to Jimmy.

'The only drawback here is that the Jesuits regard it as home ground. Still, it might have been worse, it might have been the Dominicans.' He waited for the smile of appreciation at his little joke. It didn't come so he went on. 'I come here quite often. It's not far from the Gregorian and the Ministry and, on occasion, the Quirinale. Thankfully it's just too far from the Trevi Fountain to get tourists.' He was making a last-ditch effort at charm so that Jimmy could acknowledge how very fortunate he felt to be sitting here at the same table.

'How do you know which ones are the Jesuits?'

The bland monsignor gave up.

'So, Mr Costello, I have been asked if I would help you by giving you certain information concerning cardinals.' You weren't asked, mate, thought Jimmy, you were sent. You were given no choice. 'I'm sorry I had to squeeze you in like this and ask you to meet me here. But lunch today was my only window and I understood that what you wanted had a degree of urgency.'

'This place is fine.'

'Good, the people I deal with are not the sort whom you can

163

cancel on at short notice. Their time is extremely valuable, mine of course is at the disposal of …'

'You speak very good English. You did say you were Italian, didn't you?'

The monsignor almost certainly resented the interruption, but it didn't show, not even in his eyes. He was smooth, thought Jimmy, smooth like oil.

'Yes, Mr Costello, I am Italian, Roman in fact, and as you say I speak excellent English. I also speak excellent French and Spanish. I am only passable at Russian and German. Sadly, my Mandarin Chinese is barely suitable for anything more than polite conversation.'

'I only speak English so we'll stick to that.'

The monsignor sat back. This objectionable peasant of a man had something he wanted to ask. Let him ask it. He would tell him what he wanted and then be rid of him. The waiter arrived with their food. He put it on the table and was about to leave when Jimmy spoke.

'And a beer.'

'A beer, sir?' It was another waiter who spoke. He had arrived with the wine in an ice bucket on a stand. He put it beside the table. 'Which brand, sir?'

'Anything local; Peroni.' The monsignor almost winced. 'Not cold, just as it comes.'

'All our beers are chilled, sir.'

'OK, just as it comes.'

The waiter nodded and the two of them left.

Jimmy waited. The monsignor was praying an obvious Grace before starting his meal. When he had finished he took the bottle, poured himself a glass, put the wine back into the bucket, took a long sip, then picked up his knife and fork and began to eat. Jimmy glanced at his plate. It looked good and he felt sure it would taste nice. He put his elbows on the table and leaned forward.

'Over the last two years, anywhere in the world, how many cardinals have died suddenly?'

The question didn't even get a pause.

'Do you mean died as a result of violence?'

'No, died unexpectedly, like Archbishop Cheng a couple of years ago.'

The monsignor kept on eating and took another sip.

'Does the age matter?'

'Not necessarily.'

'Then five, possibly six.'

'Including Archbishop Cheng?'

'No, he wasn't a cardinal.'

'Can you name them?'

'Cardinals Laurence Grimshaw, Felipe Obregon, Giovanni Stephano Capaldi, John Chiu Fa, Pius Mawinde, and possibly Pietro Maria Gossa.'

'Why only possibly?'

'Because he was ninety-one and died in his sleep here in Rome, but it was unexpected, in so far as a death at ninety-one can be unexpected.'

'Could the others have had anything in common?'

The monsignor stopped eating.

'Now that is an interesting question.'

He put down his knife and fork, took a sip of his wine, and then sat slightly forward with his voice lowered a fraction.

'It is a question I have been half-asking myself off and on ever since Archbishop Cheng's death.'

'Why half-asking?'

'Because of the answer.'

'A connection?'

'Leaving out Gossa on the basis of age, three of the rest have a kind of connection. Cardinals Grimshaw, Obregon, and Mawinde.'

'The connection?'

'They would have been very important if a conclave were to have been convened.'

Jimmy sat back. The answer had taken his breath away coming like it did. He had come to ask the question because it was the only question he had, not because he had any faith in where it would lead. Although he would never have admitted it, he agreed with Ricci and felt the whole thing too far-fetched. The truth was, he only wanted the investigation to continue because when it finished he wasn't going anywhere, certainly not back to any priestly training. McBride had made that clear. He wanted time to adjust, to think, and this investigation, so long as it went on, however pointlessly, gave him that time. He hadn't expected to get any sort of helpful answer, certainly not such a solid one, nor to get it so quickly.

'They'd have been important in a conclave?'

'Oh yes.'

'But not the other two?'

'Cardinal Chiu Fa was under eighty and therefore would have a vote but that is all. He would not have been an influence. Cardinal Capaldi was a Liturgist, a vital element in the changes to worship the Church is currently involved in, but that was all. In a conclave, being over eighty, he would not even have had a vote.'

'But the other three, they would have been influential?'

'Grimshaw was American and Americans are always influential; they represent money. Obregon was Central American and a liberal. He could have organised the liberal wing, the modernisers. Cardinal Mawinde was a conservative to put it mildly. He could have been a rallying point for the traditionalists.'

'How many cardinals would there be at a conclave?'

'It varies but around one hundred.'

That was a lot of cardinals.

'And Cheng? What group did he represent?'

The monsignor smiled.

'None, Mr Costello, no group at all.'

'So why is he connected to the other three? If he's spent most of his life in China and a good part of it in Chinese prisons how could he be …'

He didn't finish the question. It had clicked, and the bland monsignor saw that it had clicked.

'Exactly, Mr Costello. He could easily have become pope if a conclave had been called.'

'Are you sure?'

'That he would have been elected?'

Jimmy nodded.

'Absolutely not, Mr Costello. To predict the outcome of a papal conclave is impossible, it cannot be done. But if you mean, could he have been elected, was he the sort of man who might well get chosen? Then my answer would be, absolutely yes. He was very much papabile.'

'Papabile?'

'Suitable pope material. Archbishop Cheng was a man of great personal holiness and humility who had suffered tremendously for his faith. But he was also a gentle man, a man of prayer who had the capacity to forgive those who had treated him so cruelly. He put his Christian duty to the greater good before any personal feelings. And he was a very able administrator, during his years of freedom he proved that. I would have said he was papabile, Mr Costello, wouldn't you?'

The monsignor poured some more wine and went back to his meal. The waiter was at the table with a bottle of beer and a glass on a tray.

'Sorry about the delay, sir.' He put the glass beside Jimmy and poured some beer, then put the bottle beside the glass. 'I took the chill off it but I'm afraid I had to use my judgement as to how you'd like it.'

Jimmy took a taste. It was just beer.

'Excellent, just right. Thanks.'

'My pleasure, sir.'

The waiter left. Jimmy took the bottle and poured some more into his glass. The monsignor was eating, waiting for Jimmy to get going again.

'Doesn't the pope have to be a cardinal?'

'Technically, no, on election the pope becomes the bishop of Rome and so long as the candidate is in no way debarred from taking up that office anyone could be chosen. Technically you could be our next pope, Mr Costello.'

'Me!?'

'Yes, if you have been accepted for training to the priesthood I assume you are a baptised and practising Catholic. You are not married nor, I hope, in a state of mortal sin. You are eligible. If you were chosen you would be ordained priest, then consecrated bishop of Rome and then you would be pope.

So could I, so could millions, but as you said, the pope is now always chosen from among the College of Cardinals.'

'So Cheng would have to have been a cardinal to be pope?'

'Realistically, yes.'

The monsignor pushed away his plate and refreshed his glass of wine.

'He wasn't though, was he?'

'Wasn't he, Mr Costello?'

'He was an archbishop.'

'If you say so. I'm sure your information is more accurate than any I might have. I am, after all, no more than a humble Vatican functionary.' You're something, thought Jimmy, but whatever it is, it isn't humble. The waiter arrived and took the monsignor's plate. He looked at Jimmy's untouched meal and hovered, uncertain what to do. The monsignor came to his assistance. 'Are you finished, Mr Costello?'

'No, I'll eat in a minute.'

'But your meal will be cold, sir.'

Jimmy looked at the waiter.

'Is it any good cold?'

'Not really, sir.'

'Maybe you could re-heat it?'

'I hardly think it would be suitable re-heated, sir.'

'Mr Costello.'

The monsignor was getting annoyed. Jimmy picked up the plate and held it out to the waiter.

'Have a go anyway.'

'If you say so, sir.' The waiter took the plate. 'Will you require anything else, Monsignor?'

'No.'

The waiter left.

'If there is nothing further I can do for you, Mr Costello?'

He was ready to leave.

'There is.' The monsignor stiffened and then relaxed. His face registered indifference but his eyes told another story. Jimmy poured the last of his beer into his glass. He took his time about it and about taking a sip. He wondered how many would die in the blast when this guy finally exploded if he got pushed any further. 'If, for the sake of argument, Cheng was a cardinal, there was a conclave, and he had been elected pope, what effect might that have? How would a Chinese pope go down?'

'With whom?'

'With anybody.'

'The Church would welcome him as the new holy father with joy and celebration as they would any new pope.'

Getting his own back, is he, thought Jimmy. We'll see about that.

'Don't you know or won't you say?'

It hit home. He had been sent to co-operate, not to make a new friend nor to score points off a new enemy. His whole manner changed.

'Would you have said that John Paul II, a Polish pope, has had an effect, Mr Costello?'

'Yes.'

'Indeed, yes. When he first became pope the Soviet Union looked as if not even a nuclear attack could destroy it. And now it is utterly destroyed. What he helped start in a shipyard in Gdansk couldn't be stopped and it brought down one of the world's two superpowers, a thing the other superpower had been trying to do without success for the second half of the twentieth century. And all without a shot being fired.'

'He didn't do it on his own.'

'You could argue that he didn't do it at all. That a desire for truth, justice, and freedom did it from within.'

'Aided and abetted by rampant poverty and corruption, also from within.'

'Mr Costello, I am a busy man. If you really wish to discuss the fall of the Soviet Union, could you do it some other time with some other person?

'It would matter, you think, a Chinese pope?'

'I think it would matter very much indeed and I think the prospect of Cardinal,' he paused, 'of Archbishop Cheng as bishop of Rome would be something that might be opposed vigorously in certain quarters, most vigorously indeed.'

'Stop at nothing sort of thing?'

'Perhaps.'

Jimmy had heard all he wanted to for the moment. He needed to go and think things over.

'OK, I'm finished, you can go. I'll hang on and see what the – what was it called?'

The monsignor was getting up. He was being dismissed by a crumpled, unimportant little peasant of a man. But he didn't mind, he would offer it up as a penance for the sinfulness of mankind.

'Saltimbocca, Mr Costello. I hope you find it still edible, but I doubt it. Good day.'

He left. He forgot to say his grace after meals, thought Jimmy, as the monsignor made his way between the tables, nodding a couple of times to important-looking diners. I hope he remembers it when he next goes to Confession. The waiter was back at the table.

'Do you want your meal now, sir?'

'Did he pay the bill?'

The waiter looked after the monsignor who was disappearing through the doorway into the street.

'The monsignor has an account.'

'I see, he runs a tab.'

'Sir?'

'A tab, an account.'

The waiter smiled. He liked to pick up new English words.

'A tab, yes, sir.'

'Is it a modest tab?'

'Sorry, sir?'

'A modest tab. He says he likes to live modestly. He says to live modestly is to live well.'

The waiter smiled again.

'Yes, sir, I would say the monsignor lives well.' The smile almost became a grin, but not quite. He was talking about a good customer. 'Do you want your meal now, sir?'

'No, it won't be any good warmed up, will it? Do you do any pasta?'

'Of course, sir. If you want pasta we can give you whatever you wish.'

'Spaghetti.'

'And how would you like it, sir?'

'Just as it comes. Ask the cook to use his judgement.'

The waiter smiled.

'Certainly, sir.'

He left. Jimmy reached out to the ice bucket. The bottle was about a third full. What sort of priest has a tab at a place like this and when he orders a bottle of wine leaves nearly half of it? He looked at the label, it said Pecorino and gave the year but otherwise it was meaningless. How much was inexpensive, he wondered. He poured some into his unused glass. It was wine, just white wine.

He turned his mind back to what the monsignor had told him. Three cardinals dead unexpectedly, all influential if a conclave was held and a possible favourite to win dies under questionable circumstances. But if Cheng's death was part of something it meant it was two years into whatever was going on.

'Your spaghetti, sir.'

The waiter put the plate on the table. It was just spaghetti with a simple tomato sauce.

'Thanks.'

'Another beer, sir? I have one ready with the chill taken off, just in case.'

'Yes, thanks.'

Jimmy began his meal, it was good, just how he liked it. The waiter arrived with the beer.

'You can take the wine away; it's finished with.'

'Certainly, sir.'

'Is it any good?'

'All our wines are good, sir.'

'Is it cheap?'

'We don't stock cheap wines, sir, but if you mean is it one of our less expensive wines, then yes, it is modestly priced compared to many of our others.'

'How much?'

It didn't sound modestly priced to Jimmy. It sounded damned expensive.

171

Jimmy went back to eating and thinking. One hundred cardinals locked in one place with no outside contact and no way in. If someone wanted to fix the election they had to be got at before they came to Rome or got at once they were assembled and neither way made any sense. Before they came to Rome they were scattered across the world: any attempt to nobble them would be too obvious. Once they were together no one could get at them except someone on the inside. Which only took him back to getting at them before the conclave. He paused in his eating.

It was like some bloody stupid Agatha Christie thing. The pope will be found dead in the Vatican Library with all the doors and windows locked from the inside and a knife of oriental design stuck in his back. Then all the suspects, the cardinals, will be gathered in one room while I stand in front of them, tear off my whiskers, and say, it is I, Hawkshaw, the great detective, and I now know which one of you is the murderer.

Jimmy went on with his spaghetti. No, they didn't want Agatha bloody Christie on this or any sort of detective. What they wanted was a magician, because if it was about fixing a papal conclave it was going to be one hell of a trick.

Absolutely one hell of a trick.

TWENTY-SIX

Danny didn't look happy and when he spoke he didn't sound happy.

'I don't like this, Jimmy. I don't like what you've told me and I don't see what I can do now that you have told me.'

Jimmy signalled to the waitress. She came to the table.

'Same again?'

She was a chirpy South African.

'Just a beer, thanks, no coffee.'

She went away.

'I don't like it.'

'It gets worse.'

'I bet it does. How could it get any better?'

'I'll tell you if you want.'

Danny held up his hand.

'Too much, you've already told me too much, don't tell me any more. A Chinese archbishop who may have been murdered here in Rome, old friends in London who ordered a factory in Glasgow firebombed, an investigation that's unofficial but high-level, and a rector who did everything but kidnap you. Not to mention whoever put you into hospital.'

'That doesn't count. That was just a message from an old acquaintance.'

'Oh, fine, then I can see how that wouldn't count. What I

don't see is why you told me about it all in the first place.'

'So you could watch my back. That doesn't seem a lot to me.'

'Watch your back how, watch for what?'

'Whatever comes.'

'I'm retired, Jimmy.' The waitress arrived, put the beer on the table, and left. 'If only half of what you've told me is true then it's way out of my league. This isn't any kind of police work that I was ever involved with.'

'Just look out for me. If you see me getting into trouble call a policeman.'

'How can you get in any more trouble than you're in already?'

'I'll wear a pink carnation behind my right ear. Just keep an eye on me, and if you think I'm …'

Jimmy wasn't sure how to put it.

'If I think you're what?'

'If I seem to be losing the plot.'

'And how would I know? You left me behind on this from the start, as soon as you told me.'

'No, not that. If I seem to be cracking up. It might happen. Like you said, this is out of the frame for anything you or I ever did. I might screw up or it might screw me up. Just keep an eye on me.'

Danny fiddled with his empty coffee cup.

'I can do that, I suppose,' then he pushed the cup away, 'but that's all I can do. Don't expect me to pile in if this blows up in your face.'

'But you can call a copper if you think I need one.'

Danny nodded.

'If I can find one. You know what they say about coppers when you need one. And make it a sunflower behind your ear, that way I'll be sure to spot it.'

Jimmy laughed.

'Sure, a sunflower it will be.'

Danny's voice changed, the laughter replaced by concern.

'Listen, I have to say this. That plot you thought you might lose? Well, what if you've already lost it? All that you've told

174

me, well, it's not exactly normal is it, even for police work. Maybe you should see someone, a doctor, have yourself checked over.'

'I'm not long out of hospital. There's nothing wrong with me.'

'I wasn't thinking about your body. Look, Jimmy, I don't think you need anyone watching your back and I don't think it's a policeman I should get for you. I think you may need to talk to someone.'

'I'm talking to you.'

'Not me, someone who can help you with what's going on in your head.'

'Help me how?'

'You lost your wife, that must have been bad. You try to get over it, you think you have and decide to become a priest. You come to Rome. You're among strangers. You decide to keep yourself to yourself, a loner, a man on the outside who doesn't mix. Then you suddenly disappear and when you come back you get put in hospital.'

'So? I explained all that.'

'A message from an old acquaintance? Some explanation. You tell me a story about a murdered archbishop and a conspiracy to get you here run by none other than your own college rector. Mysterious fires in Glasgow and policemen suddenly getting sent to the US.'

'Fire and policeman, both singular. It was only one fire and one policeman.'

'This isn't a joke. Even if it was only one policeman or one fire it's already too much. Archbishop Cheng died, yes, but my guess is it was just an old man dying after a hard life. I know that you really are a Duns student and you really do have a rector, and that's all I know for sure. Everything else is just stuff you told me.'

'I got put in hospital. That was real enough. You tried to visit me there, remember?'

'OK, but it had all the marks of a mugging. Why shouldn't it be just what it looked like? The hospital bit is true but I think the rest of it is all in your head. No inspector, no fire, no conspiracy. I think you were about ready for a breakdown and when you got mugged that, on top of everything else, well, it sort of ...'

'Pushed me over the edge? You think I'm nuts?'

'I think it's like a film that's going on inside your head. To you it all seems real but you're the only one who can see it. I think you need help.'

Jimmy wished Danny was right, that it was all going on in his head and the right kind of help would make it all go away. As it was, there was a chance someone might have murdered four cardinals. That had to mean something. But then there was McBride and what she's said about his mental state. Now it seemed she wasn't the only one. He was here with Danny and had told him everything because he'd believed what she'd said, that he might go nuts, and permanently this time. But what if she was wrong and Danny was right, it wasn't going to happen. It already had. Schizophrenics believed the voices they heard were real. To them they were real. He'd interviewed one once after he'd committed a violent assault and the memory of that interview brought a chill to his heart.

The 'Ride of the Valkyries' suddenly began in Jimmy's pocket. He pulled out the phone and answered it.

'It's still Ride of the bloody Valkyries, you said you'd fix that.' He listened for a moment. 'Right. I'm in a bar, La Tosca in the Piazza Colonna on the Corso. In a few minutes then.' Jimmy put the phone away. His mind had cleared. He was back in the land of the living. This was no film inside his head. 'That was my imaginary inspector. He's coming to pick me up and he can back up everything I've told you.' Jimmy finished off his beer. 'Sorry, I shouldn't have dragged you into this but I didn't think I could do it without someone to talk to and I chose you. Sorry.'

Danny smiled a big smile.

'For God's sake, what's to be sorry for? I just got through telling you that I thought you were having a major breakdown, suffering from chronic hallucinations, that you were a mental basket case. You don't think I wanted it to be that way, do you? But if even a small part of what you've told me is true then you

176

are in deep shit, man. It's going to chew you up and it won't spit you out, not alive anyway.'

'So now you're an expert on Vatican politics? I hope you're better at it than you were at making your psychiatric diagnosis.'

Jimmy was grinning, but Danny wasn't.

'I don't have to be any sort of expert to know that if some stray bystander gets sucked in by that sort of machinery they don't get left to walk away and tell the tale when it's over.'

In the distance a police siren began to be heard.

'If it's Ricci he must be in a hurry.'

'You're going to carry on with this?'

'I don't think I get a choice.'

'Well leave me out of it. I still have a choice and if you want to meet make it somewhere other than this place?'

'Why? I like this place, I think we fit in.'

'We fit in like nuns at a strip joint.'

'Well I like it, we're not locals. We live in Rome but we don't belong. Why shouldn't we fit in with the tourists?'

'We're supposed to be here to study. We're not tourists, we're students.'

'For God's sake look at us, two men old enough to be grandads, and you think we should fit in as students? We're freaks, something the tourists ought to have a good look at alongside the Forum and St Peter's and all the other stuff. Fools for God, that's what we are, a little Roman peep-show.'

'If it's true at all it's only true about you. I'm not a freak and I'm not part of a peep show. Even if I'm leaving I'm still …'

Whatever Danny thought he still was, Jimmy didn't get to find out because a siren came down the Corso and then the big, black police Lancia pulled up outside the door to the bar. It stood there with its engine running and the blue light on the roof flashing.

'This your man?'

'Yeah, I'll let him come and get me. I want you to be sure he's real.'

The back door of the car opened and a smart young man got out and came into the bar. He saw Jimmy and came to the table.

'What are you doing? Why didn't you come out?'

'Inspector Ricci, I want you to meet my friend Danny. He's a student priest like me.'

Ricci looked at Danny, then he put out a hand.

'Nice to meet you, Danny.'

Danny shook his hand.

'We've met before, Inspector, in another bar, but Jimmy didn't mention you were a policeman.'

'Have we? Sorry, I don't remember.' Ricci turned back to Jimmy. 'OK, can we go now?'

Ricci didn't wait. He turned and walked away. Jimmy got up.

'See, real, like I told you.'

'Yeah, Jimmy, just like you told me. Go careful now and remember what I said.'

'That it's a film and it's all happening in my head?'

'That it will chew you up.'

'I'll remember, and I'll keep in touch. Pay the bill, will you, I think my man's in a hurry.'

And Jimmy left the bar.

TWENTY-SEVEN

The police siren seemed to make no difference; no one got out of the way, the traffic was just too congested and too obstinate. The driver had to push his way through like everyone else. Ricci had been sitting in silence, sulking that he had been made to get out of the car and go into the bar, or maybe he was thinking. Jimmy broke the silence.

'How come we get a car and driver?'

'Luigi's a friend, off duty. He's doing us a favour. Don't you want to know where we're going?'

'If you want to tell me.'

'Quadraro, out of the city, down the Via Tuscolana.'

'And what will we see when we get there?'

'Two days ago the police were called to a break-in in an apartment out there. It turned out the place was empty. The young woman who lived there, Anna Bruck, was away. She couldn't be traced. No problem, just wait until she gets back. Meanwhile the scene of crime is turned over, prints get taken.'

'All the usual.'

'All the usual, pure routine, no hurry, and not particularly thorough. It was just an opportunist break-in. The prints got sent off and suddenly all sorts of alarm bells started to ring.'

'A petty break-in rings alarm bells? Was the thief someone special?'

'Not the thief, the girl who lives there. It turns out she's Anna Schwarz, the only member of the Geisller Group still at large.'

'Geisller Group?'

'A German terrorist group named after their leader, Conrad Geisller.'

'What sort of terrorists?'

'Extreme, sort of right-wing.'

'Neo-Nazis?'

'No, not in the traditional sense. They admired strength. Their particular creed was that any cause that can fight its way to the top is a justified cause and any cause that wouldn't use force to achieve its aims is a weak cause and should go under. To them the law of the jungle was the natural law, the only real law.'

'Might is right?'

'Exactly, their favourite slogan translated more or less as, it's not wrong to be strong, their manifesto was headed: Conviction, Action, Victory.'

'They had a manifesto?'

'Oh yes, four pages of pro-violent nonsense dressed up in socio-political jargon. Real adolescent stuff. They were a bunch of campus hard cases. No one took any notice of them until they murdered the professor of history at the university where they were studying.'

'They did what?'

'Murdered him. Claimed he was perverting evolution by manipulating history to subvert natural selection.'

'Again?'

'That he was homosexual and thereby frustrating the natural law, that he was part of an atheistic liberal world conspiracy to suppress the divine right of the strong to assert their will and control their destiny.'

'Well you can't say fairer than that, can you?'

'I memorised it from a website. I thought it would give you a laugh.'

'Oh, hilarious.'

'They were political weirdos. They supported Israel and the

US because of their use of force and Hamas and Hezbollah for the same reason. They were on the side of the tough guys regardless of what they stood for. It was all a bit incoherent. They were just stupid kids playing at being revolutionaries.'

'So naturally they topped their history teacher. Well you would, wouldn't you? And after that show of strength what happened?'

'They went on the run. They lay low for a while until they bungled a bank raid. Nobody was hurt and they didn't get anything. Then there was a raid on a supermarket, they got away with quite a bundle of cash but a security guard got shot and died later in hospital. After that things hotted up. The media became interested and that's when they stopped being a bunch of violent young thugs and became the Geisller Group. The police turned up the gas but they all managed to get away somehow.'

'How many were there in the group?'

'Four at university, five when they first went on the run. That was when Anna joined them. Her big sister Eva was supposed to be the brains of the outfit.'

'I thought you said Geisller was the leader.'

'At university he was, but that didn't make him clever enough to get anywhere. He was muscle, not brains, and he was good-looking. At their age strong and good-looking is enough to be the leader.'

'So Eva did the thinking?'

'So it seems. What little sense there was in their ideology she put there; Geisller was just a ranter and a bully.'

'And Eva's sister joined them when they went on the run after the murder?'

'No, after they'd bungled the bank job.'

'Was she at university?'

'No, she lived at home with her parents.'

'Why did she join them?'

Ricci shrugged.

'Who knows? Maybe she had the hots for Geisller or one of the others. Maybe it was the media attention. Anyway, we know about them because after 9/11 US intelligence began to turn them up. The best guess anyone came up with was that they went on the run from Germany and headed to where the real terrorists operated, Afghanistan or the Middle East. Somehow they seemed to have hooked up to someone who was Al Qaeda or Al Qaeda related. Whoever they were they wanted European faces who could be used for fetching and carrying, setting things up. US intelligence was sure the Geisller Group were among those faces.'

'So what does that mean? They'd converted to Islam or what?'

'I doubt it. They were just doing their thing. Al Qaeda was a cause, it believed enough to do something, it had taken on the world's only remaining superpower. You don't get any tougher than that.'

'What happened to them? You said Anna was the only one still at large?'

'They surfaced again, this time in Spain, and pulled another bank job. They got away with a tidy sum but one of them was shot by a security guard and the others left him behind. When they questioned him he spilled the works so they were on the run again but this time the police had one of them on their side. French Intelligence got two of them just outside of Carcassonne in a holiday let. There was a shootout, one got killed and one got taken.'

'Were either of the sisters involved?'

'No, it was the two men. Would you believe it, Geisller was the one who survived.'

'What about Anna and Eva?'

'Nowhere, and Geisller had no idea where they were.'

'Who had the money?'

'Geisller had some but the girls had most of it.'

'I see. Do you think it was the sisters who gave them to French Intelligence?'

'No idea, does it matter?'

'Probably not.' The car was free of central Rome traffic and they were moving fast now along the Via Tuscolana. 'You said Anna was the last one left of the group, what happened to Big Sister?'

'Gunned down outside a railway station in Austria somewhere. No one knows why it was done or who was responsible. It could even have been the sister, a falling out maybe. They were just amateurs who got to play in the big time for a while. If the real terrorists hadn't needed some innocent-looking white kids to help set up their operations they'd have tried another bank job or something like that and it would probably have ended there.'

'That's all?'

'It's enough, it's a damned lot considering the time I've had to follow up on it.'

'Yes, you did well. Where'd you get it all? You're on sick leave.'

'A copy of the file was delivered by hand.'

'Police?'

'I doubt it. My guess is the minister's aide had it passed it on. Look, Anna Bruck, now Anna Schwarz, is a known terrorist. There's been no word on her since the Carcassonne thing and suddenly under her assumed name she pops up here in Rome. The file gets handed to us. It has to be connected to what we're doing somehow.'

'How?'

'I don't know but if it gets dropped in our lap we have to follow it up, don't we?'

'She suddenly pops up. That's interesting, isn't it?'

'How do you mean, interesting.'

'Why now?'

'Why not now? If what we've been given so far about the cardinals is right then whatever it is could be terrorist-related. Why not? And this has to be a better lead than what we've got now. At least this is the real thing, not some crazy speculation. If I'm going to follow a trail I'd rather it was this than anything to do with fixing a conclave.'

Ricci was back in a good mood. This was big, important, and, unlike Cheng's death, solid: something they could get their teeth into. He looked at Jimmy who was looking out of the window. He should be pleased as well but he didn't seem pleased.

'Well? What do you think?'

Jimmy was watching the buildings and trees go past.

'I think it's like a film.'

'What?'

'Like I'm being shown something, something not real, that only I can see.'

'Talk sense, will you?'

Jimmy turned back from the window.

'It was a break-in? Door forced?'

Ricci nodded.

'Yeah, but a neat job. Somebody who knew what they were doing. A neighbour in the next apartment heard some noises, knew the girl wasn't there, so she called the police.'

'But the intruder was gone before they got there?' Ricci nodded. 'Don't you think that's odd?'

'Why, the response time wouldn't be so very quick. It wasn't anything special.'

'No, not that whoever broke in was gone.'

'Then what?

'That somebody who knows what they're doing and gets in quietly, makes so much noise that they get heard by next door, then slips quietly away so no one sees anything. I just think it's odd.'

'That he got away? What did you want the neighbour to do, stand outside the apartment door and arrest him when he came out? She was frightened. She kept her door shut and waited for the police. It was the right thing to do.'

'I suppose so.'

'I know so.'

With the siren going and the roads less congested they were making good time.

'Why do we have to have that thing going, we're not in a hurry.'

'We look like we're on police business. If anyone sees us at the apartments we're just cops having another look.'

'We're going to a crime scene that's two days old. Why would we need a siren?'

Ricci leaned forward and spoke to the driver. The siren fell silent. The driver lowered the window, pulled the light off the roof, and stuck it under his seat. Jimmy watched him. He'd better be good at his job, buggering about like that at the speed they were going. The Lancia went on, slower now, just part of the traffic.

'Was Anna ever convicted of anything?'

'Never charged because she was never caught. They got prints, DNA, and a photo from her home. Other than that they never got a smell of her.'

'So Anna, late of the Geisller Group, turns up here in Rome. When did she come and what was she doing?'

'She came three weeks ago. Posed as a post-graduate student from Tübingen University in Holland doing research into Renaissance Vatican diplomacy. She wanted to have access to certain documents in the Vatican Library. Her papers checked out which is fine until the police check again after they know who the prints belong to and find that there is an Anna Bruck and she is a post-graduate student but she's studying electronic engineering and has never left Tübingen.'

'Do we have a picture of Schwarz?'

'Not recent. The only one on file is about ten years old. It was supplied by her parents when it became known that she'd gone on the run with her sister.'

'Did she ever go to the Vatican Library?'

'Not that anyone can remember. Her contacts with their administration were by phone and e-mail. They thought they were dealing with someone in Holland but she could have been anywhere.'

'You've done well, you've covered all the ground.'

Ricci decided to be modest. 'It was all in the file.'

'Yes, it was a very thorough file, wasn't it? Did you know the bloke who brought it?'

'No.'

'And he didn't say who it was from.'

'No, just said he'd been told to deliver it by hand.'

'What sort of file was it?'

'How do you mean?'

'Was it a police file?'

'Some of it was, copies of pages from a police file. Some pages weren't.'

'The envelope?'

'Plain.'

Ricci looked at Jimmy, who had gone back to studying the passing scenery. Why wasn't he pleased? He was in a funny mood today. Then he thought, what the hell, if he wants to look out of the window let him look.

The dual carriageway entered a busy suburb with apartment blocks all round, shops at street level and a Metro station, Porta Furba.

Ricci leaned forward and spoke to the driver who nodded. The car drove on then pulled over.

'This it?'

'No. I want to get some aspirins. I've got a headache. I seem to have one all the time lately.'

'It must be me.'

'Yeah, it could easily be you.'

Jimmy sat back as Ricci left and went into a pharmacy. In a few moments he returned with a small packet and a bottle of water in his hand. Once in the car he opened the packet and the bottle, took a sip, and swallowed some tablets.

'How many did you take?'

'Four.'

'That's a lot at one go.'

'It's that sort of headache.'

The car pulled away into the traffic.

Jimmy looked at the busy pavements on either side of the road. It looked a nice place to live, if you liked a view of nothing but other apartments and being treated like a sardine twice a day on the Metro.

The Lancia turned left off the main road, made a couple of turns, and pulled up outside a block of apartments that looked like all the others with washing strung across balconies and slatted shutters on the windows. Here the sun was something you kept on the porch, like muddy shoes in England, even this pleasantly warm spring sunshine.

They got out of the car, the driver leaned back, lit a cigarette, and opened his window. He wasn't interested in what they were doing. He was off duty.

'It's on the first floor.'

They went in and began to climb the concrete stairs.

'Her apartment gets turned over while she's away and the police find out who she is through a routine fingerprint check. How is it connected to what we're doing, that's the question? What do you think?'

Jimmy shrugged.

'It's like you said, considering what else we've got we live in hope. How did you get to know?'

'Got a phone call yesterday evening.'

'Did the voice say who it was?'

'No.'

'And you didn't recognise it?'

'No. I was just told what had been found and that the minister had ordered a complete information shutdown. He doesn't want the media to get any sort of line on it. But a file on the case would be sent to me directly by hand. Because the minister was mentioned I assumed the call was from the Cherub's office, that he thought we'd want to know.'

'Yes, I can see how you'd think that. A brownie point for the Cherub then.'

But Jimmy still didn't seem pleased as they turned off the staircase and went on to the apartment that had been rented in the name of Anna Bruck.

TWENTY-EIGHT

It was a small, one-bedroom apartment. A washed plate, some cutlery, and a mug were stacked neatly on the draining board by the sink. There was food in the kitchen cupboards and in the fridge, there were clothes in the wardrobe. The bedclothes were rumpled, pulled up but not straightened out. There was a four-day-old copy of *la Repubblica* on the settee in the living room. It was all neat in a sloppy sort of way. Jimmy sat on the bed. Ricci stood in the doorway looking round.

'We're not going to find much, are we?'

Jimmy nodded.

'It's all been cleaned up.'

Ricci looked around the bedroom.

'The next apartment's the other side of that wall. I don't see how he made enough noise to get the next door neighbour to call the police unless he threw something against it.'

'What sort of noise did the neighbour say she heard?'

Ricci shrugged.

'I didn't ask.'

Jimmy reached over, pulled back the bedclothes, and looked at the sheet.

'The bedclothes are rumpled but the sheets haven't been slept on.'

'So? The bed was put back together after the place got

searched.'

They went into the living room.

'How did the woman next door know she'd gone away?'

'A note through her letterbox. "Hello, I'm your new neighbour, Anna, I have to go away for a week. If anyone asks for me could you tell them I'll be back next Tuesday?"'

'Why not do it in person?'

'Because she wanted to be seen as little as possible by as few people as she could manage.'

'So has next door ever seen Anna?'

'No. No one seems to have seen her.'

'What language was the note in?'

'Italian, and I know that may be odd but it was definitely in Anna's handwriting. It got cross-checked and it matched.'

'So Anna the terrorist who is on the run sets up an alias and with this alias she comes to Rome. How did she rent the apartment?'

'All done by phone, rent paid for six months in advance. Checking references would be a formality if the money was already in the agent's account.'

'Was the money paid by a bank transfer?'

'Cash, paid into the agent's account, she used a bank in Genoa.'

'And the teller doesn't remember her?'

'She doesn't remember a thing, just another customer. There was nothing useful from the CCTV either. Two or three women who used the bank on the day the payment was made could have been her but there was nothing definite.'

'She seems to be able to move around free as a bird and yet stay invisible.'

'She's had the practice. She had the cream of the US and European anti-terrorist agencies looking for her and they never even got a sniff.'

Jimmy went to the window and looked out. Why was she here? Out of nowhere, when they needed something to breathe life into the corpse of an enquiry they got a known terrorist dropped in their lap. This wasn't like the cardinals, just something to keep him going, to put off the day he'd have to face the fact that his priest training was probably finished, that he'd have to start all over again.'

'She does actually exist, doesn't she, our invisible Anna?'

'She exists. Her parents say she contacted them twice while she was on the run, both times to tell them she and Eva were OK.'

'Contacted them how?'

'By letter. The handwriting was hers, she used a nickname she'd had when she was little, and the fingerprints checked. Fingerprints and DNA taken from her home check out with here. She may be invisible but she exists and she's been here.'

'What did Geisller and the other one the police got say about her?'

'Nothing, they never met her.'

'What?'

Jimmy turned away from the window.

'They never met her?'

'No, they never saw her.'

'Are you telling me she was part of a terrorist group and the rest of the group never met her? How the hell does that work?'

'It seems she organised things through Eva. She set up the places and passed the information to Eva. Anna always made sure they were separate with Eva and herself together; she never had any direct contact with the men.'

'Now three are dead, two banged up in prison for the rest of their lives, and Little Sister has surfaced on her own.'

'Yes.' Jimmy turned back to the window. Ricci let him think for a while but then got fed up of waiting. 'So what do you think, is it anything to do with us?'

Jimmy left the window and sat down on the settee.

'Could be yes, could be no, or it could be something else altogether.'

He picked up the old newspaper. Then put it down.

'Come on, Jimmy. Don't pussyfoot about. Do we follow this one?'

'Oh, we follow it all right,' he stood up, 'and we don't have to piss about on our own any more. Anna is a known terrorist on the run so there'll be big guns out looking for her. Get the

Cherub to give you an official hook-up to whoever is running the investigation. This flat will have been gone over by experts so we'll plug in to anything they get. Whatever she's part of it's off and running and she's busy doing what she came to Rome to do.'

Ricci didn't like the idea of bringing the police in, there'd be nothing in it for him if the whole thing turned official.

'Do we need to tell the police what we know?'

'What do we know? There's an outside chance that Cheng might have been killed, that there's also an outside chance that some other cardinals might have been killed, and on the basis of those two possibilities we have concluded that there might be a plot to fix the election of the next pope. That what we've got so far and if we told them that they wouldn't cooperate, they certify us, and they'd be right. What we have is comic cuts.'

'What?'

'Something my dad used to say, comic cuts. It was a kids' comic, silly stuff, only fit for children and people weak in the head. Anything we told them about what we've done so far will sound like a load of bollocks to any working detective.' Jimmy's manner changed. 'But Anna Schwarz isn't bollocks, is she? She's real and she's the first piece of concrete evidence we've had, a lead that we can actually follow. We were looking like clowns, chasing moonbeams, but now, suddenly, we're hooked up to something real.'

But Ricci wasn't really listening. He had other things on his mind.

'It's going to be tricky. If we don't tell them anything about what our interest is then it has to be a one-way street, their information to us and nothing from us to them.'

'Then make it the minister's problem, he brought us in so he can deal with it. If this Cheng business is so important and Anna might be part of it we have to be in. Unofficial maybe but still on the inside. Tell him to kick some backsides if he has to.'

'And what if they pick her up?'

'I don't think that's likely.'

'Why not?'

'The police can follow her if she leaves a trail but that's

about all they can do. I doubt they can stop her; she's been too good in the past to make any stupid mistakes so my guess is she'll be too good this time. Whatever she came to do will get done and then she'll disappear.'

'And what, according to your theory, is it she's come to do that can possibly be linked to Cheng's death? Kill another cardinal?'

Jimmy didn't mind the sarcasm but noted that it was still his theory.

'She's not a killer, from what you told me not even close to being one unless she shot her sister. She moved people about so let's assume that whatever she's here for must be related to what she was good at. Maybe she came to move a team. Her job is getting them in and putting them as near to their target as possible.'

'That makes sense and if we're right then the target is probably in Rome. Why else set up here?'

Jimmy noted that now it was "if we're right". If things went their way on this pretty soon it would become our theory and if they made it all the way Jimmy's guess was that when Ricci made his report it would have always been his own theory.

Well, why not, he had other things to worry about. He felt angry with himself. What was going on? Why wasn't his brain working properly? What was holding him back? Danny had said it was all a film running in his head that only he could see. Maybe he wasn't so far wrong. It was like being in a movie, playing a part. He'd once heard a story about a Chinese philosopher who'd dreamed he was a butterfly. After that he was never sure if he was a man dreaming he was a butterfly or a butterfly dreaming he was a man. That was the trouble with dreams, while you had them they *were* real. It was the same with schizophrenia, while it was happening it might be a dream to others but it was real to you.

Jimmy tried to break away from that line of thinking; it got him nowhere and if he was mad or even close to it, thinking about it wouldn't help, probably only make it worse. Whatever his state of mind Anna Schwarz was real enough, she wasn't a figment of anyone's imagination, not a character in any film. A known terrorist had surfaced here in Rome and somehow, like Alice in Wonderland, he had fallen down a rabbit hole and become part of it, so grab it with both hands and get on with it. He had to concentrate on the job in hand and push everything else out. But he didn't like doing it. He had a vague idea that in there somewhere he was pushing out something important.

'We need to know how she travelled when she left here, which means car rentals or travel tickets. She didn't know anyone would be looking for her so she will almost certainly use the same ID. Also, she's been away three nights if she put that note into the next door flat the day before the break-in.'

Ricci nodded.

'She did.'

'Three nights then. So we need to know if she has checked into any hotels.'

'What do we tell the Cherub?'

'That it's possible she's moving a team and the target could be here in Rome.'

'OK. Anything else here?'

Jimmy gave the place a look.

'I doubt it but I'm not sure. There's something at the back of my mind, something that's pulling me away from just going straight after her.'

'What is it?'

'God knows, probably nothing. Probably just that this whole thing has been screwy from day one and is getting screwier by the minute.'

'So what are you going to do?'

'I'm going to try and work out what it is, what's annoying me. Either it's important, in which case I need to know, or it's nothing, in which case I need to get rid of it. Either way I need to bring it up where I can see it. You get on and find out how things stand with the police and what they've got on how Anna travelled. I need to think, I need to go over everything from where we started through to now. Can I get back from here by myself?'

'Sure, you take the Metro. It's about fifteen minutes to Termini.'

'No. I'll need more time and the Metro is too noisy, all that piped musak. What about a bus?'

'Yeah, there's a bus. But it takes about a day and a half.'

'Slow is just what I want. I'll take the bus.'

'Where will we meet?'

'Chiesa Nuova.'

'Not a bloody church.'

'Why not? It'll be quiet, it'll be a good place to think, and maybe say a prayer. If you don't get the right sort of information we might not have anything to fall back on except prayer.'

He was smiling but he wasn't really trying to be funny. Something was happening and Anna Schwarz turning up meant that it was happening now and the truth was he didn't have a clue as to what it really was. He wasn't sure about a team, but he believed in Anna. Somehow Anna was the key, but the key to what? Anna was on the move and if she thought she was clear there was a good chance she'd leave a trail. But if this was terrorist related why recruit an on-the-run amateur? Why not someone trained and better still someone without a record?

Ricci broke into Jimmy's thoughts.

'Are we going or are you going to stand there all day? Come on, I'll drop you at the bus stop.'

They left the apartment. When the driver saw them coming he threw his cigarette out of the window and started the engine.

'Who knows?'

The question puzzled Ricci.

'Who knows what?'

'There may be a Mass on. I haven't been getting to Mass as often as I'd like since this started.'

'You're a bloody religious nut, that's what you are.'

That was what Ricci said, but Jimmy wasn't the only one with private thoughts and concerns about the way things were turning out. He was glad he'd be alone in the car. He'd also done some hard thinking about something that was worrying him. He was expected to go to the minister's aide and tell him that it was possible a known terrorist with Al Qaeda links had been sent to Rome to bring in a team, but a team to do what, assassinate a cardinal? It was mad but it was all they had so far, that there had been the unexpected deaths of those cardinals who might be connected by their importance should a conclave be convened. Which all meant? God knew. It probably meant that at best he'd get thrown out on his ear for wasting the aide's time. But if the aide thought there was a chance, even only an outside chance, that they were right he couldn't do anything once he'd been told. If there was any possibility at all it would mean, what? Putting extra security round every cardinal in Rome? If it could be done how many men would that take, for Christ's sake, and then, when nothing happened and everyone started asking questions, he'd be the one they'd be looking at waiting for the answers. And what could he tell them? An ex-London copper, who'd got early retirement due to stress and who wanted to become a priest, thought someone was out to kill cardinals.

He didn't want to think about it any more, but it was all he could think about. This was going to be a ball-breaker. If Jimmy was wrong, and the odds were he was as wrong as he could be, then Ricci's career as a copper ended. It wouldn't just stall, it would end. They wouldn't even put him in Traffic. They'd kick him into the nearest gutter and jump all over him before they went away and slammed every door they could think of on him. If he told the Cherub and Jimmy was wrong then the shit was going to hit the fan in a big way. But if he didn't tell the minister and Jimmy turned out to be right then the shit also hit the fan but in a much bigger way. Either way Ricci knew exactly who the fan was pointing at. Maybe Jimmy was right, at this point in time maybe prayers weren't such a bad idea.

The car pulled over and stopped. Ricci nodded to a bus stop.

'The X53 from here will take you in. When you get there say one for me, and maybe light a candle.'

'I was going to do it for both of us; I think we need it.'

The Lancia pulled away. The driver had attached the blue light to the roof and the siren was on. Jimmy watched it go. Ricci was in a hurry. Of course he was. He wanted to let the minister's aide know what was happening as soon as possible. He wanted to get the credit. Well, why not? It would help him and it was no use to Jimmy.

He looked at the oncoming traffic. There was no bus in sight.

What are we doing? Jimmy tried to go over it but he was confused. He'd always been a good detective. He could look at the facts and put them into some sort of order and see if they pointed to anything. But in this thing what were the facts? An archbishop had died …

No, it was no use going over it all again, he'd been over it and over it and it never went anywhere. Or did it? It had led them here, to Anna Schwarz, but where was that? He looked down the dual carriageway. There was still no bus in sight. He went back to his thoughts.

TWENTY-NINE

Jimmy was in luck, there was a Mass about halfway through when he arrived at the church with a small congregation gathered together in the front two or three rows.

Chiesa Nuova had been built at the beginning of the seventeenth century as the Oratorio di Ssn Filippo Neri and was the imposing Mother Church to oratories which had spread world-wide. But in this city of ancient churches it had always remained Chiesa Nuova, the 'New Church'. Jimmy didn't like it, the interior was too ornate, crowded with paintings and statues, with flourishes of gold leaf on endless decorative stone carving. To Jimmy's London-Irish sense of Catholicism, with its solid streak of puritan Jansenism, it all conspired to distract the eye from what should be the central focus: the altar.

He sat down in the back row of the pews far away from the congregation. The priest saying Mass wore red vestments. It must be the feast day of some martyr, red was for blood, for violence and death.

He sat searching for words.

'Dear Lord …'

Dear Lord what? Dear Lord, why is Anna here? No, not that. God knew, but he wasn't about to share the information. Dear Lord, keep me good as a detective. No. Dear Lord, keep me bloody good as a detective. No, it wasn't that. You got it by

199

working at it. It didn't come any other way. Dear Lord, make me wrong about the film in my head, keep me sane. But God didn't change things. He wasn't a slot machine, put in a prayer and get out what you want. If God had been like that then all he'd ever get was, Dear Lord, please give me a winner with long odds for the 2.30 at Kempton Park. So, what were the right words? Jimmy switched off his mind, and when he did, the words came.

'Dear Lord, keep in your mercy, compassion, and forgiveness Bernie and Michael, and take them into the love of your everlasting kingdom of peace and happiness.'

You didn't ask for yourself, you knew what you were. You left yourself to God and hoped for mercy and maybe, if you were lucky, other people prayed for you. The ancient formula, spoken without thought, came automatically to his lips.

'May their souls and the souls of all the faithful departed, through the mercy of God, rest in peace. Amen.'

He looked at his watch and realised he was hungry. He'd had no lunch and it was now three o'clock. When the Mass was finished he would go somewhere and get something to eat. If Ricci hadn't come by the time Mass was over he could phone him to say where he was. He turned his attention to the priest and switched off his mind. The priest was speaking rapidly in some language that wasn't Italian. He was oriental. Jimmy looked at the people in the front rows. They were oriental, probably pilgrims with their own priest. He looked back to the priest and had no difficulty in following what was being said. He knew the words of the Mass almost by heart, but from constant repetition not from any study or interest in what it all meant. The interest had come after Bernie and Michael's deaths, when he had tried to leave his old life behind him in London and went to the west of Ireland to search for a new life. There he had started to listen. Why had he waited for them to die before he had begun to listen?

Jimmy sat and watched the altar.

It was something someone had said. The thing he wanted to bring out into the open was something someone had told him. No, not someone, more than one person. He had been told something very important and told more than once and by more than one person. He concentrated and as he did so whatever it was slipped further away.

He gave up. It would come when it was ready, if it came at all.

He got up and quietly walked to the nearest candles. They were in a black, wax-spattered affair by a massive round pillar and above them, on a plinth, the statue of a saint looked down. Jimmy put some coins in the money box, picked up two candles, lit them, and put them among the others. There were always candles burning. People always wanted something from God, a big favour, a small favour. When only God could help you reached out to him and you did it like you did to all the powerful ones. You got an insider to put in a word for you. Jimmy looked at the stone saint.

'Whoever you are, if you were ever in trouble, please pray for me.' Pray for what, what was the message he wanted this saint to slip to God? 'That I can find a way of going on, if not as a priest then as something. Amen.'

He crossed himself and looked back into the church. The priest had come down from the altar and was distributing communion at the altar rail. It was nothing to do with him, he was a spectator, uninvolved. It was their Mass after all, not his.

Jimmy went out of the church into the sunshine. It had only been a little prayer to a very minor saint whose name he didn't even know. But it was something. It was the best he could manage in the circumstances. Now he could go and get something to eat and try to work out why Anna and why now? Or perhaps he could dredge whatever was at the back of his mind out into the open.

Chiesa Nuova was on the Corso Vittorio Emanuele just opposite the entrance to the narrow street with the café where he met Danny and Ron, so he knew the area quite well. He had a choice of places to eat but he just wanted a simple meal in quiet so he went round the back of the church into a maze of back streets where he could find the kind of place he wanted.

It was something he'd heard, just one thing, like Anna was just one thing. One thing that might tell him what he needed to

201

know, but what? What had he been told?

He found a place where the locals ate, not unlike the bar he, Danny, and Ron used. He ordered spaghetti and a beer and sat down. He put his mind into neutral. He'd tried thinking and it hadn't worked so now he just sat and drank his beer. His spaghetti came and he ordered another beer. The spaghetti was good, he was ready for it.

When he was about halfway through his meal the 'Ride of the Valkyries' jangled in his jacket pocket and the man at the next table, smoking a cigarette with a glass of red wine in front of him, looked across.

'Shit.' Jimmy put his fork on his plate, took out the mobile and answered it. 'It's still playing bloody Wagner, when are you going to …' He stopped and listened. 'Why won't they?' He listened again. 'Oh, fuck.' If the solitary drinker at the next table spoke English he didn't seem to mind the language, but it wasn't much of a place, so it probably didn't matter one way or another. 'Look, we'd better meet, this needs sorting. Where are you now? I'll be there in about ten minutes.'

THIRTY

Cars weren't allowed in Campo di Fiori because of the busy market square but Ricci's big black Lancia was outside the bar with the blue light still on the roof to identify it as a police car. There was no sign of the driver. Ricci was sitting inside holding his usual campari and soda, and there was a beer ready on the table. The waiter nodded as Jimmy walked past him, he didn't smile, but he definitely acknowledged his arrival. Progress there at least, thought Jimmy as he went and sat down.

'He nodded at me.'

'Why not? He's seen you before.'

'He used to ignore me.'

'Maybe now he thinks you add a dash of something to the place. To be so out of fashion in a place like this might be the way to be in fashion. Who knows, crumpled scruffy might be the new black.'

Jimmy took a drink and noticed the pack of aspirins was on the table.

'Still got the headache?' Ricci nodded. 'Why not see a doctor?'

'I've seen one, remember? I'm on sick leave.'

'Maybe you really are sick.'

'It's a headache, that's all. Leave it alone.'

Jimmy left it alone.

'Why won't they co-operate?'

'Because I'm unofficial. I'm on leave pending a medical report and when I'm at work I'm nothing to do with terrorists. As for you, you don't exist.' He paused, picked up his drink, thought better of it, and put it back on the table. 'I found out who was on the team and phoned one of them off the record. I told him I was working for the minister in an unofficial capacity and asked for a contact inside the investigation so we could share information. Fifteen minutes later I get a call which slams the door on me.'

'Why didn't you go to the minister's aide and let him pull the strings?'

'If Anna's on the move we're in a hurry and going through the minister would have taken too much time. I thought my way was best. I was wrong.'

It was a lie and not a very good one. He'd tried to bypass telling the Cherub what they'd come up with and it hadn't worked. Now he waited to see how Jimmy would take it. He took it surprisingly well.

'Well we still need access to progress reports, to information as it comes in. We need to ask questions and get them answered.'

'I put a message in to the minister's aide. He should get back to me.'

'He might get back to you? You just left it at that? We're sitting here with no police hook up, Little Sister is on the move, and all we've got is that Charlie Cherub might get back to you?'

'Well, what else could I do? And he was quick with the Anna stuff in the first place.'

Jimmy wasn't happy with it, but he left it. Ricci should have gone through the aide, not buggered about with unofficial requests; that way they would have got what they wanted. If the Cherub believed them. But would he have believed them? Maybe Ricci was right to leave him out of it, even if it hadn't worked out.

'We've got to phone McBride.'

'Why?'

'Well, who the fuck else is there?' Ricci looked around.

Jimmy had let his voice rise and in this place just about everybody spoke English. 'She must have a direct line to whoever set this up with the minister. When we asked for a Vatican contact we got her. Whoever she is she's more than just a simple academic and part-time rector. She's a player of some sort. So if we ask her for a police contact inside the investigation she might be able to get somewhere. We need access. We need to get up to speed on what the police have on Anna's movements and we need it now. If she's bringing a team in she wouldn't move until she was needed, and she wouldn't be needed until the team were about to arrive. She must already have a safe house for them.'

'We don't know that, maybe that's what she gone to do, not pick up the team.'

'Oh yes? You said she arrived three weeks ago, what do you think she's been doing since she arrived, sight-seeing? If she's moving, they're moving, and that means a timetable. I don't know how these things work but I'd say day one, the day she left, would be to get where she's going and check that everything is OK. We know she's careful so she'd want to make sure that there were no unwelcome spectators to see her meet the team when they arrive. Day two she would take delivery of the team and get them to the safe house. Day three, yesterday, her job's done and she's finished. The team's in place so Little Sister will have flown. What do you think?'

'Sounds all right but I don't know how these things work any better than you.'

'We need to know how she travelled. If she hired a car the team might still be using it.'

They both sat in silence for a moment with their own thoughts and both were thinking about the same thing: their future, what happened to them when this ended, however it ended. It was Ricci who broke the silence.

'Look, whatever's going on is a long way from Cheng's death. It might be a blind alley for us even if we get inside the information loop. Why don't we give it up and let the police sort Anna out? We're tying ourselves in knots on something that's probably nothing to do with what we're supposed to be looking at.'

'Then why were we given Anna in the first place?'

'She was a coincidence, she's not connected to Cheng or anything we're doing. And even if she was we'd never be able to sit here and work out what it is.'

Ricci was right, but Jimmy wasn't going to agree. Cheng and the other cardinals might be a dead end but finding Anna Schwarz was all that stood between him and having to face rebuilding what was left of his life.

'We could try.'

'For God's sake, stop being Sherlock bloody Holmes and let's go back to Cheng. That's what the minister wanted us to do, not chase phantom terrorists.'

Jimmy nodded and picked up his beer. Ricci was right but he wasn't going to drop it so easily. 'All right, but at least let me get in touch with McBride.'

'Why? We don't need McBride, we don't need to know what the police have got or what they'll get. We need to drop the fucking thing.'

This time Ricci didn't look round. He didn't care what anyone might think. Jimmy finished his drink and ignored Ricci's outburst.

'I'll go to my apartment and phone her.'

'Oh, Christ, I don't believe this. Why do you have to be such a stubborn bastard?'

'Just the way I am I guess.'

'God give me strength.' Ricci reached for the packet and dropped the last three tablets into his hand. He swallowed them with the last of his drink. 'Come on, if that's the way you want it I'll drive you.'

Jimmy got up slowly. 'You sure about that headache and a doctor?'

'I'm sure. I know what's causing it: you.'

'OK, but I still think you should see a doctor.'

'Go to hell.' And they left the bar.

THIRTY-ONE

Ricci sat in a chair and watched Jimmy put the phone down.

'What did she say?'

'I told her what we'd got so far, how Anna turned up, and our theory about bringing in a team.'

'Your theory, Jimmy, you're the brains, the leader, remember?'

It was back to being his theory.

'I told her Anna was on the move and what we think might be happening …'

'What you think might be happening.'

'… and she just said stay where you are, give me your number, and I'll phone you back as soon as I can.' Jimmy sat down; his manner seemed far away. Ricci waited for a second.

'So we wait here?'

'You don't have to. I'm the one who wants to see where this goes.'

'No, I'll see where it goes, if it goes anywhere.'

'Funny though, she didn't seem interested, she just listened. Why didn't she have any questions?'

'You told her what you think and then told her what you wanted, an urgent message passed to the minister. What do you expect her to do, spend time cross examining you? She's getting on with it, doing what you asked her to do.'

Ricci wasn't wrong, but he wasn't completely right either.

'I suppose so.'

Ricci stood up and wandered about the room. He was restless. Waiting, doing nothing wasn't something he was good at, especially when he didn't like the nothing he was doing.

'Shall I make us coffee? Do you want a coffee?'

Jimmy gave him a vacant stare. He wasn't really listening, he still seemed far away. He managed an answer.

'No, no coffee.'

'Neither do I. Do you have any aspirins?'

'Somewhere. You had some not so long ago.'

'Where are they?'

'Try the kitchen.'

Ricci went to the kitchen. After a few minutes he came back.

'I can't find any.'

'I still say you should see a doctor. Headaches shouldn't last that long.'

'All right, I'll see a doctor.'

It wasn't easy, trying to think with Ricci just standing there. He wasn't going to settle until he was occupied. Jimmy dragged himself away from his thoughts.

'I'm not happy about this.'

Ricci gave an ironic laugh.

'Not happy? That's a bit of an understatement, isn't it?'

He went and stood by the window looking out.

'Tell me, did you ever want to be in a movie?'

'What the hell are you on about now?'

'Well that's what this all feels like. It's like we're following a script, like someone's …'

'For Christ's sake, don't.' Ricci came back and sat down heavily. 'Don't make it any worse than it already is with another of your crazy ideas. We're not in a movie, there is no script. Anna Schwarz is real and the police looking for her are real and Cheng died, that's real. Stay away from Hollywood and stick with what's real.'

'OK. Let's stick with Anna. She's a known terrorist and apart from being invisible what she's good at is moving other terrorists around. If she's here for anything it's to move people,' bring someone in, probably more than one. Why Rome, what's so special about Rome?'

Ricci had sat forward, his elbows on his knees and his head in his hands. He didn't look well but Jimmy couldn't help. Telling him to see a doctor had used up all his medical knowledge.

'Go on, tell me what's special about Rome.'

'Do you remember what we were looking for, a connection?'

Ricci sat up. He definitely looked bad.

'Sure, you thought you'd found one, fixing the next conclave.'

'And to get a conclave you have to have a dead pope.'

'Is that it? They're going to kill the pope? Of course it is because everything has to fit your theory or it can't be right, can it? If Anna's bringing in a team it has to be to kill the pope.'

Jimmy looked at him.

'Finished?'

'No, I'm not finished. I feel like I'm being sucked into your head, that everything I do and think about is crammed inside your head but I have to go along with it because it's where you want to go and I was told to follow. All right, let's say that Anna Schwarz really has come to bring in a team and they have a target. Why not a sports event or pop concert, anywhere that would be crowded? If it's terrorist related it could be almost anything. Why do you have it that it must be killing the pope?'

'All right, it could be a bomb, but if it is why did we get given Anna? Before Anna it was all Vatican related, Cheng was Vatican, whoever put pressure on the minister was Vatican, our information on Cheng's funeral and confirmation he was a cardinal were both Vatican. If we've been given Anna it's because somebody thinks that whatever she's here for is to do with the Vatican. And maybe you're right, it won't be an attempt on the pope, it may be a bomb, a bomb in the Vatican.'

'For God's sake, why?'

'Why not? Put a bomb on the Metro and who do you kill? Civilians, nobodies, innocent bystanders. Bombing the Vatican would be as big as hitting the Twin Towers, bigger depending

209

on how many die and who they were. Imagine it. They get a plane, stuff it with explosives, and fly it into the dome of St Peter's during a papal Mass. The dome collapses and everybody inside dies and it would all be televised. It doesn't just hit Italy, it hits the whole Catholic world. It would be like a declaration of war against Christianity. '

Ricci made an effort. A bomb. It could be a bomb. If it was terrorists a bomb was the best bet and that was his idea, not Jimmy's. This time he wasn't following, he was leading. He felt a bit better; it showed in his voice.

'Bombing the Vatican is better than killing cardinals and fixing a conclave.'

'A damn sight better even if I can't see how it ties into Cheng.'

'Sod Cheng. Now we stick with Anna. If there is a connection it'll show at some point.'

Ricci pushed his headache from the forefront of his mind. A terrorist bomb made sense. But in Rome, in the Vatican. His mind went back to the TV pictures of the Twin Towers being hit. He tried to imagine something similar here in Rome as Jimmy had described it. He found it all too easy.

'Thank God we can get it stopped.'

Jimmy looked surprised.

'Oh yes, and how do we stop it? We haven't told anyone what we think except McBride and with her only that a team may be coming in. At this moment in time the minister doesn't even know that we think the Vatican may be a target. Nobody's told him.'

Ricci felt uncomfortable. He should have done better than just that message with the minister's aide.

'No, I know we haven't. Look, I thought I'd get nowhere with the minister's aide. All we'd actually got was that maybe the deaths of some old cardinals might be suspicious. Maybe they were connected if a conclave were to be called. I mean, when you come right down to it, before Anna turned up, what did we have, what concrete evidence was there?'

Jimmy looked at him. He was tired, not in good shape, it was time to leave it alone.

'Well, we've gone as far as we can. All we can do now is wait for a call from McBride and see if she gets anywhere.'

'Well I hope she's operating with more than we have.'

'And what do we have?'

'Prayers, candles, and hope.'

Jimmy smiled.

'I have great faith in prayer, candles, and hope, especially when they're mixed in with Professor McBride.'

THIRTY-TWO

They had been waiting an hour, Ricci had taken to wandering in and out of the kitchen trying to find some aspirins. He had even looked in the fridge. It was something to do. Jimmy was sitting at the table staring at nothing. Ricci had begun to hate the room. Now he was ready to hate Jimmy because apparently he could sit still forever doing nothing.

'Are you thinking or have you just switched off? Maybe you're dead. Should I close your eyes?'

'I can't believe I played along with it for so long. It was all there in plain view. I even got told and more than once but I still didn't see it.'

'See what?'

'It's all in my head, you told me that, you said it was like being sucked into my head and you were dead right. Danny said the same thing, it was like a film someone was running inside my head.'

'Danny? Your black friend? For Christ's sake tell me you haven't told him anything.'

Jimmy brushed aside Ricci's concern.

'We've been part of a bloody movie, everything so far has been scripted and directed. We get brought in and given Cheng's death. When it was obviously going nowhere we get the cardinals?'

'That was your idea, no one fed us that. You thought up that little fantasy.'

'I did, didn't I? I knew it was rubbish but I didn't want the investigation to stop. I wanted it to go on so I forced a connection where there couldn't be one and when I ask for someone to tell me all about it what happens? I get a monsignor who invites me to lunch and there it is, all the confirmation I need to turn a piece of nonsense into a possible lead. Sure there are some cardinals whose deaths might be suspicious and guess what? It might be something to do with a conclave, and guess who might have been elected pope in that conclave? Only Cheng. My God, I must have been sleepwalking. From Cheng's death to fixing a conclave. It's all been nothing more than a film show, Killing cardinals, a fantasy movie playing in a head near you: mine.'

'And who's supposed to be behind all this elaborate conspiracy? The minister, the pope, the president of the ...'

'I don't know, but McBride is involved. She has to be.'

'Your rector.'

Ricci couldn't restrain a burst of laughter.

'Now that *is* a joke.'

'Is it?'

'She's a bloody academic, a professor, a temporary rector. All right, she has Vatican connections, but who doesn't in Rome if they matter at all?'

'She's American. It could be something to do with the CIA.'

'No, that's enough. Not the CIA on top of everything else. Forget the Americans and any movie in your head or anywhere else because there's one thing that blows your stupid theory right out of the water: Anna Schwarz. She's real, she's not part of any script. Nobody made Anna up.'

'That's right. And that's what all this fucking crap of play-acting has to have been about, to lead us to Anna. Someone knew she was here. Once she was out of the apartment and on her way to do whatever she's doing they arranged a break-in and made sure the police got called. Then Charlie Cherub kindly tells you all about it and lo and behold there's a file on Anna with everything we need to know and it gets handed to you nice as pie.'

'But why? Why the hell would anybody go to all that trouble?'

'Because we're not detectives on this, we never were. We're going to be the bloody evidence. We're witnesses. Whatever happens from now on will be as carefully managed as all the rest. We'll be fed enough, but just enough, to be able to say at the end that it was definitely a terrorist attack aimed at the Vatican, that we stumbled on it as part of an investigation into Archbishop Cheng's death. What we started out with might sound like a fairy story but no one will care about that after a bomb has gone off. All anybody will be interested in will be the bit about Anna and that will be all too believable. Mind you, if I'm right there's one good thing about it all.'

'What?'

'If I'm right then whatever happens we'll survive, we need to be alive afterwards if we're going to tell our story.'

Jimmy said it like a joke but Ricci couldn't see any funny side. Jimmy had thought it out and made his case. Ricci wanted to laugh at it, to tell him it wasn't possible, another stupid idea. Unfortunately he agreed with it.

'But who would know about a bombing and yet still let it happen?'

'Someone who stands to gain from it all. It must be. Somebody who knew about the attack, wants it to go ahead, and be able to prove it was terrorists.' A thought occurred, 'Or better still, someone who's set up the attack and when it's done wants to be able to prove it was terrorists, and before you ask I have no idea who that might be or what they stand to gain. What I do know is that we've been used and will go on being used.'

The phone rang. Ricci stood up and watched as Jimmy picked it up and listened.

'Thanks.' He rang off. 'We've got a briefing in one hour.'

'Police headquarters?'

'No. The Duns College rector's office.'

They stood for a moment.

'Jimmy, do you think you could be wrong about this, about a

bomb aimed at the Vatican?'

'It fits what we know and I can't think of anything else that does.'

'And the bomb? What sort of bomb? A plane like you said?'

'Maybe; I don't know, but something that sends out the right message; we can do it and we can do it anywhere because we've done it in New York and now in the heart of your Christian world, we've done it in Rome.'

'Christ. So what do we do?'

'We do whatever we can.'

'Which is?'

'Assume I'm right and pray that I'm wrong.'

Ricci waited for the rest, but there was no rest.

'It's not much.'

'No, it's not, is it? But at the moment it's all there is.'

THIRTY-THREE

Jimmy's apartment was close enough to the Vatican for them to walk. The evening was pleasant, they had time before their appointment and both wanted to talk. Jimmy wanted to find a way forward and Ricci wanted to find a way out.

'Why don't we just tell the minister what we think? That the whole thing has been a set-up?'

'And what will that do?'

'Well, if he knows that we know then … then …'

'Then we all know we know?'

Ricci gave him a look. It was no time to try and be funny.

'Then maybe we'd be no good to them any more. If they know we've worked out that it's all some sort of set up then maybe they'll let us drop out of it.'

'For Christ's sake think, will you? If we tell them that the whole thing was a set up by somebody who wanted it to look like terrorists do you think we get to walk away from it, to stay alive and tell whoever we like?'

They walked on. A bomb, not a terrorist bomb but one that could be made to look like it was. Who would do that? Who would benefit? Jimmy had to ask the questions but didn't like the only answer he could come up with. If it wasn't terrorists but had to be made to look that way it meant the thing was planned by someone supposedly on our own side.

The dome of St Peter's became visible as part of the skyline. Ricci broke his silence.

'Could we stop it?'

'How? We aren't even sure it's happening. If it is, we don't know when or how. We don't know where the device will be or what it will be.'

'All right, all right. So what *can* we do? There must be something we can do, someone we can tell.'

'Like who, and what would we tell them? Whoever set this up has got us by the balls. What's happened all makes sense to us because we know it all happened. Say we went to the police. The minister, McBride, your China-watcher, everyone we could name wouldn't even have to deny anything, just tell a slightly different version and we'd look a couple of idiots. We'd probably get locked up for wasting police time.'

They walked on. There were still plenty of tourists about, everything was as normal as it could be. It was Rome on a beautiful spring evening.

'So what do you think we should do?'

'We go on. What else is there? The way I look at it, it has to be something big, a suicide bomber in a vest or a car bomb would be just another atrocity, nasty but not unique.'

'So you think it has to be big, bigger than anything before?'

'Maybe.'

'How big?'

'No idea.'

'You think your plane idea will be the way they do it?'

'No, hiring a plane shows them and gets recorded. Then they'd have to load it with explosives. It's too risky. I also doubt if an unidentified aircraft can just swan over central Rome and the Vatican. But it has to be big enough to do the job. How do you get something really big close enough to the target? How do you get, say, a lorry-load of high explosives right next to St Peter's?'

'You don't. You can't.'

'That's right and if you're not close, not in Vatican Square, just nearby, what do you get? You blow up some shops and offices and kill bystanders? That's bad, very bad, but it's still not the Vatican and that has to be the target.'

Ricci could tell from the way Jimmy spoke his mind had got to where he wanted it to go.

'Then how?'

'If it was a small nuclear device,' Ricci was too stunned to say anything. It had moved from fantasy to nightmare, 'it would do the job. If the Vatican stood it would still be contaminated, it would be finished, and the pope would die, maybe not straight away, but he'd still die.'

'Christ, and so would others, how many others?' Ricci's mind baulked at what it saw. 'No. No one would do that.'

'Some people would do anything and that way it works. It's about the only way it works.'

'Christ, you think that's it?'

'I don't know, do I? I'm as much in the dark as you and all I have to go on is what we've been told. It's far-fetched, almost impossible, but so was what happened in the States. No one could hijack all those planes and navigate them into Manhattan and to the Pentagon. But they did.'

'Christ.'

'If I'm right the safest way would be to bring it in is by sea. Road or air have to be too risky. That means that Anna may not be picking up a team. They might be coming in by themselves and she's gone to pick up the bomb. If she has then she'll have gone to a port and it will be one near Rome. She'll use the same name so long as she thinks it's safe.'

Ricci didn't say anything for a moment, he was trying to think it through, to spot some fatal flaw, something, anything, that made it wrong, that made the whole idea impossible. But nothing came. It could happen the way Jimmy had figured it. This wasn't dead cardinals, this might be real, as real as Anna Schwarz.

'And you think it would come in by sea?'

'Who would try to bring that sort of kit in by road or air?'

'So the best line of enquiry is to check hotels in ports, starting with those ports nearest to Rome.'

'Yes.'

They walked and talked until they came to the Swiss Guards

219

at the security fence. There they went through the usual routine and were admitted.

When they arrived at the rector's office door Ricci knocked. A man's voice answered. They went in. From behind the desk the bland monsignor who liked to live modestly and, when asked, thought that only three cardinals to his knowledge may have been murdered, smiled at them. He gestured to two chairs at the desk.

'Come in and sit down, please.'

'I was told we were getting a briefing from the team who's looking for Anna Schwarz.'

'And so you are, Inspector, so you are. The minister asked for an up-to-the-minute report and I have been asked to deliver its contents to you.' They sat down. The monsignor picked up a sheet of paper from the desk. 'I was told you would only want relevant information. Needless to say I was not the one who decided what was and what was not relevant.' He looked at the paper and began to read. 'A woman calling herself Anna Bruck hired a red Fiat Punto from Hertz Rent-a-Car at their Rome central office four days ago using the address of her apartment in Rome and a current European driving licence. This afternoon at 17:15 the car was located by Hertz at their Florence airport office. It is now being examined but first reports say there were no fingerprints nor any other traces in the car to make an initial forensic confirmation that the woman who hired the car was actually Anna Schwarz. Descriptions from Hertz in Rome were vague, a young woman of about the right age, about the right height, who wore dark glasses and a yellow headscarf. Her hair may have been blonde. The staff concerned were shown a photo of Anna Schwarz but were unable to confirm it was the woman they dealt with, it may have been. The car was left at the Florence airport office with the papers and keys in it. No one saw who returned the car. No further trace of the woman known as Anna Bruck has been found and no female of the name Bruck or Schwarz flew out of Florence after the car was returned. Enquiries are continuing.'

The monsignor put the sheet of paper on the desk and sat back. Ricci looked at Jimmy.

'Now what?'

'If she picked up what we think was coming she took it to Florence airport and handed it over some time this afternoon before taking the car back to the Hertz office. That means that whoever took delivery probably came into Florence by air, hired a car or van, met her, and took delivery. Once that happened her part was finished. They won't find her now.'

'So our package is on its way to Rome?'

'Yes, or it's already here.'

Ricci felt a cold sweat forming on his brow. He had thought Jimmy was wrong, had forced the thing further than it could reasonably go. Now it looked increasingly as if he was right. Or was he letting himself be sucked into his mad movie idea? Either way Anna had sat tight until her team was due then gone to Florence and handed over whatever she had collected for them. It could be anything, any sort of bomb, but if Jimmy was right it could start World War Three, setting Islam against the West and probably with America shouting "charge".

The monsignor waited patiently until Jimmy spoke.

'Can you get a message to the officer in charge of this investigation?'

The monsignor pulled out a phone and began to key in a number.

'What is your message?'

He finished dialling and held the phone to his ear.

'Get the car checked for any signs of radioactivity. If it's there then check for anyone who flew into Florence today and rented a car or van. Tell him it's terrorist-related and it's as bad as it sounds. That he should take whatever action he thinks fit.'

Somebody answered the monsignor's phone.

'Hello. Yes it is, I have a message which is to be passed to the officer leading the search for Anna Schwarz. He is to check the car she used, the one she left at Florence airport, for radioactivity and if he finds any he is to cross-check the names on passenger arrivals with car or van rentals at the airport.' He listened for a second, then looked across at Jimmy. 'How long before?'

'Up to six hours, that should be enough, but if they turn up nothing then keep going to twenty-four hours.'

The monsignor passed on the answer.

'If there is radioactivity present in the car the threat is real and present and whatever action thought fit should be taken.' He held the mobile away from his mouth and looked across again. 'Anything else?'

'If he finds any likely matches among the rentals the vehicle and its contents will be headed for Rome or will already be in Rome.' He looked at his watch and turned to Ricci. 'How long to drive here from Florence?'

'From the airport it would be three to four hours depending on how fast you drove and where in Rome you wanted to get to.'

Jimmy worked out the timing. They got the bomb before five p.m., it was now eight thirty.

'If the radioactivity test is positive they should start turning Rome inside out.'

The monsignor passed on the message then looked back.

'I'd like to know the outcome of the test as soon as they have it.'

'Do you have a number they can reach you on?'

Ricci gave the monsignor a number and turned to Jimmy.

'It's the mobile I gave you.'

The monsignor gave the number then slipped his mobile inside his jacket.

'Is there anything further, gentlemen?' They couldn't think of anything. 'In that case I will wish you good evening.' He stood up, picked up the paper from the desk, put it into an inside pocket, and went to the door. He looked at his watch. 'I'm meeting friends, drinks and *Il Trovatore*. I'll just make the interval.' He smiled and left, pulling the door shut behind him.

'Who the hell was that?'

'He's my monsignor, a man who thinks to live modestly is to live well.'

'Look, stop playing fucking games. Who the bloody hell is he?'

'He's the one McBride sent to give me the information on the other cardinals, the one who confirmed the link between

222

them and Cheng, that they would be important in a conclave. He also dropped me the bit about Cheng being pope material. He was very helpful and had everything ready at his fingertips just like he did tonight, everything we wanted, ready to hand to show us we're right.'

'And?'

'And what?'

Ricci rubbed a hand across his forehead. Jimmy thought he looked worse. The strain was really beginning to show, or the headaches, probably both.

'You OK?'

'No I'm not OK. I've still got a bloody headache and my back hurts.'

'You should take something.'

'I am taking something, aspirin. Look, stop fucking me around, will you? We tell that guy to pass on a message that something radioactive could be on its way to Rome, that it's terrorist-related and as bad as it can be and he doesn't bat an eye. Then when he's finished he tells us he's off to drinks and the opera. No shock, no questions, no nothing? That makes no sense.'

'It doesn't, does it? But somehow I'm not altogether surprised.'

Ricci got up angrily and began to walk around the small office.

'For Christ's sake stop being cryptic and give me a straight answer and I don't want to hear any more of that movie shit. My family live in Rome, for God's sake: parents and a sister. What should I do if those guys you're so sure are coming set off their bomb before they can be picked up?'

'What do you think you should do? They're your family.'

Ricci slumped back down into his chair. He was tired and his head felt like someone was driving a spike into it.

'Headache bad?'

'Never mind my headache. Why do you think he wasn't interested in a nuclear bomb about to arrive here in Rome?'

Jimmy gave a shrug. Ricci asked too many dumb questions to answer them all.

'He knows something that we don't; also I think he was trying to make a point.'

'What point?'

'That he doesn't like me.' There was no more outburst, the headache and frustration combined to silence Ricci. He leaned forward with his head in his hands. 'You should see a doctor.'

Ricci ignored him so Jimmy sat back and waited.

The monsignor didn't like him and he guessed the monsignor was the kind of man who let people know when he didn't like them. But in Jimmy's case he couldn't do much about it because he was under orders to help. So the drinks and opera with friends could have been an "up yours", which would become clear later. And he did it because he knew something they didn't. If he really didn't care about the bomb was it because he knew there was no bomb? If that was the case then what was the whole fucking game about? He could see why Ricci had a headache. This whole shambles almost gave him one.

Ricci sat up again. He looked dreadful but he was ready to get going again.

'How long before we hear? You think less than an hour?'

'The police have the car, all they need to do is get something to test with. They'll start looking for names from flights and rentals straight away, not wait for results. I don't know how many vans get rented from the airport or cars big enough to carry some sort of crate but I hope it's not so many. Once they start checking names from rentals against passenger lists they should turn up something fairly soon and that gives them the type of vehicle and registration. After that it shouldn't be too difficult.'

'So, shall we wait here?'

'No, I need some air. They've got the mobile number so it doesn't matter where we wait and this dump depresses me.'

Jimmy looked round. It was a dump, and yet from the outside it was what the tourists wanted the Vatican to look like. It was just as well that they never got into the place. The inside would have been a real disappointment. It was like the Catholic Church really. What you saw from the outside was impressive, but it wasn't what you got if you came inside.

Ricci was standing by the door waiting.

'Well, are you coming?'

'Sorry, I was thinking about something.'

'You think too much, you know that? You spend too much time in your own head. No wonder you think they show bloody films there. Come on, I need a drink.' Jimmy stood up, there it was again. People had been telling him that almost from day one but he wouldn't listen. Well, now he'd listened and it all made sense. He joined Ricci, switched off the office light, and walked towards the stairs. 'I'll leave my car at your place and get a taxi home. I'll pick the car up tomorrow.'

'If there is a tomorrow.'

'No, you're wrong, it's all too weird. There'll be a tomorrow, there's always a tomorrow. You're good, Jimmy, very good, but I think you're wrong on this. Dead wrong.'

No I'm not, thought Jimmy. I was wrong, but now I think I'm right. In fact I know I'm right.

226

THIRTY-FOUR

'You know my trouble, Danny, I don't listen to people. People keep telling me things and I just don't listen. I guess I try to live in my head too much.'

'I told you there was nothing I could do.'

'I know. You told me. You told me more than once but I just wouldn't listen.'

Jimmy took a sip of his beer and Danny reluctantly took a sip from his coffee. The barman read his paper and the few regulars talked, smoked, or stared into space. The bar was just the same, dull and shabby, and the sky still didn't get any further than being a narrow ribbon of blue between the apartment roofs. Jimmy liked it.

'Where's Ron?'

'A lecture.'

'But you've bunked off?'

'I do sometimes. It doesn't matter now, does it?'

'I suppose not.'

'We're starting on Dogmatic Theology.'

'Good.'

'What do you mean, good? You wouldn't say good if you'd just started on Dogmatic Theology.'

'So what's your favourite?'

Danny thought about it.

'Maybe Church History. Know what happened and why it happened and you begin to get some idea about why things are the way they are. Church History helps.'

'I know what you mean.'

Danny got up.

'Back in a minute.'

He walked away towards the toilet.

Jimmy liked Danny. In many ways they were the same. They both wanted to know why things were the way they were. With Danny it was the Church, with Jimmy, just at the minute, it was the investigation. He thought about how Ricci had reacted the previous night in the bar when the call had come through. The test had been positive, there had been something radioactive carried in the red Punto. Florence airport had turned up a van rented by two Asian men travelling on British passports who had flown in from Pakistan via Frankfurt. Ricci had gone all nervous on him and had ordered a large whisky.

'Christ, Jimmy, I was wrong and you were right. Christ, Jimmy.' He had put his mobile on the table. He wanted to call somebody, his family probably. He wanted to say, 'Don't ask questions, just pack a small bag and get out of Rome as fast as you can and as far as you can.' But if every copper who was looking for the men and the van did that Rome would be in total panic inside one hour and the chances of nailing the culprits would have gone. Jimmy remembered watching him. He hadn't made any call. He'd drunk his whisky, picked up his phone and put it away, and asked what they should do. What did he think there was for two men sitting in a bar in central Rome to do? The police had all they needed.

And he had been right. There'd been nothing for them to do.

Ricci was the one they'd phoned to say they'd got them. They'd been picked up as they approached Rome. Now they were somewhere being interrogated. It was all simple and straightforward. Jimmy smiled, remembering how Ricci had been really pissed off after the danger was over. He had banged on about how they had been cut out of it, as though it had all been done deliberately to spite him.

'I should have been there. It was us who worked out what

was going on. We did the detective work. We worked it out all the way from Cheng to Florence airport.' Jimmy liked how it was "we" now, how they had done it all together and Ricci had never had any doubts. 'They just took our message and watched the Florence to Rome road, for God's sake. Traffic probably made the collar.' Christ, was he pissed off, and he wouldn't leave it alone. He had kept on about it. 'This way we get nothing and the team chasing Anna gets it all. They get to be heroes, and the best of it is, they didn't even do what they set out to do. They missed Anna. She's free and clear, but they're still the bloody heroes and no one even knows who we are. We get nothing.'

Jimmy reflected that he could have asked Ricci whether saving Rome from a terrorist-sponsored nuclear attack was getting nothing. But Ricci hadn't been in the mood to appreciate the irony. Maybe he had wanted a James Bond movie ending with him as the hero. What they got was what you always get, the bad guys got picked up and the good guys went home. And that's what he had done, finished his drink, gone home, and left Ricci in the bar. For Ricci, last night it was over, but not for Jimmy. He knew it wasn't over.

Danny came back.

'You want another beer?'

'No, I'm OK with this one. Don't much feel like drinking or talking. I'm not good company today.'

'Thinking about the investigation? I thought you said it was sorted.'

'I know.'

'Then for God's sake leave it alone.'

'I guess I still live in my head too much.'

'What time's your meeting?'

'Two o'clock.'

'You'll tell her how it went?'

'I think she probably knows.'

Danny looked at his coffee trying to make his mind up whether to say what he was thinking. He decided he would.

'Jimmy, you told me it was all over, finished. But you didn't tell me what happened. You didn't tell me how it finished, and

229

that's OK because I don't want to know. But I'm still worried about you. One minute you're telling me some weird story and saying how you want me to watch your back because it's all big deal stuff and very hush-hush. Then all of a sudden it's finished. Everyone's gone home and the show's over. Whatever this is about it's not that bullshit about Archbishop Cheng. I think this is about you, and that's me as a copper speaking as well as a friend. I think you're still in trouble. The machine is still chewing you.'

Jimmy looked at him. Was he a friend? When had that happened, if it had happened? Or was it just words? What the hell, friend or copper, either or both, he was right. Jimmy knew he should have listened to him from the beginning. In a way it *was* all about him, and he should have seen it long ago. God knew it was pointed out often enough.

'No, Danny. It really is finished and it's not something you need to worry about. Not as a copper, not as anything.'

Danny gave a shrug.

'OK, if you say so. But you're going to pack it in, aren't you? Whatever it was, it's made you change your mind about becoming a priest.'

'I don't know. Let's just say I'm asking the question, although whether I still have a choice may be in someone else's hands.'

He looked at his watch; it was nearly time to go but all he wanted was to stay and sit. He'd been up all night going through the whole thing from beginning to end and now he was worn out. Now he just wanted to rest. He picked up his glass and finished his beer. He began to rise.

'I better get going.'

'OK, see you around.'

Jimmy put his hand in his pocket pulled out some coins and put some on the table.

'You won't be having another, will you?'

'Do I ever?'

'See you, Danny.'

'See you, Jimmy.'

Jimmy picked up the bottle and glass and took them to the

bar and walked away. The barman glared at Jimmy's back, then went back to his paper. Danny watched him go. Just before he reached the door the 'Ride of the Valkyries' jingled. Jimmy stopped, took out his mobile, and held it to his ear and walked out of the bar into the street. As he walked past the window Danny could see he was listening to someone. God go with you, he thought, then added, not that it will change anything even if he does.

THIRTY-FIVE

It was the same attic room, shitty as always.

'Come in, Mr Costello.' Jimmy came in and sat down. 'You asked to see me. Was it to bring me up to date?'

'I think you're pretty well up to date, Professor. Wouldn't you say that you were pretty well up to date?'

She was still neat, still just back from the laundry, and Jimmy was right, she wouldn't say. She sat and waited. He had asked for the meeting, it was up to him.

'What happens now, Professor?'

'In what way?'

'Now that the Vatican has become a nuclear power,' he paused just long enough to know that he had scored, 'which you realise puts it in breach of the UN Nuclear Non-Proliferation Treaty and I don't know how many others?'

She didn't say anything and her expression never changed. Whatever had been there, in her eyes, had flickered and gone. But it had been there and she knew he had seen it. She didn't try to be clever. If he knew, he knew.

'When did you know?'

'I worked it out last night.'

'May I ask how?'

'Detective work, just straight detective work. You'd laid it all out nicely for me in your script, the one Ricci and I have

233

been acting out for you. All I had to do was go over it. That's the problem with movies, they're like dreams, while you're watching they all seem fine, the plot always makes sense. But afterwards, if you go over it, you spot the holes, the weaknesses, the places things don't quite fit.'

'Something gave it away. What was it? Do you mind me asking?'

'No, it's why I wanted to meet, I wanted you to ask. I wanted us to talk. It was the red Punto that finally did it, but I think I was on my way for a while. Certainly after Anna went walkabout I knew there was something I should have been seeing. But it was the Punto that really did it, that told me I was right. There was something I'd missed, something that was there all along but I couldn't see it, not while the movie was running. But after it was all over it was just a matter of going back over the whole thing and looking at it in the right way, which we both know was not the way it was shown to me in the first place.'

She turned it over in her mind. Then she relaxed.

'You just can't get the staff, and you can't do it entirely by yourself, can you? There's always some little thing that you delegate and that's where it all starts to unravel. Some little thing like hiring a car.'

'The guys who came in rented a van so whatever they picked up wasn't carried to the airport in a small car. There wasn't enough room.'

'Yes, I should have thought of that myself, but however thorough one tries to be there's always some little thing that slips through, isn't there?'

Jimmy nodded.

'A red one, maybe it was her favourite colour, whoever she was.'

McBride made a dismissive gesture with her hand.

'A secretary. She was fair and the right sort of age. I had a false Italian driving licence made up in the name of Anna Bruck. On the day I needed the car to be hired I told the secretary that a Sister Bruck had a problem. She needed a hire car quickly but had been called to a meeting and she couldn't be in two places at once, could she? Would she phone Hertz and rent a vehicle in Anna's name and then go and pick it up using her driving licence, which Sister Anna had left with me. I gave her cash to cover the hire.'

'I would have said you were taking a chance, but if the whole thing was straightforward and payment was in cash I suppose you figured no one would look too closely and no one would be any the wiser. Did you drop it off at Florence?'

'Yes. It was a nuisance but I couldn't delegate that. I left it near the Hertz office with the paperwork and the keys in it. No one saw me but it was there when they started to look.'

'What about the name?'

'What about it?'

'Bruck. It's not exactly Italian is it?'

'No, but names don't mean much. The secretary spoke like a Roman, dressed like one, and the licence had a Rome address. The name wouldn't matter. She was supremely ordinary, nothing would go wrong.'

'Except she wore a yellow headscarf and kept her sunglasses on even in the office, that got remembered.'

'Yellow! She wore a yellow headscarf and sunglasses?'

Jimmy nodded.

'You can't blame her, she wasn't a professional, just someone you used, but a woman who's an expert at staying invisible doesn't wear a yellow headscarf and dark glasses to rent a car.'

'No, she certainly does not. But I couldn't very well have edited her choice of clothes even if I'd thought about it. Yellow, how unfortunate, no wonder it set you to thinking.'

'It was just one more thing, but it meant she wasn't the real Anna Bruck, whatever the forensics said. Wasn't it all a bit risky, so late on in the whole thing? The renting of the car in Anna's name, was that so important?'

'Yes, but it wasn't risky as you put it. I'd done it before, you see, so I knew it could work. We really did have a sister, a Nigerian missionary sister, who was visiting Rome and needed a car and suddenly got called away. She lent me her driving licence and I rented the car in her name. No one looked too closely, and my black face wasn't so different from her black face so no one made a fuss.'

'What if the secretary had said no?'

'I knew her, she's a nice girl, co-operative and always keen to help. If I asked in the right way and said how much the imaginary Sister Anna needed the car I knew she would agree, and she did.'

'I see, a simple but effective lie.'

'A lie, Mr Costello? How was it a lie? In a sense, a very real sense, Anna was in Rome and I needed her to rent a car.'

'But she wasn't a sister.'

McBride let that one pass.

'She did what I asked her to do, she rented a car for Anna Bruck. Unfortunately she rented a Fiat Punto and wore a yellow headscarf to do it. Oh well, as I said, I couldn't do everything myself, could I? And it served its purpose.'

'You used what came to hand, Cheng, me, Ricci, the China-watcher, the monsignor, and the secretary. You looked around and used what was available.' She nodded, a bit smugly, Jimmy thought. He could use that. He would use it to get the leverage he needed. 'What are you really, and don't tell me you're a simple academic.'

'I am an academic, Mr Costello, but also I occasionally get asked to do things that need to be done, and this needed to be done.'

'What about the traces of radioactivity planted? How did you do that?'

He was almost there now. She was enjoying herself, showing him how clever she'd been. All he had to do was wait for her to get sloppy.

'When the secretary came back from renting the car I told her to put it in my parking space which would be empty and bring the keys to me. I had already arranged for someone from the Instituto de Technica to pick up the car, plant something that would produce suspiciously high levels of radioactivity, and bring it back when I needed it to go to Florence airport. I don't know what he used. He said it would show up clearly but wouldn't be at all dangerous when the car was used again.'

'Didn't he ask why you wanted him to do it?'

'Of course. I told him to mind his own business.'

'That's it? You just told him to mind his own business?'

'More or less. I told him that if he wanted to know he should enquire from the minister direct. Naturally he chose to leave it alone.' She allowed herself a smile as she went on. 'I see now, of course, that I should have told the secretary that Anna needed a station wagon or something like that. But you can't think of everything, can you, and we were so close to the end.'

'Who told you the bomb was coming?'

'The Chinese.'

'The Chinese!'

'Chinese Intelligence. I'm afraid I don't know what their official name is. Two years ago a government scientist was approached to sell a small amount of weapons-grade plutonium. He was probably approached because he had already sold bits and pieces of know-how. Chinese Intelligence were on to him and had him under surveillance so when he was approached they quietly picked him up and told him they wanted the sale to go through.'

'Go through?'

'Yes. If an organisation was looking to build a bomb they assumed it had to be terrorist-related. With the way things are today if they didn't get what they wanted in China they might very well get it elsewhere. A decision was made to sell the plutonium and then track what happened to it, where it went, who was involved, and what was the probable target. It was not an ideal situation but the alternative was to arrest their man which would make the organisation who wanted the material look elsewhere and perhaps succeed. A small nuclear device set off in a major Western city has been a prime aim of terrorist groups for some time. One day it would happen: the materials and expertise were becoming increasingly available. This way the Chinese stood a fair chance of preventing such an attack and if they failed, well, the target wouldn't be a Chinese city, would it?'

'It's still a big risk. Why take it?'

'The Chinese economy was booming, they were about make

it into the very top grade of economic nations, they didn't want all the economic tables to be kicked over at the moment of their greatest opportunity.' She could see Jimmy wasn't convinced. 'Let me put it this way, Mr Costello, that we are having this conversation and are not dead should be confirmation enough that they made the right choice.' When she put it like that, thought Jimmy, you could see she had a point. 'Once they'd decided on their course of action they needed to alert someone in Europe to deal with this end of things.'

'This end?'

'They were sure the target city was going to be European.'

'Why certain?'

'They were certain, that's all.'

'All you know or all you'll tell?'

'It works out the same for you either way.'

Jimmy decided not to press the point. He had his own ideas about it anyway.

'OK, so who did they contact?'

'People here within the Catholic Church.'

'The Church? Why the Church?'

'They were enabling someone to build a nuclear device aimed at a European target. They were prepared to take the risk but how many European governments do you think would have agreed with them?' She didn't wait for an answer. 'They needed someone who would have a significant presence already on the ground wherever the bomb turned up. Someone who could support their agents, who would be already there in sufficient numbers to get information and move freely. They needed to be absolutely sure that once the bomb arrived they could keep close to it and get hold of it before it was delivered to whoever was going to set it off. The Catholic Church is the only organisation which fits the bill. We have personnel, a great many personnel, in every European country that would be on the bombers' list. We have the communication infrastructure. We could provide transport and all the non-specialist resources they would need. They would have the specialists, the people who knew how to handle the bomb when they got it, and the intelligence resources to make sure they could track it while it was on the move from wherever it was made. They needed our resources so they came to us.'

'How? How did they come to you?' She was about to answer when it dawned on Jimmy. 'Wait, I know. They sent Cheng. He was their messenger.'

'He was being rehabilitated, he was available. They were prepared to trust him and they knew we would trust him. He was ideal. Also, who would notice another archbishop coming to Rome, even a Chinese one. He delivered his message but then died.'

'From natural causes?'

'Quite natural. Fortunately contact had been made and an agreement was eventually reached.'

'Did he get his red hat?'

'Not that I know of.'

'And the funeral?'

'I have no idea.'

'That was just something to keep us going.'

'As you say, something to keep you going.'

'And the cardinals, the dead ones.'

'That was a nuisance. I didn't expect such an odd request so I did what I thought best and gave you what you wanted.'

'Another story.'

'Not quite. The three cardinals named all died unexpectedly, though not suspiciously.'

'And the conclave.'

'All cardinals influence a conclave so not really a story, just selective truth. You asked for a connection so I gave you one. I needed to keep you involved until I was ready to move you.'

'What did they ask for, the Chinese?'

'That as soon as they knew the destination we should help in making sure the bomb could be intercepted without involving the local police until it was absolutely necessary. We agreed, the necessary communications were set up, then we waited. They tracked the plutonium to Pakistan where the bomb was to be assembled by a government nuclear scientist who was willing to sell his services. From Pakistan it was sent by lorry to Lebanon in a packing case marked as machine parts. In Beirut it was delivered to a man who had been recruited to arrange for the shipment of the case by sea.'

'A terrorist?'

'Perhaps. He was a shady character, part gangster, part fighter, part middle-man. A man who was paid by many groups to do anything from arms smuggling to car-bombing. He had the experience to handle a job like shipping the goods and not get caught. The crate was held in Beirut for some months, obviously they were waiting for something, but finally it was loaded onto a ship bound for Italy. Then man then flew to Italy where he thought he would take delivery of the packing case and get it to the handover.'

'Thought he would?'

'The Chinese knew which port and the arrival date, so they waited until the boat was due to dock. They let him pick up the crate and then moved in and took it off him. They interrogated him, got the details of where the bomb was to go and how the handover would be made and what the final target was.'

'He just volunteered that information, I suppose?'

'We never asked. It was something we were prepared to leave to the Chinese. Whatever methods they used they were able to give us all the information we needed. With their information we knew how to finish what they had started. We told the Chinese how we thought it could be dealt with. They agreed, so we put our plan into action. We arranged for everything to be in place.'

'And everything included me and Ricci?'

'Yes.'

'And Anna's stuff? That was all part of it?'

'Yes. We had you and Inspector Ricci ready to move when we needed you by arranging for you to be looking into Cardinal Cheng's death. That meant we could feed you information as and when we wanted. When we were ready we arranged for it to appear as if a known terrorist was in Rome which brought in the police. After that I was going to provide you with the information about the high radioactive traces. It was to have been a piece of last-minute information that had suddenly come from an intelligence source. You, however, beat me to it. You put the last pieces together and alerted the police to the fact that there might be high levels of radioactivity which of course there were. Once you had done that the police could take over and arrest the men who thought they were carrying the bomb. All very simple, very straightforward. It was just a matter of bringing everything together at the right time.'

'It was all your plan?'

'The matter was entrusted to me. I had help, of course, but basically, yes, it was my plan.'

'Did the Chinese know who the bombers would be?'

'No. The Lebanese go-between had been given an airport and flight number and was told to wait at Arrivals holding a card with a name on it.'

'What name?'

'Does it matter? It would certainly have been false. It was merely to allow the bombers to make the correct contact. Our job was to provide a replacement for the Lebanese who would use his papers to make the handover at Florence airport. We had the police already mobilised looking for Anna, you and Inspector Ricci were our trigger to move them in. It was a pity the car chosen by the secretary was too small to have carried the bomb but its only purpose was to provide the evidence of a nuclear device, which it did, so no real harm was done. I doubt the police will spot the mistake in a hurry. They'll be too busy congratulating themselves on the arrest. When they find out that the radioactive traces are the wrong sort it won't matter, everything will be over.'

'So it was all a set-up from beginning to end?' McBride had the good grace to give an apologetic smile. It was an excellent plan and she was right to be proud of it. 'Even getting me here so I could supposedly train for the priesthood?'

The smile went.

'No, as I have already told you, your application was processed by the selection panel in the normal way. My interest was, shall we say, parallel to theirs.'

'So why me?'

'We needed a detective but not one on active service. My attention was drawn to Inspector Ricci. He had just been put on sick leave. However, we needed someone else, another trained mind to help him. He wasn't a well man and he might not have stayed the course. I looked around and found you.'

'And the state of my mind? What brought on that little episode?'

'Having met with you several times I was worried that you might see through the whole thing. You struck me as rather astute in a plodding sort of way. You must have been a good detective. I decided to try and divert your attention somewhat, not hamper you mind too much, but sow enough doubt to slow you down. As a matter of interest all I told you I believed could be true but, as I said at the time, I have no formal training in that field. I tried never to lie to you, to always base what I said on the truth.'

'Are you telling me you tried to be honest with me?'

'Oh no, not honest, but to stay as close to the truth as possible so that you could never be sure what was true and what was false. I must say I was pleased with the way things went, except for that business of you being put in hospital. I hadn't anticipated that.'

'Ricci got caught looking into my record.'

'Yes, I was told.'

'So you arranged for his mate to get invited to America?'

'Yes. It wasn't difficult; art crime is an interesting subject. I understand his talks were very well received and he will probably be invited back. Just as a matter of interest what was the attack on you about? I presume it was related in some way to what you were doing?'

'You weren't the only one who got told Ricci had been looking. Some old acquaintances of mine got some hooligans to throw a petrol bomb into his uncle's factory in Glasgow to warn him off. He asked me to go and check it out.'

'But if your friends in London were protecting you why the attack when you returned?'

'Putting me in hospital was someone else's way of warning me off, saying I shouldn't think about coming back to Scotland, ever.'

'Well, thank goodness no lasting harm was done.'

242

Jimmy had been listening but as he listened his brain had been working and he was finally beginning to understand. There were no outright lies, that was the key. She was telling him facts, but she was still at her old game, she was muddying his mind so he wouldn't see the joins in her story where she'd left the truth and slipped into storyland.

'The Anna thing was clever, I liked that. She was never here, was she?'

'No.'

'But you did it neatly. It was real enough to get your police team up and running. Where is she?'

'Does she have to be somewhere?'

'Oh, yes. You may be good but not even you could just reach out and lay your hands on her fingerprints and DNA.'

'At this moment she is about to take her initial vows in an enclosed convent. She is, and has been for some time, in Bavaria.'

'So what was the story there?'

'There is no story. No story for you, that is.'

Jimmy paused for a second. He wanted to stand up and shout out. He had her. She had finally made her mistake. She had told him a fact she couldn't spin. Now he knew he could get it all, the truth, the whole truth, and nothing but the truth, so help him God.

'So, Anna Bruck, real name Anna Schwarz, a known terrorist wanted by several governments, is in a convent in Bavaria. That's interesting.' A look of concern flitted across Professor McBride's face. 'I would guess there are plenty of people who would think it worth the time and effort to check which convent.'

'There are plenty of convents, Mr Costello. I don't think anyone would find anything.'

'But if someone tells the intelligence community she's there somewhere they'll start looking. I don't say they'll find her. I'm sure your nuns will be as good as the monks were when they moved Nazis around after the war. But she'll have to give up any idea of a settled religious life. Is that what you want for her?'

She wasn't so pleased with herself any more.

'No.'

'Then tell me about her, where she fits in.'

'She's not part of this; she wasn't ever in Rome.'

'You made her part of this, not me, and if you made her a part of it I want to know what that part was.'

'Why, Mr Costello? Why is it so important for you to know? It's all over now.'

'I need to know where I stand in all of this. If what you've told me is true then there's been some very powerful people involved and my guess is they wouldn't think twice about what happened to one individual they thought had information they didn't want shared with anyone else. You got me involved so I want you to tell me what I was involved in, which means you tell me about Anna.'

It didn't take more than a couple of seconds for her to decide.

'Eva and Anna were chalk and cheese. Eva was wild from being a teenager, Anna was always quiet. Eva's parents hoped her going to university would help her settle down, as we know it did the reverse. Anna was pious, wanted to be a nun. She was waiting until she was old enough and was sure she had a vocation. She used to go and stay at a convent and talk to the other nuns and the mother superior. She was pretty close to being admitted when Eva and her friends did what they did and went on the run. Eva turned up one day and got Anna on her own. She demanded her help and gave Anna no choice. Help or I'll kill Mummy and Daddy and then I'll kill you. What could she do? She helped. She got the men places to stay and got herself and Eva into a retreat house. It was perfect. The men didn't know where the sisters were, and who would look for a murderer in a Catholic retreat house? Then that idiot Geisller tried the bank business. Eva realised at once that if he tried again without her, they'd be taken. They met up and she planned the supermarket robbery. Once that was over they had enough money to travel so they set off to find the real strong men, the ones who were organised and ruthless. Anna went home and her parents arranged for her to go into a convent.

They realised they'd effectively lost one daughter, they didn't want to lose the other to a long prison sentence so they pretended she was on the run with her sister. In the convent she was safe and they could visit her if they were very careful.'

'And the mother superior agreed to take her?'

'Of course; Anna had done nothing wrong.'

'Nothing wrong! She acted as transport officer for a gang of murdering thugs.'

'I mean she had committed no sin. No doubt under criminal law she could have been charged with complicity after the fact in a murder and for actual complicity in armed robbery. But she had been given a choice between two evils: help her sister or see her parents murdered and be murdered herself. She chose the lesser of two evils. To do that is not a sin. She may have been guilty according to the law but to the Catholic Church she had not sinned.' Jimmy the policeman would have laughed at such reasoning, but Jimmy the Catholic could see how it worked, if only for a truly Catholic mind. 'The Geisller Group dropped out of sight and Anna settled down to a life in the convent but she never felt safe. At any time Eva might have turned up and demanded her help again. Then Eva was shot outside a railway station and the threat was gone. For Anna and her parents the nightmare was over.'

'Do you know who did it, the shooting?'

'No, but given who she was running with it could have been anyone.'

'But with Eva dead Anna could pick up the threads?'

'That's right and when the mother superior felt that emotionally and spiritually she was ready she agreed to let her begin her training.'

'And she was to hand when you needed a known terrorist for your piece of drama.'

'Yes.'

'And that's all of it?' She didn't answer. Jimmy waited, but she still didn't answer. 'Only the thing is, I got a phone call as I was coming here from Inspector Ricci. He's been following up on things. The two men, it turns out, were British Asians, one from Manchester and one from Luton. Both were students at

245

Birmingham University and both sang like canaries as soon as they were questioned. Yes, they were would-be suicide bombers and yes, they had tried to detonate the bomb when they were stopped by the police. But the bomb didn't go off.'

If this information surprised her, she didn't show it.

'Didn't it? Maybe the fuse or whatever it was failed.'

'Do you want to know why I think it didn't go off?'

'If you want to tell me?'

'Because there was no bomb in the van. What they got at the airport was a case, a packing case marked machine parts but to them it was their bomb. The man who gave it to them had the right identification so they just took delivery. Then they set off for Rome and ran straight into the police who were waiting for them, just like you'd planned.'

'So you think there was there no bomb?'

'Oh yes, there had to be a bomb for this farce to have happened. And now you've got it.'

'I assure you that ...'

'Wriggle all you like, piss me about with half-truths and fancy words. You personally haven't got it but the Vatican has it, or knows where it is.'

McBride let the thing go. If he'd worked it out he'd worked it out. Just listen to what he thought he knew and then find out what he wanted.

'This only makes sense if you switched the bomb when it was picked up in Italy. After the bomb was safely in your hands you could let things go on because nothing bad could happen. The bombers would get caught and everything would be neatly wrapped up.'

'Neatly wrapped up?'

'You had the proof, the proof of who was really behind it. You had the bomb, you had the Chinese who had sold the plutonium, the Pakistani scientist who had put it together, and the Lebanese who was supposed to collect it and pass it on. You even had the men who were supposed to have done it. There was a beautiful trail from Pakistan down to Lebanon and on to Italy where a couple of radicalised young British Muslims were to have carried out the actual attack. It comes out as a straight

Al Qaeda-sponsored attack.'

'But you think something else?'

'I know it was. It was set up by to put the Christian world against the Muslim, to make everyone take sides.'

'And who do you think might want such a thing to happen?'

'The Americans. This was all a CIA operation so their War on Terror could be fought to a conclusion.' She was about to speak but Jimmy didn't give her the chance. 'If I wanted to radicalise every Muslim you know what I would do? I'd bomb Mecca, preferably during the Hajj. That would hit every Muslim across the globe, moderates, secular, Westernised, the lot. Turn it round, make Rome the target, and you get the same result, only with Christians, not Muslims.' She looked at him with genuine surprise as he went on. 'You didn't get anything from the Chinese. Somehow you got wind of it, someone leaked the plan to you so you had to see that it never happened but you couldn't afford to point the finger at the American government. The only way was for you to let it happen and then step in at the last minute and take the bomb. Then you'd be in a position to say, "We know all about it and we can prove it, so don't ever try anything like it again, anywhere." The Chinese choosing the Vatican to help out was just crap, like the target could have been in any European country was crap. The Vatican was the target from day one.'

The surprise had left McBride's face. Now there was a slight hint of worry. She had been right to find out what he thought he knew. He was indeed a good detective, but he had gone too far, he had overshot. He hadn't let her point his nose for him, he'd gone where he wanted to go, not where he was supposed to go. Now he posed a real danger.

'I'm afraid you're quite wrong, Mr Costello. The American government, I assure you, through their intelligence services or in any other way, would never contemplate using a nuclear device against Rome, against the Holy Father.'

'No lies, remember. Don't take to sinning at this stage of the game. The truth, the whole truth, and nothing but the truth. You said you started digging into my past when I resurrected my application. That was when you were looking to recruit. But that had to be wrong, the timescale didn't fit did it?' He paused, he was just about sure. 'You told the Chinese that an approach would be made to their man to get plutonium. You told them, they didn't tell you.'

Her reply was quiet.

'Yes.'

'And Cheng was acting for you both. He was your secure line of communication?'

She nodded.

Now was the time. Now he could tell her what he knew, what he had worked out.

'It was the Americans, wasn't it? Unite the West against Islam. One billion Catholics world-wide baying for blood and the Americans leading the pack.' Jimmy was trying very hard not to let his anger take over. He wanted to be right more than he wanted to be angry. 'For Christ's sake, it's like,' he struggled for words, 'it's like stealing God. Only the Americans would be so fucking arrogant as to think that they had the right to …'

She didn't interrupt because of Jimmy's language. She interrupted because he needed to know the truth, the real truth, and he needed to know it now.

THIRTY-SIX

'We were told very early in the planning. But it wasn't as you think.'

'What is it about you Americans, why is it never your fault? Why can your people never be the bad guys?'

'I assure you, Mr Costello, it is not some patriotic, blinkered view which makes me say it was not America.'

Jimmy sneered at her. His anger was taking over. He wanted it to.

'America, always banging on about being leader of the Free World. America doesn't want to be leader of the Free World, it wants to be the bloody owner of the Free World, to do anything they like with the Free World so long as it suits their interest.'

'Mr Costello.' There was a sharpness in her voice that stopped Jimmy. 'Mr Costello, it was not the Americans.'

Jimmy shut down his anger. This woman was hard to call. She said she'd told him the truth and in a way she had, in a twisted sort of way. Was she telling the truth now or was she still trying to give him a run-around? No, he was sure. It had to the Americans.

'Prove it to me. If not the Americans, who? And don't try to give me terrorists.'

'Just as a matter of interest, why not?'

'Because from start to finish no real terrorists were used.

Real terrorists would have used their own people. They would have to buy the scientist but they would have used their own to move the bomb from Beirut to Italy, not some freelancers. The two British students were probably why the bomb sat in Beirut for so long, while they were given some sort of training. They were new recruits, stooges, who only needed to collect the crate, drive it to Rome, then sing the right song when they got picked up. And why target the Vatican? If terrorists had a nuclear device and could move it they'd send it to an American port and let it off as soon as the ship docked. They wouldn't even have needed to unload it. They would have made their point. We can get to you, nowhere is safe now. For terrorists the target would have been America, not the Vatican.'

'Very well, Mr Costello, not terrorists, at least not what people call terrorists in the current sense.'

'So if not America then who?'

'I can't tell you, Mr Costello.'

'Can't or won't?'

'Can't and won't. I am not allowed to tell you. I have undertaken to keep that information secret. There is no way I will give you a direct or indirect answer to the question. I'm afraid it is something you must work out for yourself.'

The awful part, she thought, is that now I have to make him believe me. He only has my word for it that it is not the Americans, but he has to believe me enough to work it out. And please God he's good enough to work it out. She waited.

'OK, I have to ask you a straight question and I have to have a straight answer. Maybe then I'll know enough to decide what I might do, if I do anything.'

She nodded. She knew what was coming. If she answered his question properly, he might finally accept he had made a mistake. Although whether that was better than how things stood at the moment was very much a moot point.

'Were the Americans involved?'

McBride was ready for it.

'There are extreme Christian groups in America who believe that the Second Coming of Christ can only take place after Armageddon. They would welcome anything that brings that

250

day closer. They might very well view the prospect of the Middle East conflict going nuclear as one way of bringing about Armageddon, thereby bringing the Second Coming. There are also elements on the American Right who would welcome any action which polarised opinion between the Muslim and non-Muslim world and allowed the War on Terror to be waged without restraint to a conclusion. This is all common knowledge, Mr Costello, you do not have to have spent a lifetime watching the international political scene to know that these realities are at work, but any unholy alliance between military hawks and Christian fundamentalists would not be supported in any way by the government.'

'Or the intelligence agencies?'

She knew it had to be the truth this time, just the truth.

'One cannot rule out that within the intelligence community such an option has been discussed.'

'So?'

'So, yes, there were almost certainly people in America, important, influential people who would not have been party to planning such an operation but could have known about it and done nothing to stop it. Such people would have been ready and waiting to persuade the American government that, if it had happened, it should be used to the benefit of America, that what was done could not be undone and the best use should be made of the situation on the ground. It would have been a powerful argument but, as it is, we will never know what might have been the ultimate outcome.'

Suddenly something she had said switched a light on in Jimmy's brain and he could see his mistake. He had become convinced it was the Americans because he wanted it that way. Now he could see who else benefited.

'This wasn't about starting Armageddon, was it? It was about stopping it.' She sat in silence. He was there. 'It was the bloody Israelis. If the world thought terrorists had nuked the Vatican the Israelis could call it a first strike and reply in kind by hitting Iran. They're shit-scared of the Iranians going nuclear. If they took out an Iranian development facility with a strategic nuclear attack that would send the message from Egypt

251

to Syria and beyond: we will use a nuclear response to any attempt to create nuclear weapons in the region. No western government would object. After what had happened to Rome the Israelis would be the good guys, showing they'd take out any facility in the region they thought was being used to develop a nuclear weapons capacity. They'd be making sure the status quo remained, with Israel as the only nuclear power in the region. The bloody Israelis. Why didn't I see it?'

'Because you wanted it to be the Americans, Mr Costello. So many people want the Americans to be the bad guys and you've just found you are one of them.'

'The bloody Israelis.'

'No, Mr Costello, you're close, but it wasn't the Israelis, not the government anyway. It was a combination of a radical splinter group in their military and an extreme religious political group. Between them they dreamed up the plan and set it up. Fortunately for us one of the military involved told his wife. She couldn't accept that the loss of so many innocent lives justified what they were planning to do. As it happened she had specialised in classical history when she was at university and spent some time in Rome. I'm sure that the loss of so many historical treasures weighed with her just as much as innocent lives. Anyway, whatever her reasons, she didn't dare go to her own people because that may have placed her husband in danger so she went to a priest friend and asked him what to do. He contacted, well, never mind who he contacted. The matter arrived at the Collegio Principe and we took it from there.'

'The Collegio Principe, your college?'

'Yes, my college, not the Vatican. It was a matter of politics, power, and religion, so it came under our remit of action.'

Jimmy sat trying to see it.

'But, surely, Fr Phan, the monsignor, surely ...'

'The Collegio enjoys excellent relations with many institutions in Rome as it does with many academic institutions, governments, and government agencies. They are always willing to assist if the project in hand seems to justify support.'

She waited and gave him time.

'So what are you, some sort of Vatican secret service?'

'I told you, Mr Costello, we study politics, power, and religion. What good would all those centuries of study be if they resulted in nothing but yet more words? Study leads to knowledge and the proper use of knowledge is action, right action. What good would the CIA or any other intelligence service be if all it did was put its knowledge into words and never take any action. We knew the people planning the attack were going to approach the Chinese because she told the priest they had identified a nuclear scientist who was known to have sold bits and pieces. We acted on our knowledge and took the necessary right action. We warned the Chinese. The rest you know.'

'The rest I found out.'

'If you prefer it that way. If the attack had gone ahead the political group which sponsored the attack would have pressured the Israeli government to follow it up, to, as you said, make the best use of the situation on the ground.'

'What's done is done, let's make the best of it.'

'Yes.'

'And would they have gone ahead?'

'Oh I think so. It was a very good idea and very well done. It would certainly have been taken as an Islamic terrorist attack and it gave them a way of justifying strikes against any nuclear weapons facility their neighbours in the region tried to build.'

'Now they'll all have to go on killing each other with conventional weapons?'

'Regrettably yes. As far as the Israeli-Palestine conflict is concerned our success changes nothing.'

'What about the Chinese, won't they want the plutonium back?'

'They can have it any time they ask for it, but they have plenty. I think they'll prefer it to stay where it is and do the job we want.'

'Why did they want Chinese plutonium? Couldn't they have got some from inside Israel?'

'I don't know, but they couldn't have used it. If the bomb had gone off it would have left a nuclear footprint. The radiation could be examined and the source of the plutonium identified. If they used their own plutonium the Americans would have recognised the footprint as Israeli because they gave Israel the bomb in the first place. The source had to point to a terrorist bomb which meant it had to come from somewhere like China, India, or Pakistan. It had to be an illegal sale.'

Jimmy sat back and the professor relaxed. Now it really was all over. 'What will you do now, Mr Costello? You have some dangerous and very powerful information. There are those who would pay well for what you know.'

'I don't need any more money.'

'A sentiment as refreshing as it is rare. So what will you do?'

'Can I go on studying for the priesthood?'

'Perhaps, if I do not share what I know about you with the relevant authorities. I'm afraid if they knew the sort of person you really are they would insist on your departure.'

'Will you tell them?'

'Does it matter? Can you still see yourself as a priest?'

'I don't know. What does a priest look like on the inside?'

'A good question but not one to which I have any answer.'

'What about Ricci?'

'He was satisfied it was all over when the bombers were intercepted.'

'But when he finds out that the crate doesn't contain any bomb – what is in it, by the way?'

'Tractor machine parts, as it said on the manifest.'

'Well, he'll find out and he'll start thinking. He's not such a bad detective. He might very well get as far as I did.'

'I doubt it. I doubt anyone will. The two students were targeted because they could be radicalised. As you said, they were unsuspecting young men carefully selected and trained well away from any real Islamic group. They'll admit to everything. They'll glory in what they tried to do. The police may even give them a real but conventional bomb, with a faulty trigger of course, and let them have their day in court and their years in prison. It would seem to be the best ending all round. They get to be heroes of jihad, the police get to be heroes of democracy, we get our evidence. Only the fanatics lose out.'

'For the moment.'

'Sadly, yes, only for the moment. The search for a nuclear capacity in the region by those states determined to remove Israel from the map will continue. Our success, I agree, can be looked on as a mixed blessing.' Jimmy stood up. 'Are you going, Mr Costello?'

'If you've told me everything I should know. Have you?'

'You were not supposed to know anything, Mr Costello, other than what you were told.'

'No lies, remember; have you told me everything I should know, yes or no?'

She paused before answering. He was asking a direct question and it required a direct answer. God, she hated telling the truth, the whole truth and nothing but the truth. It made things so very difficult. Sometimes you just had to give in to temptation and take the easy way out.

'Yes, Mr Costello, I have told you everything you should know. But you still haven't told me what you intend to do.'

'No, I haven't, have I?'

And he turned and left the office.

McBride sat for a moment then picked up the phone, dialled a number, and waited for it to be answered.

'Come to the Duns College rector's office.' It was an order. 'I don't care who you're with and what you are talking about. I want you here in no more than half an hour, understand?' She listened for a second. 'I don't care if the minister will think it rude. Tell him anything you like, tell him your wife just had twins, tell him you've just been elected pope. Just get here.'

Across Rome in a splendid office the bland monsignor stood up, made embarrassed excuses, and left. How he hated that woman. Why, oh why had the Church allowed women into positions of power and influence? As he hurried through the marble halls he longed for the days of his youth when women cooked, cleaned, had babies, and it was a simpler, easier world for men.

Professor McBride sat back. She would not leave the office until she had seen the monsignor. It was silly perhaps, bordering on the superstitious, but even going down stone steps could be fatal. A slip, a fall, who knew? As a child she was told that God watched out to take you unawares in your sin. It had been a way of frightening her into going to confession. It was just a silly tale, she knew that, but things from your childhood stuck.

She would sit and wait and not leave the office until the monsignor had come and heard her confession and given her absolution. As she sat she prepared for her confession. It had only been a small lie but the trouble with lies, even small ones, was that you never knew what they might lead to. A lie linked you to consequences over which you had no real control. Better to be on the safe side.

THIRTY-SEVEN

Jimmy got up from his chair, went to the door, and opened it. Ricci was standing there.

'Come in.'

Jimmy closed the door and followed him into the room. Ricci turned and looked at him.

'I went to the doctor. He gave me the results of the tests they were doing.'

His voice was flat, almost dazed. 'Can I sit down?'

'Sure.'

Ricci went to an armchair and almost fell into it. He held his head in his hands for a moment. Jimmy began to feel worried. Ricci raised his head. There were tears running down his cheeks.

'I'm going to die, Jimmy. He says I'm going to die.' Jimmy didn't doubt what he was saying for one second. Shit, he didn't need this, he had his own troubles. Ricci wiped his face with a hand. 'I didn't know who to talk to so I came to you. I don't know why, we're not friends, we hardly know each other. I have no right to …'

'That's OK, you needed to tell someone. Tell me.'

Jimmy went to the table and pulled a chair round so he faced Ricci, and sat down. Ricci pulled out a handkerchief and wiped his eyes and cheeks.

'You know I've been getting these headaches then pains in my lower back and over the last few days I've started to be nauseous so I went to see my doctor today. He said he was glad I came because he'd just got my medical report and the news wasn't good.'

'The report you said was a cover?'

'That's right.' Ricci put his head in his hands again. Jimmy waited until he was ready to go on. 'I told him I thought the report was just something he had been asked by the police to pretend to have done, and he said, no, there really was a report and the police hadn't asked him to do anything.'

'Tell me what happened.'

Ricci began, he wanted to talk.

'I go for a check-up every six months, I don't have to but I do. I like to stay on top of things, take care of myself. Not the last check-up, but the one before that, I was OK except my blood pressure was high. I'm fit, I work out, there was no reason why it should have been high. The doc said it wasn't anything I should worry about and he would check it again next time. Six months later it was still the same so he said he wanted a blood sample to send away for tests. I told my boss about it. He didn't need to know but I told him. I wanted him to know I kept in shape, that I looked after myself. Anyway, I forgot all about it until I was told I'd been given leave and the minister's aide wanted to see me. I was going on special assignment and I would be put on indefinite paid leave with a story that I was awaiting the results of medical tests which might indicate a serious illness. I assumed it was just a cover story, but now the report's come back. The doctor said ...'

But Jimmy wasn't really listening any more. He needed to work out timings.

'How long was there between you giving the blood sample and getting told about the assignment?'

'What?'

'How long?'

'I don't remember.'

'Remember, it's important.'

Ricci's head went back into his hands, then he suddenly
258

stood up. He was very pale. He looked like he was going to throw up.

'Where's your …'

Jimmy pointed and Ricci went, holding a hand over his mouth. He came back wiping his mouth.

'It's nausea, it makes me retch, nothing comes up. The doctor said it was to be expected.'

Ricci sat down again.

'How long between the blood test and getting the assignment?'

He couldn't afford to let it go. Ricci forced himself to concentrate.

'About two weeks, maybe more, it's hard to remember. I didn't take much notice.' The tears came back. 'I don't know what to do. What do you do when they tell you you're a dead man?' He was lost, bewildered. Jimmy looked at him. Yes, you're a dead man, and you may not be the only one. Jimmy's mind was running fast. It had to be connected, this had to be part of things. Ricci was chosen because someone knew he wouldn't be around for very long after it was all over and he'd been chosen in case Ricci deteriorated more quickly than expected. But he hadn't got any terminal illness so what was the plan for him? Ricci tried to pull himself together. 'I'm sorry, I don't know why I came here. I just needed to talk to someone. I don't want to tell my family, not yet, not while I'm like this. The doctor says there'll be a lot of pain but they can control it. For Christ's sake, I've only got a few months.'

He started to get up.

Jimmy leaned forward, put a hand on his shoulder and gently pushed him back into the chair.

'It's all right, you needed to talk to someone, I understand.'

Ricci was breaking apart. Jimmy didn't like that, he needed to know what was going on. He didn't want him in pieces.

'There's so much I was going to do, there's so many things. I have a girl, you know, a nice girl, not just someone to sleep with. We've talked about getting married, having a family.' Ricci wasn't looking anywhere, he was talking to himself. That was fine, thought Jimmy, let him talk. It's good to talk.

So Ricci talked about a future that would never be and Jimmy sat and thought about whether or not he had a future.

Did they have Ricci sorted from day one? Was he was chosen because he was already taken care of, because nature had done it for them? Or had it been neatly arranged? Slip him something that would finish him and fix it all in a medical report. All very sad but all very neat and tidy.

'The doctor said it was some sort of …'

Jimmy nodded but he wasn't really listening, Ricci was saying something about dying in a haze of morphine. That was tough, but he had other things on his mind.

This was the last little bit and he hadn't seen it coming. But he should have seen it coming. There was no way McBride was going to leave loose ends around. In a couple of months Ricci would be shot so full of drugs he would do well to remember his own name and in the meantime he wouldn't give a damn about what was in the crate. He wasn't a threat to anyone. He was already dead.

'The doctor says he can arrange …' he was better now, talking himself through it, '… but it won't help, it will just confirm …' soon he could get rid of him and get on. Now he knew about Ricci he knew what had to be done.

Ricci took out his damp handkerchief again and blew his nose hard. Then he wiped his eyes. Jimmy noticed because he did it the wrong way round and that meant he was on autopilot, but that was OK because it also meant he was trying to pull himself together and getting ready to leave. He was sorted, it was tough on him, but he was sorted. But what about him? Ricci's troubles would soon be over, Jimmy's were just beginning. Ricci was sitting in the chair staring at the floor. What the hell was he waiting for?

Suddenly Jimmy thought of Bernie. Bernie would have been beside Ricci. She would have an arm round him and she would have listened, really listened. And Michael, Michael would have found some words, the right words. And what had he done? He'd thought about Jimmy Costello. This guy was going to die, he could die in a haze of morphine or die conscious and screaming at the pain, that was some shitty choice and all he did was close the book on him and think, how does this affect Jimmy fucking Costello? Oh God, would he ever change? Jimmy got up, stood beside Ricci and put his arm around his shoulders. Ricci didn't move, didn't respond in any way, he just looked at the carpet. Jimmy wanted to think of the right words, he wanted to listen, he wanted to help. But Jimmy's mind wasn't having any of it. Jimmy's mind was running. It didn't care what this new Jimmy wanted, it was running and Jimmy knew he'd soon have to join it. He wasn't Bernie and he wasn't Michael, he was Jimmy Costello, and would be for the rest of his life.

THIRTY-EIGHT

Jimmy was waiting when Danny came into the bar, walked to the table, and sat down. There was a whisky in front of Jimmy, and a bottle of beer and a glass. Jimmy pushed the beer and glass towards Danny who looked at them before he spoke.

'I hope this is as urgent as you made it sound, man. I had to miss a Christology lecture, an important one. I was looking forward to it. "What was the nature of the Word before the Incarnation?" Did Jesus' nature only become human when Mary conceived?'

'Deep stuff, I'm glad I'm out of it.'

'So, you're out of it? You made up your mind?'

'Somebody made it up for me.'

'Your rector?'

'In a way. Cheers.'

Jimmy took a sip of his whisky. Danny looked at the beer.

'I drink coffee, Jimmy.'

'You hate coffee.'

'Maybe so, but it's what I drink.'

'This is special, this is goodbye. Drink your beer, or would you prefer whisky? Or maybe white rum?'

Danny smiled his big smile.

'You know damn well I'd prefer white rum, but I guess I'll settle for this.' He took up the bottle and glass and carefully poured the beer. 'Cheers.' He took a large sip then closed his eyes for a second and Jimmy waited. 'The first in over five years, man. That's how much I'm doing for you.'

'I appreciate it.'

'You damn well better,' and Danny took another small sip. Jimmy put his hand inside his jacket and pulled out a brown paper envelope. It was thick. He put it on the table and pushed it across. Danny picked it up and opened it. It was full of Euros. He put it back on the table. 'Who?'

'Who what?'

'Who do you want me to kill? Your rector?' Danny laughed. 'I'll do it, of course, but you don't need to pay me. It'll be a favour to a friend.'

They both laughed.

'It's to pay off my apartment to the end of the tenancy. It was finished in under two months anyway so there shouldn't be any trouble.' Jimmy put his hand into his pocket and pulled out some keys which he put on the table. 'I want you to clean it out. Get rid of anything, absolutely anything of mine that could help anyone who might come looking for me. Clean the place out, Danny, and I mean really clean, like a dealer expecting a bust.'

There was no laughter now. Danny looked at the black holdall on the floor beside Jimmy's chair. He was on the move and travelling light.

'You're running?' Jimmy nodded. 'I understand. I'll see to it.'

'Slow them down, Danny, make them work for it.'

'Who is it? Who's going to come looking for you?'

'Someone I won't see coming and someone I can't stop.'

They sat in silence. Jimmy took a sip of his whisky and Danny took one of his beer.

'Listen, Jimmy, there's nothing really keeping me here. I could leave tomorrow if I wanted. Why not come to Jamaica with me? I have friends there who could look out for you.' He smiled, 'I could even watch your back like you asked me to.'

Jimmy thought about it. Maybe they'd leave him alone, maybe no one would come for him. He was small fry, not important. He looked at his glass. And maybe he'd get made bloody pope. If they came they would ask around, ask among the mature students and find that he'd hung around with Ron and Danny. If Danny had left suddenly and gone home about the same time he'd gone that should take them to Jamaica, and if he was somewhere else, somewhere far away …

'It's a thought, Danny. Do you think your old police buddies could really make it safe for me? I think the people who come, if they come, will be tough nuts and good at what they do.'

'I think it may be the best chance you've got, if you really are in the kind of bind I think you are.'

'OK, Danny, I'll do it your way. I'm going today, as soon as I leave here. How long will it take for you to clean up my stuff and get away?'

Danny thought about it.

'Maybe three, four days if you want it done thoroughly.'

'Right. How will I contact you in Jamaica?'

'When you get in, ring this number and I'll come out to the airport.' Danny pulled a small notepad and a pen out and he jotted down a mobile number. He tore out the page and handed it to Jimmy who took it, looked at it, and then stuffed it into the side pocket of his jacket. 'Any time of the day or night, just call and I'll come and get you.'

'Thanks.'

'Why didn't you get out when I told you to, man? I told you they would chew you up and they wouldn't spit you out alive. Why didn't you get out when you could?'

'I know, you told me, but I just wouldn't listen. I never listen.'

Jimmy picked up his drink and finished it. Then he stood up. Danny was a good friend. Going to Jamaica might slow them down; he hoped Danny didn't get too chewed up in the process.

'You think they will follow you to Jamaica?'

Jimmy knew they would come. He was a nothing, but what he knew about them wasn't nothing. They would come all right.

'Maybe not, Jamaica's a long way away. So long, Danny. I'll see you in about a week, two at the most.'

Danny didn't get up, he just stretched out his big hand.

'Go carefully, Jimmy, and God go with you.'

265

They shook hands.

'Light a candle for me.'

'I'll light two. We'll need them.'

Jimmy turned and walked out.

Danny pushed the beer away; it was better than coffee, but only just. He got up. He would go to church and light those candles, although he knew two weren't enough. There probably wasn't enough candles in all the churches in Rome to make sure Jimmy was going to be alright. But what could you do? Jimmy was Jimmy, and he always would be.

Epilogue

'If that tide of money they say washed over Ireland got as far as Mayo it didn't do as much as wet the soles of my boots.'

'The trouble with the Celtic Tiger was that its mouth was over in Dublin, that's where what money there was got swallowed. The west of Ireland was at the other end of the beast and we all know very well what the other end deals in.'

'Shite.'

'Is that a comment, Noel, or are you agreeing with him?'

'Neither.'

'Maybe it's a bit of both.'

The four men sitting together at the table laughed.

'It was bloody foreign charity that's what it was and what's worse, it was charity that went to the wrong people. Charity is for the poor, and it certainly wasn't the poor who got it.'

'Well it's been and gone and we're all back to square one so there's an end to it.'

There was a pause until one thinker asked a question.

'But tell me, if we're the arse end of Ireland, where's the tail? There's nowhere after us until New York.'

'The Celtic Tiger never had a tail, it started to run short of money somewhere in Roscommon and wasn't able to afford one by the time it got here.'

But the answer only made the Thinker ask another question.

'So wouldn't that have made it a Manx Tiger, not a Celtic one?'

'What?'

'It's Manx cats that have no tails.'

'And I have no beer in my glass so if none of you mean buggers are buying there's nothing for it but to use my own money.' The speaker got up and took his empty glass to the bar. 'Another pint please, Ned.'

The three thinkers left at the table in Maloney's Bar lost interest in European finance and, as the talk had been of money, the conversation naturally turned to farming. The man at the bar looked around. It wasn't a busy night. He nodded to the only other customer, a crumpled, middle-aged man in an old tweed jacket sitting at a table by himself with a half-finished glass of Guinness in front of him. The man nodded back, but without any real enthusiasm. When the pint came the man asked the barman quietly,

'Do we know yet who he is or why he's here?'

The barman waited until a note had been handed over for the pint of Smithwicks before he answered.

'He's an Englishman, London by the sound of his voice, and he doesn't seem to be here for anything in particular.'

'Doesn't fish?'

The barman shook his head.

'Golf?'

Another shake.

'Maybe he paints.'

'Well I hope it's watercolours because we've seen nothing but rain for the past month.'

'Maybe he's a writer. I can't see why anybody would come here from England if it's not for the fishing or the golf, so maybe he's a writer. I wonder what he writes. What did you say his name was?'

'I didn't, but it's Costello.'

The barman put the man's change on the counter. The Smithwicks drinker continued to speculate.

'I've never heard of anything written by anybody called Costello, but he might write under another name.'

'Maybe he's come here to be left alone and not have people poking around finding out who he is and what he's doing here.'

The drinker took his change and his pint.

'Well he's made a poor choice if he has. There hasn't been a secret kept in Eriskenny since Cromwell was a Catholic.'

And he rejoined his friends.

From his table the solitary Englishman glanced at the group of thinkers and drinkers. They were locals, friends, and neighbours having a drink together. They probably met like this most nights of the week. God knows there wasn't much else to do in this town except stay home and watch the TV. His mind reflected on the place he had fetched up in: Eriskenny. An ugly little town on the main road to nowhere, it had a run-down, hopeless air about it. It survived on an agriculture which itself struggled to survive the wet, rocky, heather-strewn land. The wide main street was a collection of shabby little shops selling everything a householder might ever need, from paint and paraffin to lace curtains and china tea sets with the odd funeral wreath and First Communion dress here and there.

Among the shops were scattered no less than seven bars. The man took a sip of his Guinness. He didn't really like it, that was why he drank it, that way the pints lasted longer and he could get through the night on just three. Maybe he would change to Smithwicks. It might be all right, and if he took a good long walk in the mornings and again in the afternoons maybe after three pints of bitter he would be ready to sleep.

He took another glance at the men at the table. They certainly weren't furious drinkers. Their pints seem to last longer than his and he was deliberately slow. How could a place like Eriskenny support seven bloody bars? He did a quick calculation. Allowing fifty per cent of the population were women and it seemed like three-quarters of what was left were kids that meant there was one bar for about every twenty adult males. That couldn't be right. Yet that seemed to be how it was. Suddenly the man who had just bought a pint got up and came to his table.

'I hope you don't mind me coming over but, as you've been here a few nights, we thought we should say welcome, like, and maybe buy you a drink.'

The drinker stood and waited. The crumpled man looked at him then at the group. They were all looking at him, the youngest, a man of about twenty, gave him a big smile and called across.

'Welcome to Eriskenny.' The others nodded, endorsing the sentiment, but they didn't smile, as if to distance themselves from the impetuosity of youth. The crumpled man seemed

269

reluctant to speak and looked back to the man standing at his table who realised it was his initiative so he had to make the next move. 'What'll you have, sir?'

'No.' The man standing blinked at the sharp emphatic response, but the crumpled man's voice changed as he went on. 'Let me buy you all a drink, that would be better. You've said welcome and I appreciate you saying it, so let me say thank you and buy you all a drink.'

The young man shouted across again.

'Good luck to you, sir,' then to the barman, 'mine's a Bushmills, Ned, a double.'

The oldest man of the group, eighty if he was a day, looked at him.

'Yours is a pint like it always is, Seamus Dooley.' Then he turned to the crumpled man. 'All pints, thank you, two of Guinness and two of Smithwicks.'

The crumpled man looked to the bar.

'And you, you'll join me?'

The barman nodded. This was turning into a big night.

'Thank you, sir, I'll have an orange juice.' The crumpled man started to get up. The barman stopped him with a gesture. 'No need, sir, I'll bring them over.'

The man standing at the table made the invitation which would cement the night and turn it into an occasion.

'Would you care to come and join us?'

'Thank you but if you don't mind I'll pass on that tonight. I'll be going soon and I have a few things I have to think about before I go, but thank you for the offer. Another night, maybe.'

'Any time, sir, any time at all, and thank you for the drinks.'

He returned to his friends where the talk subsided to whispers and sly glances. A writer. The consensus was definitely a writer of some sorts. Someone in the cultural line anyway, an educated man, properly educated, like a priest.

Jimmy sat with his thoughts, not that they were particularly good company, but he sat with them anyway. He didn't hear the lowered tones or notice the glances, he was doing his thinking. Six weeks had passed since he caught a train out of Rome to Milan. From there he had flown to Paris then travelled to

Roscoff where he caught the ferry to Cork. Now he was back in the same part of the west of Ireland where he'd run to last time. Then it was people in London who wanted him dead and here he was again, still running. Was he safe? He was not. Was he happy? He was not. Did he have any idea what he was going to do? He did not. He had a small piece of information lodged in his brain and it was going to kill him as certainly as if it was a malignant tumour. He was on the run, but he was no Anna Schwarz, he didn't have the Catholic Church to hide him away where no one would ever find him. The question he thought about was the same one he had started with on the day he left Danny in the bar. What next, where to go next? The door of Maloney's Bar opened and an old man in a black cap and black raincoat walked in. Jimmy recognised him at once as he walked to Jimmy's table and sat down.

'Hello, Jimmy. How are you?'

'Well, thank you, Father.'

'Good. I've come across to give you something.' Jimmy looked at him. How many times had they talked over cups of tea in the comfortable presbytery in another dead and alive little town on some other main road to nowhere? It was the old priest who had finally persuaded him to write off and enquire about the priesthood, who had waited patiently with him while Rome took so long to process his application. 'I've something for you. It came today and I thought you should have it right away.'

He began to fumble around inside his raincoat.

'How did you know I was here?'

The priest stopped fumbling.

'This is a very small part of the world and I'm a parish priest. People talk to me and I listen. How would I not know you were here?'

The barman brought the drinks to the next table where they were taken and raised to Jimmy with various toasts to their benefactor.

'To you, sir.'

'Cheers.'

'God bless you.'

The barman came to Jimmy's table.

'Can I get you something, Father?'

'No, no, I'm in and out, Ned. Just talking to my man here and then on my way.' The barman left them to their talk and the priest began to fumble again. 'It's in here somewhere.' Finally he pulled out an envelope and passed it to Jimmy. 'It was in a letter sent to me from Rome and I was asked to pass it on if I knew of your whereabouts.'

'And of course you knew of my whereabouts?'

'Thirty-odd miles, Jimmy, just thirty-odd miles between us, why wouldn't I know? If a cow farts or a sheep coughs I know about it.' Jimmy took the envelope and put it in his jacket pocket. The priest stood up. 'Well, I've done what I came to do, goodnight, Jimmy. You know where I am if you need me.'

He turned and headed for the door.

'Goodnight, Father.'

The old priest nodded to the barman and left. After he had gone Jimmy sat for a while then finished his Guinness, said his goodnights, and left. Back at the small hotel he sat on his bed, pulled the envelope from his pocket, and looked at it for a while. Then he tore it open and took out the sheet of paper.

Duns College
Vialle Santo Maria Magdalena 21
Vatican City
00 135 Rome

Dear Mr Costello,

I have no way of knowing whether this will reach you but I have sent copies of this letter to three places I think safe enough to be trusted where you might be found.

I feel you are owed an apology. I apologise. I regret that, like Anna Schwarz, I was given a choice between two evils but I think I made the right choice. Nonetheless you were used and have been put in harm's way as a result.

I assure you that all records of your presence in Rome have been erased from any file or storage system to which I have access. Officially, you were never a Duns student and never in

Rome. However, I cannot erase memories, so your existence as a student in Rome remains with those who knew you while you were here.

Before I met you I only knew you as you had been, as you were remembered by the people who had known you as a policeman in London. You know better than I what picture that would have drawn of you. But having known you a little as you are now, I think you are trying to change, to live a life your late wife might be proud of.

I know it is not easy and I also know that what I did has made it that much harder for you, perhaps impossible.

I cannot undo what has been done. What was done had to be done. But now I can offer my help.

If you would like some time to think again about the priesthood I would be happy to arrange a placement for you with a parish priest. It would be somewhere discreet but I cannot promise total anonymity. Alas the Collegio Principe has many resources, but not a witness protection programme.

I know that a parish placement is not much, but it may help you to get closer to where you thought you were going when you first applied to Duns College.

If you take up the placement and decide to reapply to Duns College I think I can assure you that acceptance for training will be a formality. Further than that I cannot go.

Concerning the other matter, I regret I cannot help you. It is not that what I have in my possession is not enough to help you, unfortunately it is too much.

However, if you ever came back to Rome I assure you there would be the fullest co-operation of all agencies with which we have influence to ensure your safety while training.

With my prayers and every good wish,
Professor Pauline McBride

Jimmy put the letter on the bed. He couldn't make her out. Had she been responsible for Ricci's death or had it been natural causes? Or what? He gave up, he didn't want to think about it tonight. He didn't want to think about the priesthood, Rome, or any of it. If it was going to be part of anything in his life then that was still in the future. He would leave it for tonight. But despite himself he thought about Danny. Had they found Danny yet, had they come and watched him? Had they talked to him or hurt him trying to get information he didn't have? Or maybe he'd picked up with his old partner, the white rum. Maybe now he drank and slept well and had given up on his friend from Rome.

Jimmy got up, picked up the letter, folded it, and put it in his pocket and slowly began to get undressed with one simple thought.

Forget Rome. Rome was yesterday and yesterday is finished and gone. Think about today and get ready for tomorrow. You do what has to be done in whatever way you can. You use whatever comes to hand. Whoever comes to hand. You …

And then the words stopped and thinking finished. You did what you did and you tried to live with it. He switched the light out, got into bed, and tried to pray. 'Dear God, take Bernie and Michael into your mercy and …' But he still didn't know if he was talking to nothing and there was no Michael and Bernie any more. Was there a God? Maybe when you died that was it, no eternity, no Heaven, no Hell. Nothing. How could you know? Well, whatever Bernie and Michael had got, he would settle for the same and fuck all the rest of it, God, eternity, the Church, the whole lot. Fuck you and …

And nothing. You couldn't turn life off at the switch. So he lay still and waited for sleep in the full knowledge that soon he would wake up to another day, and it would all go on again, day by day, until it ended. He began again to pray. 'Oh my God, I am sorry and beg pardon for all my sins …'

It wasn't what you wanted, but it was all that was on offer, so you took it, and you did what you had to do.

James Green

Agents of Independence Series

Another Small Kingdom
A Union Not Blessed
The Eagle Turns
Never an Empire
Winston's Witch

For more information about **James Green**

and other **Accent Press** titles

please visit

www.accentpress.co.uk